MAGGIE CHRISTENSEN

Finding Refuge in Bellbird Bay

Copyright © 2023 Maggie Christensen
Published by Cala Publishing 2023
Sunshine Coast, Qld, Australia

This publication is written in British English. Spellings and grammatical conventions are conversant with the UK.

The moral right of the author has been asserted.

All rights reserved. No part of this book may be reproduced, stored in a retrieval system, or transmitted by any means, electronic, mechanical, photocopying or otherwise, without the prior written permission of the author.

This is a work of fiction. The locations in this book and the characters are totally fictitious. Any resemblance to real persons, living or dead, is purely coincidental.

Cover and interior design: JD Smith Design
Editing: John Hudspith Editing Services

ISBN: 978-0-6455285-5-8

Dedication

To the memory of a dear writer friend, Toni, who was an inspiration to my early writing and who departed this life in 2022.

Also by Maggie Christensen

Oregon Coast Series
The Sand Dollar
The Dreamcatcher
Madeline House

Sunshine Coast books
A Brahminy Sunrise
Champagne for Breakfast

Sydney Collection
Band of Gold
Broken Threads
Isobel's Promise
A Model Wife

Scottish Collection
The Good Sister
Isobel's Promise
A Single Woman

Granite Springs
The Life She Deserves
The Life She Chooses
The Life She Wants
The Life She Finds
The Life She Imagines
A Granite Springs Christmas
The Life She Creates
The Life She Regrets
The Life She Dreams

Mother's Story

Bellbird Bay
Summer in Bellbird Bay
Coming Home to Bellbird Bay
Starting Over in Bellbird Bay
Christmas in Bellbird Bay

One

It was a cool July day in Bellbird Bay. Bev Cooper, owner of *The Pandanus Garden Centre and Café*, had just returned home from a busy day at work when her twin brother, Martin, and her best friend Ailsa burst into her kitchen hand-in-hand, clearly eager to share some news.

At first Bev couldn't believe her ears, then, 'A wedding?' she said, gazing at Ailsa and Martin, who were grinning sheepishly, her delight tempered by a stab of regret. 'You're getting married?'

'An October wedding,' Ailsa confirmed. 'We thought…' she glanced at Martin. '…we thought it was a good idea. It's been more than two years and my divorce has been through for over a year.'

'How wonderful.' Bev tried to inject a note of enthusiasm into her voice as she hugged her twin brother and her best friend. Of course she was pleased, delighted, even, but she couldn't suppress the memory which surfaced whenever someone she knew chose to tie the knot. She knew it was foolish, and she was always happy for them, despite the small voice that whispered, Why not me?

At fifty-five, Bev knew marriage wasn't for her. She'd watched Ailsa find love twice, the second time with Martin, who Bev had despaired of ever settling down. And she'd seen other friends in this small coastal town of Bellbird Bay find love in later life. But, scarred by an experience when she was only twenty, Bev was happy to remain single and avoided feeling lonely by keeping busy.

'This calls for a celebration,' she said, putting as much energy into her voice as she could and hoping the pair hadn't noticed her initial hesitation. But, she realised, they were too wrapped up in each other to notice anything or anyone else. What must it be like to feel that emotion for someone, and to have the feeling reciprocated? The memory of the one time she had felt that way swamped Bev as she took a bottle of champagne out of the fridge and three champagne flutes from the cupboard. 'This has been waiting for a special occasion,' she said with a smile.

'Thanks Bev.' Ailsa hugged her.

'Careful.' Martin grabbed the glasses from Bev and, placing them on the benchtop, retrieved the bottle and proceeded to open it. The foam spurted everywhere, making them all laugh.

'So, an October wedding,' Bev said, when they were seated on the deck of her renovated beach shack, the house she'd bought after the death of their parents over thirty years earlier. It looked out over the ocean, and today they could see the swell of the waves and a few surfers taking advantage of the last vestiges of daylight. It had become her refuge over the years, the place where she could shut out everyone and everything and retreat into her own little world.

But, almost three years earlier her peace had been shattered when her best friend from uni, Ailsa, had accepted her invitation to visit, and the visit had morphed into a lengthy stay, while Ailsa considered her future. The visit had coincided with the arrival of Martin, Bev's twin brother, taking a forced break from his world travels as a photographer. The two had hit it off, and now there was to be a wedding.

'We thought perhaps towards the end of the month, after the triathlon, and we wondered...' Ailsa glanced at Martin again. 'We'd love to have it in the garden centre.'

Bev drew in a breath. *The Pandanus Garden Centre and Café* was her baby. She had started it when she'd returned to Bellbird Bay to care for her aging parents. She didn't regret it; she'd had no option. Martin was tied up in some distant spot doing what he did best. So, it fell to her to do the right thing.

Over the years, the garden centre had grown, a café had been added, and it was now a highly profitable business, of which she was proud. It had never hosted a wedding, but recently, Bev had been entertaining the idea of offering one secluded corner as a venue for wedding ceremonies.

'What do you think?' Ailsa asked breathlessly, when Bev didn't immediately reply.

'Sis?' Martin asked.

'It… it sounds like a good idea,' Bev replied. *How did they know she'd been toying with the idea of doing just that?*

Martin grinned and hugged Ailsa. 'We knew you'd agree,' he said.

'And I'm sure Cleo could manage to cater it,' Ailsa said, referring to the woman who managed *The Pandanus Café* attached to the garden centre.

'Oh!' Bev hadn't approached Cleo with her idea as yet, but she knew the manager of *The Pandanus Café* was not only very skilled and professional but flexible, too.

'It seems you've thought of everything,' she said, trying to sound upbeat.

'Not quite. I'd like you to be my maid of honour. Will Rankin will be Martin's best man, and I'll ask Nate to give me away.'

'I'd love to, Ailsa. I'd be honoured to witness this brother of mine getting hitched.' Bev nodded. It was what she'd have expected. Will was Martin's oldest friend. The two had reconnected when her brother returned home. And Nate was one of Ailsa's sons, the one who lived here in Bellbird Bay.

Her mind wandered, imagining hosting Martin and Ailsa's wedding in the corner of *The Pandanus Garden Centre*. It would be a perfect way to launch her new project – if it could be ready in time. October was only three months away.

*

When Ailsa and Martin finally left with more hugs and good wishes, Bev was left with a sense of loss. She always joked she could never find a man who'd put up with her, but the truth was she had once felt the spark others talked about. It was so long ago she'd almost forgotten what it felt like.

There hadn't been anyone since. Deciding she wasn't intending to be part of a couple, Bev had put all her energy into building her business and making it into the success it was today. And she'd been happy. Bellbird Bay was a great little community. She was well-known and respected here. She didn't need anything or anyone else in her life.

It was only at times like this, seeing her brother and best friend so happy, planning their wedding, that she wondered what her life would have been like if only things could have been different.

Now, she stifled the memories, pushed them to the back of her mind where they'd been for the past thirty-five years. She had a wedding to plan.

Two

Iain Grant rubbed a hand across the top of his head, his grey, cropped hair feeling like bristles under his fingers, and stared out at the traffic heading across Sydney's Spit Bridge, as the aroma of his morning coffee rose to fill the kitchen. Normally, he'd be dressed in a suit and tie, preparing to join the line of traffic himself. But not today. Never again.

Soon, he knew, he'd have to wake his son and granddaughter, and the day would begin. But he could enjoy a few moments of peace and quiet first.

He thought back to the meeting with Paul Connor the day before and gave a sigh. It would be a wrench to leave the architectural practice they'd established almost twenty-five years earlier. But he could think of no other solution. Staying here in Sydney wouldn't help Bryan recover from the depth of depression he'd sunk into when Nadia died. The city held too many memories. And it wasn't good for Mia either. At six, his granddaughter couldn't understand why her mother had left them.

Early retirement and a move to the small coastal town of Bellbird Bay on Queensland's Sunshine Coast would provide a much-needed fresh start for all of them.

'Dad.' Bryan shuffled into the kitchen. The man who used to be a leading sports journalist on one of the dailies was a shadow of his former self. This morning, like most mornings recently, Bryan looked as if he hadn't slept, his hair unkempt, his face unshaven, still wearing the board shorts and the old Crowded House tee-shirt he'd worn for the past three days.

'Bryan, do you remember what we talked about last night?'

'Uh?' Bryan helped himself to a mug of coffee from the batch Iain had just brewed, pulled out a chair and dropped into it, clutching the mug as if it was a lifeline. 'Something about leaving work.'

'Grandad!' Mia raced in to wrap herself around Iain's knees.

He ruffled her auburn curls, so like her mother's a tear came to his eye. If seeing Mia could have this effect on him, what must it do to Bryan?

'Are you or Daddy driving me to school today?' She looked at his outfit, the jeans and tee-shirt he'd dragged on after his shower making it clear he wasn't intending to go to the office.

'I'll take you today, sweetheart. Coco Pops for breakfast?'

'Yum.' She slipped onto the chair next to her dad and reached up to give him a kiss on the cheek. 'Good morning, Daddy.' Her voice held a note of caution, as if unsure what Bryan's reaction would be.

Today, Bryan merely nodded.

Iain gave a sigh of relief.

Breakfast over, Iain glanced over at his son before he left to take Mia to school. 'Get yourself showered and dressed before I get back, Bryan. We need to talk.'

*

By the time Iain returned, he was pleased to see Bryan had taken his advice and was now washed, shaved and dressed, wearing a pair of track pants and a clean tee-shirt.

'Coffee?' he asked, going to the espresso machine without waiting for a reply.

When the kitchen was once more filled with the aroma of coffee beans, Iain felt able to broach the subject with his son again.

'Okay, Dad. What do you have to say that's so important?'

'As I said last night, I've decided to take early retirement. We both need a fresh start, to get away from Sydney and its memories.'

'Leave Sydney?' Bryan's eyes widened. 'Why?'

'I've thought and thought about what I can do to help you recover from Nadia's death.' Iain saw Bryan's face take on the closed expression it had held for the past weeks, ever since he'd heard the news his wife had been killed in a freak accident. He cursed himself for mentioning her name, knowing it was like sticking a knife into a wound.

'Nothing can do that.'

'I know, but I thought… maybe… if you weren't faced with memories every time you ventured out…' Iain's voice faltered at the realisation Bryan had scarcely left the house since the funeral. That was part of the problem.

'Move where?' There was no interest in Bryan's voice.

Iain took a deep breath. 'Remember the holidays we took on the Sunshine Coast when you were little – not much older than Mia is now?' As there was no response, Iain felt encouraged to continue. 'I checked out Bellbird Bay and, although it's grown since then, it's still a relatively small coastal town, pretty much untouched by developers. It would be good for Mia,' he added, playing what he considered to be his trump card.

'Was that the place where there was a boardwalk and a stairway going down to the beach?'

'That's it.'

'I remember. The sun always seemed to shine. It was hot. We spent every day on the beach. You taught me to swim. Mum hated it.' Bryan's sudden burst of interest died away and his eyes once again glazed over.

'I've rented a house there for six months… on the boardwalk. It will give us time to look around, decide if we want to stay, find somewhere to buy. I can rent out this place while we're gone, or put it on the market. What do you think?' Iain held his breath.

'Whatever. Sounds like you've already made up your mind.'

Iain heaved a sigh of relief. While it wasn't an unqualified agreement, at least Bryan sounded as if he was willing to go along with him. When he'd seen the house to rent, it was as if it was meant to be. A house opposite the beach in the small coastal town could be exactly what all three of them needed.

Three

Bev stretched her arms above her head and yawned as the morning sun filtered through the plantation shutters on her bedroom window. She'd dreamt of weddings – weddings with masses of flowers, and a gigantic bottle of champagne. She shook her head and rose, determined to dispel the images still swirling around in her head with a cool shower.

The shock of the chill water cascading over her tall, wiry frame helped bring Bev fully awake. Then, dressed in a pair of cut-off jeans and a white tee-shirt with the green pandanus logo, her faded blonde hair pulled back into an untidy ponytail, Bev went through to her sunlit kitchen and made herself breakfast. She carried her morning cup of lemon and ginger tea outside to where the morning sunshine was already sending its rays across the stained boards of the deck and drank in the view of which she never tired. It was going to be another glorious day.

An hour later, she was donning the green apron bearing the pandanus logo and was ready for work.

It was a busy morning in the garden centre, with the arrival of several loads of new plants, all of which had to be entered into the database, priced, and put on display. Although Bev had a group of skilled and reliable staff, most of whom had been with her for years, there were some things she preferred to do herself. So, it wasn't till almost one o'clock that she managed to take a break.

She dropped into a chair in *The Pandanus Café* with an exhausted sigh.

'Busy morning?' Cleo, the dark-haired woman who managed the café, appeared almost immediately, carrying a cup of peppermint tea, exactly what Bev needed.

'How did you know?'

'Instinct' Cleo tapped her nose with one finger. 'Though I can't claim to possess any of Ruby's uncanny insight.'

They both laughed at the reference to Ruby Sullivan, the woman who not only provided the café with a never-ending supply of delicious cakes, but also seemed to be able to read minds, as well as making her weird predictions about the future – many of which came true.

'Talking of Ruby,' Bev said, taking a welcome sip of the refreshing tea, 'I wanted to ask you something.'

'What?'

'I'll tell you when I have something to eat.'

'Sorry! Salad?'

'Please.'

Cleo left, to return a few minutes later with two plates, on one of which was the café's salad of the day.

'Now.' Cleo settled herself opposite Bev and took a bite from the ham and cheese panini she'd chosen for herself.

'Ruby.' Bev repositioned her knife and fork before continuing. 'Do you think she'd be able to make a wedding cake?'

Cleo's eyes widened with surprise. 'Who's getting married? Not...?'

'Martin and Ailsa,' Bev confirmed. 'They plan to get married and want the ceremony to be here, in the garden centre.' Saying it aloud suddenly made it all seem more real. 'What do you think?'

'Oh!' Cleo's face reddened. 'I wonder if Will knows.'

'If he doesn't already know, he will soon. Martin wants him to be best man.'

'Oh!' Cleo said again.

Bev peered at her friend. It was just over a year since Cleo and Will had become a couple and, while she was pleased for them, and thought them well-suited, she knew their relationship hadn't been smooth sailing. Was Cleo envious of Ailsa and Martin's decision to marry? Bev could understand if she was. It would only mirror her own selfish thoughts. 'Isn't it wonderful?' she asked quickly. 'I expect Ailsa will be talking to you about catering, which is why I wanted to ask about Ruby.'

Cleo didn't immediately respond. 'Where would you hold it?' she asked.

'I've been thinking. There's the area towards the back of the centre – where we usually store the garden ornaments. We could distribute them around the place.' It was the area she'd already earmarked as a potential wedding spot – where they'd held a wreath-making class the previous Christmas.

'Right.' Cleo appeared to have recovered from the shock of Bev's announcement. 'It'll be fun to cater for a wedding, and I'm sure Ruby will rise to the occasion. When exactly?'

'The end of October. No definite date as yet. It's a few months away. We can do it, though it would have to be after the centre and café have closed. It would mean extended hours for you.' She picked up her cutlery and focussed on eating lunch, allowing Cleo to do the same.

*

Back home that evening, Bev felt the warmth of her home enfold her, the way it always did, and blessed the day she'd bought this house, one of several along the boardwalk whose value had increased exponentially in the past few years. Although she'd been offered an unimaginable sum to sell it, she knew she'd never move.

She poured herself a glass of wine and took it out to the deck, surprised at how Ailsa and Martin's news had revived memories she'd relegated to the back of her mind. Strangely, they hadn't resurfaced when the pair got together. Maybe it was the talk of marriage that reminded her of the time when she had been planning her own wedding. A pang of what she had lost shot through her, and a tear slid down her cheek. Angrily she wiped it away. It was all so long ago… another lifetime. Her son would have been thirty-five now, a man. It was her secret. No one knew. Not her parents, not Martin, not even Ailsa her best friend with whom she shared everything. When she left uni suddenly, everyone believed it was to care for her parents. But at that time, they were both in good health. Bev was pregnant.

Coincidentally, at the same party at which Ailsa and Martin had first met, Bev had met Phil. He was studying at the Australian Military

Academy, training to become an officer, his military career all mapped out for him. Born into a military family, he was destined to continue the family tradition.

Theirs was a romance carried out in secret, the secrecy giving it a more poignant romantic flavour than would otherwise have been the case. When she discovered her pregnancy, they decided to marry, intending to tell both sets of parents in the next semester break. But it wasn't to be. A fatal car trip, a drunk driver, and Bev's future had been shattered. She had no intention of telling anyone. Knowing she couldn't deal with this on her own and being both totally opposed to abortion and desperate to bear Phil's child, when she began to show, she fled to Sydney, to her godmother, the one person she knew wouldn't reject her, telling everyone her parents needed her.

In Sydney, she took a casual waitressing job and stuck it as long as she could, trying not to think what she'd do when the baby was born. Then, one wet October night, she gave birth to a perfectly formed baby boy who had only lived for two days. Bev couldn't believe her last link with Phil had been torn from her. For days and weeks, she ranted at the cruel fate which had taken both her lover and her child.

Fortunately, Bev's godmother was there to support her through the grief till the day came when she vowed to stand on her own two feet, never to allow herself to get close enough to anyone again, never to be in a position where she could suffer hurt like this again. It was then her father became ill, and Bev was able to make good on her earlier explanation to go home to help her mother care for him.

Now, rising, she went to the bedroom where, on the top shelf of the wardrobe, was the box she rarely opened. It held photos of that happy time when she and Phil were together. Carefully, she took it down and dropped onto the floor, her legs curled up under her, the box cradled on her lap. Then with a sob, she took off the lid.

First, she took out the photo of Phil in his army uniform. He was such a handsome guy with a wicked sense of humour and a grin that could charm the birds off the trees. She smiled as her finger stroked the face she'd never completely forget and remembered his delight when she told him she was pregnant. Below this was a strip of photos of them together taken in one of the instant photo booths that had sprung up in shopping centres. She was smiling at the camera while

Phil was gazing at her. Bev dropped it to the floor. There, at the bottom of the box, was the only photo she had of her baby – from the ultrasound. She hugged it to her chest as the tears trickled down her cheeks.

Four

'How much further, Grandad? I can see the sea.' Mia's excited voice broke the silence which had filled the car for most of the drive. It had been a busy two weeks. It had taken all Iain's persuasive powers to force Bryan to pack up enough clothes for their stay, and the last two days had been a trial. But they were almost there.

'Not far now, honey,' he said with relief. Was this really a good idea or a mad attempt to help his son? And had it been wise to take Mia out of school in the middle of the school year? But the trip seemed to have helped her, at least. She had spent most of it on her iPad watching movies or singing along to her favourite tunes. But now, like Iain, she was tired of travelling.

Bryan had scarcely spoken all the way. From time to time, Iain had glanced over at his son, trying to gauge his mood, without success. He could only hope Bellbird Bay would prove to have the healing power he anticipated, and Bryan would emerge from this abyss of grief which was sapping his strength.

'Look!' Mia pointed to the sign at the side of the road. 'It says there's a McDonald's in Bellbird Bay. Are there really bellbirds? My teacher told us about them when I said we were going there. Will I have to go to a new school after the holidays?'

'One thing at a time, Mia. I believe there are still bellbirds living in some of the trees, and about school, we can check it out, too.' Mia was going to be a lot easier to settle than her father. Iain wasn't sure how he was going to motivate Bryan to start living again.

*

It had started to rain when they left Brisbane, and by the time they reached the sign proclaiming they had arrived in Bellbird Bay, Iain could scarcely see out the windscreen. Not a good start, he thought, as he navigated through the streets, first to the real estate agent to pick up the keys, then to the house which was to be their home for the next six months.

'Ooh, it looks cute! Look, Daddy!' Mia called out, as Iain drew into the driveway of the blue and white painted weatherboard house.

The realtor had told him it was an old beach shack which had been renovated and was quite modern inside. He hoped so, but cute wasn't the word he'd have used. The rain made the house appear bedraggled and the driveway was awash with puddles. Only the garden looked as if it had been well cared for.

'Is this it?' Bryan roused himself enough to ask, as Iain turned off the engine.

'Can we go in?' Mia was bouncing up and down in her seat.

'Let's make a run for it. We can unload the car and trailer later.' When he realised how much they'd need for such a long stay – including bikes and all the toys Mia decided she couldn't live without – Iain had hired a trailer. Luckily, he'd also hired a tarpaulin cover so, hopefully, their belongings would have stayed dry.

Iain helped Mia out of the car, and he and his granddaughter hurried through the gate to the front door, Bryan following more slowly. After fumbling with the key, Iain finally managed to push the door open to reveal a long hallway painted white with tile flooring.

Mia ran ahead, the two men following till they reached a large family kitchen at the back of the house. The little girl immediately ran to the floor-length French windows and, putting both hands on the glass, stared out. 'Look, Grandad! I can see the sea.' Her voice was shrill with excitement.

Sure enough, the house looked out onto the boardwalk Iain remembered, and on the other side of the boardwalk was the ocean, which today was a seething mass of white-topped waves.

'Hungry?' Iain asked. It was only four o'clock, but the sky was darkening, and he judged they were all in need of something to eat.

When only Mia nodded, Iain headed back outside to fetch the esky and the bag of groceries he'd bought on the way. Then he found the key to the garage enabling him to put the car and trailer under cover.

When they were all seated around the kitchen table with bowls of beef and vegetable soup and slices of toasted cheese, Bryan said, 'Thanks, Dad. I remember this place. We were happy here.'

Iain patted his son's arm. 'Maybe we can be happy here again, son. Nadia wouldn't want you to spend the rest of your life grieving.' But it was the wrong thing to say.

Bryan brushed off his hand. 'You don't know what she'd want. She…' Bryan pushed back his chair and rushed out of the room.

'Daddy?' Mia gazed after him.

'I'll go, Mia. You finish your soup, then we'll see about a bath.' Iain hurried after his son, finding him in the living room, curled up on the sofa, tears streaming down his cheeks. Iain started towards him then checked himself. Despite Bryan's descent into depression, this was the first time Iain had seen him give way to tears. Maybe it was a good sign. He tiptoed away and closed the door behind him.

An hour later, Bryan still hadn't emerged.

Iain had partially unloaded the car and trailer, Mia had had her bath and was tucked up in bed with a favourite book, and Iain had poured himself a much-needed glass of whisky, when he heard the living room door open, and Bryan appeared in the kitchen doorway.

'Sorry, Dad. I don't know what came over me. Can I have one of those?' He gestured to the glass Iain was holding.

'Sure, son. Sometimes it helps to cry. It's nothing to be ashamed of.'

'Hmm.' Bryan accepted the glass of whisky and took a sip.

Iain watched his son as the fiery liquid took effect. Despite – or perhaps because of – his breakdown, he looked less distraught than he had in weeks. 'Would you like me to reheat your soup?'

'No, I'm good. Where's Mia?' He looked around the room.

'Bathed and in bed. She was tired after the long drive. The beds are made up in our rooms, too, and the water's plenty hot if you want a bath.'

'Thanks, but I think I'll just turn in. Thanks, Dad. This may have been one of your better ideas.'

Alone again, Iain poured himself another measure. It was a relief to hear Bryan's approval, but now they were here in Bellbird Bay, he wasn't sure what they were going to do. It had been a spur of the moment arrangement, the need to get away from the city fuelling his decision. Now he was beginning to doubt his judgment. What if he'd upended all their lives for nothing?

Five

Two weeks had passed since Ailsa and Martin made their announcement, and it had rained solidly almost every day. Bev couldn't help wondering if the whole idea of holding a wedding – or weddings – in the garden centre was madness. It would be wonderful on fine days, but if it rained, it would be a disaster.

But this morning, the sun was shining and, although cool, it promised to be the sort of day she had come to expect here in Bellbird Bay. After a quick breakfast, Bev headed to the garden centre, eager to repair any damage the days of rain had wreaked on the plants she considered to be her children, the children she would never have. Plants were so much easier to cope with than people. She'd decided that long ago and had never had cause to change her mind.

The air was fresh with just a hint of the day to come as Bev pulled on her green apron. It was still early. The centre wouldn't open for another half hour, so she made her way along the aisles checking her babies, pleased only a few had suffered from the downpour. It was only when she came to the area she'd designated as the wedding site that she frowned.

'Problems?'

Bev turned quickly to see Ruby Sullivan gazing at her.

'Morning, Ruby. Not really, but…' She bit her lip.

'What you need is one of those glass roof things to keep out the rain. No, not glass, what I mean is…' the elderly woman fumbled for the word, '…a cover to let in the light but keep out the rain.'

'Plexiglass,' Bev said, her face clearing. 'I wonder…' It would need to cover the entire area and Bev wasn't sure if that was possible – or what the cost might be. It would take quite a few weddings to cover the expense.

'You won't be out of pocket,' Ruby continued. 'It's the perfect site for a wedding.'

How did she know? But then, how did Ruby ever know?

'Mmm.' She knew she had to ask Ruby about the wedding cake but didn't want to broach it just yet.

'There are other changes ahead for you, too, and a surprise. Don't allow the past to dictate your future,' Ruby said, before turning on her heel and leaving.

Bev gazed after her, perplexed. She knew Ruby had this way of making her weird pronouncements – predictions, some would say – but till now, she had never been subjected to one. *What on earth did she mean? How could she possibly know anything about Bev's past?* Despite the two weeks since she'd been reminded of the past, the memories were still fresh in Bev's mind. *Was it possible Ruby was a mind reader? It would explain a lot.*

Bev was still turning this over in her mind when she reached the entrance to the café, set on one side of the garden centre. Deciding what she needed to counteract Ruby's words, Bev walked through the still dripping hedge of plumbago to be greeted by Cleo, who was holding out a mug of coffee.

'How did you know?' Bev asked, taking the mug and a gulp of the welcome liquid before dropping into a chair. 'Mmm, tastes so good.'

'I saw Ruby heading your way. What did she want this time?'

'To advise me we need a covering for the wedding area. Not such a bad idea, actually, but I'd need to investigate the cost.' Bev decided there was no need to mention Ruby's other comments.

'Mmm.' Cleo cradled her own mug. 'Will has some sort of clear cover over part of his courtyard. I can ask him about it. You still plan to go ahead with the wedding idea, then?'

'I do. I can use Ailsa and Martin's to launch the centre as a venue.' Her forehead creased. 'I wonder what sort of permissions I need.'

'There will be other things to arrange, too – seating, music, and the setting. I presume you'd want a flower arbour for the couple to stand under.'

Bev's eyes glazed over, imagining what it was going to look like. She felt them moisten and blinked rapidly, reluctant to let Cleo see her emotion. She sensed her friend was looking at her oddly. 'Yes, of course. I'll speak with Ailsa and Martin. I have no idea how many they intend to invite. We can hire chairs for their wedding but if things take off, we'll need to get our own and to arrange storage.' Thinking of the logistics was more comfortable for Bev. This was something over which she had some control. She'd talk with Ailsa and contact the council. Bev drained her mug and stood up, glad she now had a plan of action. 'Thanks, Cleo. You've been a big help.'

'What…?'

Bev didn't wait to hear what Cleo was going to say. The centre would be open soon. She had a lot to do.

*

It was after six when Bev finally set off for home. It had been a busy day; it seemed half of the inhabitants of Bellbird Bay, encouraged by the better weather, had decided to restock their gardens. This, along with the need for Bev and her staff to do their own maintenance, meant she hadn't had time to do any of the things she'd planned about the wedding.

She was deciding whether she could be bothered to cook a meal or whether she'd make do with bread and a hunk of the local cheese she'd picked up at the market the previous Sunday, when her phone rang. Seeing Ailsa's number, she picked it up immediately.

'Hi, Ailsa. How are you?'

'Bev. You sound exhausted. Martin and I guessed you'd be flat out today after the rain. Why don't you come over and have dinner with us? I have a roast in the oven, and Martin is about to open a bottle of red.'

'You're a lifesaver. I was just debating whether I had the energy to cook. I'll freshen up and be there in the next half hour.'

'Perfect. See you then.'

Half an hour later, Bev was pushing open the gate of the tidy brick home where Ailsa and Martin lived. It was on the outskirts of town, away from the tourist area. The house had been in need of renovation when they bought it, but the couple had turned it into a comfortable home.

'Hey, sis.' Martin greeted Bev with a hug and kiss on the cheek. 'Come in. Glad you could make it. Ailsa's dying to have a chat about the wedding. I have to go out later so you two can have some girl time.'

Bev raised an eyebrow.

'Men's business.' Martin said. 'Now Will's got me on the surf committee, I have to turn up to meetings. We have the triathlon to organise.'

'You taking part?'

By this time, they had reached the kitchen where the delicious aroma of roast beef filled the room.

Ailsa, hearing Bev's question laughed. 'I doubt he'd make it these days,' she said, linking her arm in Martin's. 'But he'll be the official photographer.'

'For my sins,' Martin said. 'Who'd have thought I'd come to this?' He pulled on one ear and chuckled,

'A bit of a comedown from taking shots in the Amazon jungle,' Bev agreed. But she knew her twin didn't regret giving up his carefree lifestyle to settle down in the town where he'd grown up. Meeting Ailsa had tamed his adventurous spirit.

'He may complain about having to go to the meeting tonight, but it's really an excuse for those old surfers to get together to talk about old times, then retire to the club for a few beers.' She gave Martin a nudge.

'You got me.' Martin held up his hands in mock submission, and they all laughed.

'You look in need of a glass of wine, Bev,' Martin said when they calmed down. 'Red, okay?'

'That would be great. Thanks.' Bev took a seat at the table which was covered with a red and white checked tablecloth and set for three. 'It's been a hectic day and...'

'No more shop talk till after dinner. Then I want to have a good chat about the wedding,' Ailsa said. 'We'll wait till Martin's gone so he can't make any of his crazy suggestions.'

'Who, me?' Martin grinned.

Bev took a sip of wine and relaxed for the first time that day. It was good to be here with Martin and Ailsa, the only real family she had. Although she'd been sorry at the breakup of her best friend's marriage, it had brought Ailsa to Bellbird Bay… and had brought her and Martin together. Bev couldn't have asked for more.

*

The meal over, Martin kissed both women and headed out, and Bev and Ailsa took coffee and a platter of cheese and biscuits into the living room.

'Now,' Ailsa said, taking a seat on the sofa and curling her feet under her, 'let's talk weddings. Well, one anyway,' she laughed. 'I can't believe it's really happening. I never thought Martin would want to make the commitment, or that I'd ever consider getting married again. But…' she wound a strand of hair around one finger, '…it's what we both want.'

'You've spoken to the boys?' Bev asked, referring to Ailsa's two sons by her former husband.

'They're good about it. They like Martin, especially Nate.' She smiled, no doubt thinking of her younger son who had followed her to Bellbird Bay and was now part of the community. 'He and Cleo's Hannah are still seeing each other. They may be the next wedding in the family. I thought Pat…' She gazed into space. 'Sorry, he recently broke up with his long-term girlfriend, Vee. They seemed to be getting serious, but…' she shook her head. 'Who knows how the younger generation think? Certainly not me.'

'Okay.' Bev placed her coffee cup down and took her iPad from her bag. She'd expected Ailsa to want to talk about wedding plans and had come prepared. 'Have you decided on a date?'

'We thought maybe the third Saturday in October. The triathlon is on the first week, so it'll give the athletic members of the group time to recover, and Martin and Will time to tie up all the loose ends. Does that work for you?'

'Should do.' Bev went into her calendar and made an entry. 'Now, what else have you decided? Have you settled on a celebrant, flowers, format of the ceremony, number of guests?'

'Not yet. I've checked on the internet for celebrants and there are a few in and around Bellbird Bay, but I'm open to suggestions.'

'I'll see what I can find out. One of my young staff members had a beach wedding last year and seemed happy with the celebrant she used.' As Bev made another note, she remembered that the staff member was now pregnant and about to take maternity leave. She'd have to find a replacement. One more thing to take care of. Sometimes she felt there weren't enough hours in the day. And here she was, planning to add one more responsibility to the list. Some might say she was a glutton for punishment, but she'd always liked to keep busy. Initially, it had been to prevent her from focussing on the past. Then it had become a habit. Maybe she needed to hire an administrative assistant too. But it would depend how much revenue the weddings brought in.

'As to the flowers, they're more your bag than mine,' Ailsa said.

'No, I think you need a florist. I've never done wedding flowers, and I'm too old to start now. But I did think an arbour would be nice, something we could replenish with fresh flowers each time. And I'm investigating some sort of cover to cater for bad weather.'

'You're really serious about adding a wedding venue – not just holding *our* wedding there?'

'It's been in the back of my mind for some time. You and Martin have just helped me push it to the front. Number of guests?'

'Oh, heck. We haven't made a list. There are the boys, Mum, my sister and her partner, friends I've made here… probably no more than twenty. Neither of us wants a big do at our age. What do you think?'

'Sounds good.' Bev was relieved. It would be simpler to plan for a small event, easier to iron out any problems. 'Have you thought of anything else?'

'Not at the moment. As long as none of the guys injure themselves before then, we should be right. I still can't believe it, Bev. Who'd have thought, when I arrived in Bellbird Bay trying to put my life back together, we'd be sitting here planning my wedding and about to become sisters?'

'Life is certainly strange.' As she spoke, Bev remembered what Ruby Sullivan had said to her only that morning. *What did the old woman mean? What could she know of Bev's past? And how could what happened back then possibly affect her future?*

'You, okay?'

Bev realised she'd been frowning. 'Sure. I can get back to you when I've sorted out a few things. I need to check with the council, too, to find out what I need to do to satisfy their requirements.'

'Let me know if there's anything I can do to help.'

'Thanks, Ailsa. I will.'

The rest of the evening was spent pleasantly, reminiscing about their university days when Ailsa and Martin had first met. It was only when Bev was driving home that her own memories of that time hit her again. By the time she drove into her garage, her face was wet with tears.

Six

'Look at this, Dad.' Bryan had been lying around the house since they arrived, only venturing out to the beach when Iain and Mia begged him to join them.

Iain had repeatedly suggested he contact the local newspaper in the off chance *The Bellbird Bugle* might be able to use his skills, but Bryan had refused. It was a free paper, unlike the popular daily he'd worked for in the city, but Iain was keen to see his son make an effort to get back to normal. He couldn't lie around for ever.

'What is it?' Iain peered over the top of his glasses to see Bryan flourishing a copy of the local paper. This was a start.

'There's a job here, in the local garden centre. I might give it a whirl. You keep telling me I need to do something. It would get me out of your way.'

'It's not that, Bryan. But… we came here in an attempt to get you back on your feet, to make a fresh start, to…'

'I know all that, Dad. And I'm grateful. But I can't go back to being the person I was before…' He paused, took a breath. 'This would be manual work, outside. It would take my mind off… other things.' He handed Iain the paper open at the Situations Vacant page.

Iain read the advertisement. It was as Bryan said. A local garden centre – *The Pandanus Garden Centre* – was seeking someone on a temporary basis to help out. No knowledge of plants was required, and the position would entail some heavy lifting. He looked up. 'You'd like to do this? It's very different from sports reporting.'

'That's why. I'd be outside, busy. The new beginning you keep banging on about.'

Iain bit his tongue. Bryan was right. It would get him out of the house. Mia would be starting school soon, too. It would leave Iain alone to… What would he do? It had been easy to make the decision to take early retirement, to move here. But he hadn't thought any further ahead.

'Can we go to the beach?' Mia appeared, carrying the bucket and spade they'd bought a few days earlier.

Iain glanced at his son.

'You go, Dad. I'm going to ring this place.' He sounded energised for the first time in months, so Iain agreed.

There were only a few people on the beach, a couple with two boys who were engaged in building a sandcastle and a woman with a dog who smiled and said, 'Hello'. Iain and Mia made their way along the sand till they came to what Mia determined was an appropriate spot. Iain took a seat in the shade and, making sure Mia was wearing her hat and slathered in sunscreen, settled down to watch her and reflect on Bryan's new lease of life.

He had been sitting there for half an hour when the woman and dog reappeared. This time, the dog ran over towards Mia who dropped her spade and put out a hand to the animal. Iain rose, ready to rescue her if the dog proved a problem.

'He won't hurt her,' the woman said. 'I'm Libby, and that's Milo.' She pointed to the dog. 'I haven't seen you here before. Are you visiting?'

'Iain Grant,' Iain said. 'I'm renting one of the houses up there for a few months, while I look around for something to buy. It's a lovely spot.'

'It is a lovely spot. That's where I live. Your granddaughter?' she asked, nodding to where Mia and the dog were making friends, both running around in circles. Mia was laughing in delight.

'Mia.' Iain nodded.

'My granddaughter is about the same age. Clancy turned five earlier this year.'

'Mia's six.'

'So she'll be going to school after the holidays? Clancy started at the beginning of the year. Bellbird Primary is a good school. The teachers are very caring. Your granddaughter will be happy there.'

'I hope so.' Iain was reminded he still had to enrol Mia and equip her with her new uniform. Bryan had left it all up to him. Maybe that would change now he was looking at finding work, but if he was successful, he wouldn't have time to run around organising Mia.

'Nice to meet you. You and your family must come round for a drink with Adam and me sometime, and we can arrange for Mia to meet Clancy, too.'

'Thanks. That's very kind of you.'

'Milo!' Libby called. The dog responded immediately, and they set off along the beach.

'Who was that lady?' Mia asked.

'Her name is Libby and she's one of our new neighbours. Her dog is called Milo.' Iain watched as the pair reached the steps leading up to the boardwalk and disappeared from view

'I like Milo.'

'She also has a granddaughter only a little younger than you called Clancy,' Iain said, still somewhat bemused by the encounter. It had taken him some time to meet and make friends with his neighbours in Sydney. 'She says you'll like the local school. We'll drop by this afternoon to get you enrolled and see about a uniform.'

'Will Daddy come, too?'

'Hopefully. Now we should be getting back for lunch.'

On the way back, Mia scampered along beside Iain, chattering about her new school and wondering what colour her uniform would be. 'I didn't like my old one. It was red,' she said in disgust. 'Maybe this one will be blue… or even green.' These were her favourite colours at the moment. They were subject to change depending on her favourite television characters.

'Daddy!' Mia burst into the house while Iain was still in the doorway, 'I met a dog called Milo.'

Iain walked into the kitchen to see Bryan with a faint smile on his face. It wasn't his usual broad grin but was a start. He raised an eyebrow.

'I called, Dad. Spoke to a woman called Bev who owns the centre. I'm meeting with her this afternoon at two. She sounded nice.'

'Well done, Bryan.' Iain clapped his son on the shoulder. 'I promised to take Mia to school this afternoon to get her organised. We can wait till you're available…'

'No, Dad. Go ahead. I don't know how this will pan out but if I get the job, I'll be tied up.'

Adam sighed as he saw Mia's lower lip tremble. He knew she had been hoping her dad would accompany them, would take an interest in her new school. Before Nadia died, Bryan had been an active member of the parent group at her previous school, an ardent supporter and fundraiser. 'Daddy's busy this afternoon, sweetie,' he said, 'and school starts on Monday. Maybe we can find somewhere to have an ice cream afterwards?'

At the promise of an ice cream, Mia's face brightened. 'You can see me in my new uniform when we get home, Daddy,' she said.

'Okay, peanut.'

Iain glanced at his son quickly. Bryan appeared unaware of what had happened. This was the first time he'd called Mia by the pet name he and Nadia had for her since his wife died. It was a good sign, a sign this move may have been the right one after all.

Seven

'You look happy.' Cleo placed two bowls of pumpkin soup and a platter of sourdough bread on the table and took a seat opposite Bev. 'A good morning?'

'An ordinary sort of morning, but I had a reply to my ad for help. I was doubtful of being able to get anyone at this time of year, and Andrea will be going on leave soon. It's a guy who's new to the coast. Doesn't have any experience with plants but seems keen enough. He's coming in this afternoon.'

'Was he the only applicant?' Cleo broke off a piece of bread.

'Sadly, yes. But I only need one good one, and it would be helpful to have another male in the place to share the heavy lifting and…'

'And to climb ladders,' Cleo finished for her.

'That, too,' Bev said, remembering the accident she'd had a couple of years earlier. But it had helped bring Ailsa and Martin together, so there had been a bright side to it.

'Anything more about the wedding plans?'

'Not yet. But that reminds me. I should contact the council to find what they need from me. I checked their website, but it only refers to fees and approvals for weddings on the beach or in other beauty spots. I don't think we quite fit into either of those categories. I'll do it before this guy arrives.'

Lunch over, Bev rose to leave. 'Another delicious meal, Cleo,' she said. 'Did I detect a hint of citrus?'

'Orange zest and juice. I always think it adds to the pumpkin. Good luck with the interview.'

'Thanks.'

*

Unable to contact the council by phone, Bev emailed her query. She was closing her computer when she looked up, and the breath seemed to leave her body. The young man standing awkwardly in the doorway whisked her back over thirty-five years. It could have been Phil standing there. She shook her head and blinked to dismiss the image, but he was still there. It was as if her old boyfriend had suddenly returned from the dead, his chestnut hair had the same wayward curl, his eyes the same deep blue, his…

'Are you all right? You look as if you've seen a ghost.' The apparition spoke, and the young man's voice was completely different to Phil's.

What had she been thinking? Of course it wasn't a reincarnation of Phil, her first and only love.

'Bryan Grant,' he said. 'We spoke on the phone. You asked me to come in for an interview.'

'Of course. Just give me a minute.' Bev retreated to the office behind the counter. She closed the door behind her and, standing against it, took a deep breath. The man did resemble Phil, but he'd been on her mind lately. She'd been thinking about him after Ailsa's wedding announcement, followed by Ruby's strange words. She took another deep breath and walked back out.

'Sorry about that. You took me by surprise. You look very like someone I used to know. Come through to the office and we can have a chat. Then I'll show you around the garden centre. We have a café here too.'

'Thanks.' The young man – Bryan – seemed unfazed by Bev's explanation and followed her into the small office.

Bev's stomach was still churning, but she smiled at the young man. 'Take a seat. Would you like tea, coffee, water?'

'Water, thanks.'

Bev went to the water cooler and filled two cardboard cups. She needed some herself. She took a gulp before handing a cup to the young man.

'Thanks.' He took a sip, before placing the cup on the low table beside him.

Bev could see he was nervous, so set about putting him at his ease by asking him what brought him to Bellbird Bay.

His face blanched and a drop of moisture formed in the corner of his eye. 'My... my wife died,' he said, staring down at his clenched hands.

'Oh, I'm so sorry.' Bev's stomach lurched. She gave him a few moments to compose himself, then tried again. 'Perhaps you could tell me what you've been doing till now?'

'Of course. I was a sports reporter with a Sydney daily paper covering local and regional fixtures. After...' he swallowed, '...I couldn't continue. Dad suggested we move up here for a fresh start.' He snorted. 'Sorry. This may have been a mistake. I don't think...' He started to rise.

Suddenly, Bev was filled with sympathy for him. He was so young to have suffered such a loss – though, she thought, he was older than she had been when Phil was taken from her.

'No, don't go,' she said. 'Let me tell you about the position.'

While Bryan attempted to regain his composure, Bev described the various parts of the job, finishing with, 'Can you see yourself doing that? It's very different from what you've been used to.'

'It's what I need... something completely different. Sorry I fell apart like that. I promise I won't do it again. I wasn't expecting to have to tell you... Dad and I came up here – with my daughter – because we used to come to Bellbird Bay for holidays when I was small. He remembered it as being a place where we'd been happy, saw it as some sort of refuge, I think.' He attempted a smile which didn't quite reach his eyes, but Bev could see how handsome he'd look when he was in a better frame of mind.

Did she want to employ someone who was clearly grieving and suffering from depression? But there was something about Bryan Grant that tugged at her heartstrings. Bev wasn't sure whether it was his likeness to Phil, or the similarity of their stories – though *his* child was alive – but she was tempted to give him a chance.

'Let me show you around,' she said, getting up.

She took him on a tour of the centre, pleasantly surprised by the interest he showed and his intelligent questions. By the time they reached the entrance to the café, she had almost made up her mind to employ him. 'This is our café, *The Pandanus Café*,' she said, gesturing to the archway. 'Would you like a coffee?'

'Oh, there's no need…'

But Bev could see him gaze longingly at the small tables which, at this time in the afternoon, were beginning to empty. 'I often have one at this time,' she lied. 'Please join me.'

As soon as they were seated, Cleo appeared with a cappuccino for Bev. 'What would you like?' she asked Bryan, after Bev introduced him saying, 'This is Bryan who may be joining us in the garden centre.'

'Black, thanks.' He shuffled his feet awkwardly.

Bev wondered if he had always been so awkward but, given his background as a sports journalist when he'd have had to confront all types of sportsmen and women, she doubted it. Grief did strange things to people. If she hadn't been able to retreat to Bellbird Bay, hadn't been forced into caring for her elderly parents, she dreaded to think what *she* might have been like.

'How old is your daughter?' she asked, once Cleo disappeared into the kitchen again.

'Mia's six.' His face brightened slightly, showing Bev how he could look when not weighed down with grief.

She felt a pang. He could have been her son. If only… She took a drink of coffee. 'She'll be going to school then.'

'My dad's enrolling her this afternoon. I… I should have taken her.' He drew a hand across the top of his head and gazed around as if he wasn't sure where he was, or why he was here. Finally, his eyes met Bev's. 'She reminds me too much of her mother…' His voice broke. 'It's difficult.'

Bev's heart went out to him. She knew what it was like to lose a loved one. If her son had lived, if he had resembled his father, would she have felt this way each time she looked at him?

Cleo returned with Bryan's coffee and gave Bev a slight, almost imperceptible, nod before disappearing again. She clearly approved.

Bev nodded to herself. Her mind was made up. 'I'd like to offer you the job,' she said with a smile. 'The work's not easy, but it can be very rewarding. And it will keep your mind occupied. It seems to me that's what you want. This place has saved me many times when I thought I couldn't go on.' It was Bev's turn to gaze around the area, surprised at herself. She had never revealed this to anyone else, but it was true. Without the garden centre, she'd have been lost. At first, it was her way of keeping busy when first her father, then her mother followed Phil and her son. Then it became a habit, a lifesaver. Now it was her life.

'Thanks, thanks so much.' Bryan reached out to shake Bev's hand. 'You won't be sorry. I won't let you down. When would you like me to start?'

Bev was about to say, "Monday" when she remembered his daughter. 'Tuesday would work for me. It will allow you to take your daughter to school on her first day. I'll team you with Andrea to start with. She's the one you'll be replacing and will show you the ropes. But I would like you to take on some of the heavier work she hasn't been able to manage. Dean or I can show you that part. I look forward to working with you, Bryan. If you let me have your email address, I'll send you an employment contract. Then, if all looks good to you, I'll see you on Tuesday. We start early. I'll expect you here at half-seven. Okay with you?'

'Very okay.' Bryan jotted his email address on a napkin and stood up, seeming to stand taller than he had before.

As he strode off, Cleo reappeared from the kitchen and stared after him. 'Good decision,' she said. 'I'm assuming you offered him the job. He has the look of a man with a weight on his shoulders. You may often sound brusque, Bev, but you have a kind heart. *The Pandanus Café* proved a blessing to me when Hannah and I arrived in town weighed down with grief. I recognise the signs. What's *his* story?'

'His wife died... and he has a young daughter.'

'Poor guy. Is he on his own with her?'

'He mentioned his father.'

'So he has some support. That's good.'

'Mmm. I guess so. Maybe I'm getting soft in my old age.' Bev chuckled. But she knew part of her reason for employing Bryan Grant wasn't because she felt sorry for him – though that did play a part.

He looked so much like Phil, she couldn't have turned him down no matter what his circumstances were. She just hoped she wouldn't come to regret her decision.

Eight

Iain and Mia's visit to Bellbird Bay Primary School went without a hitch. The infant mistress, Mrs Pardon, was welcoming and showed the pair around the school before taking them to what would be Mia's classroom and introducing her to her class teacher. Miss Hodge was a young woman in her early twenties. She was wearing a pair of jeans with a bright, flowered top and her dark hair was tied back in a high ponytail. Mia immediately warmed to her.

'She's much nicer than Mrs Black at my other school,' she told Iain when they left, 'And the play equipment here is much better. I'm going to like it here. But I miss my friends, I wish Bella was here.'

'I'm sure you'll soon make new friends,' Iain said, relieved it had gone so well.

Next, they went to the uniform shop where a delighted Mia discovered her new uniform was a blue and green checked dress – her current favourite colours.

'Wait till I show Daddy this,' she said with a grin. Then her lip drooped. 'Do you think he'll be pleased, Grandad?'

'I'm sure he will,' Iain said, but he knew as well as Mia that it had been a long time since Bryan had expressed pleasure about anything.

'Can we have ice cream now?' Mia asked, when they were back in the car.

'I guess so,' Iain laughed. Trust Mia to be more interested in an ice cream than her father's moods.

They parked close to the esplanade and headed to *Bay Gelato* which promised to serve *hand crafted Gelato made with milk from a local Jersey herd*. Iain hadn't been aware of any local farms but was happy to patronise the café, and Mia was pulling him towards the glass-topped counter where a wide variety of flavours of ice cream were on display.

He was glad to see they also offered coffee and they were soon seated at one of the outdoor tables, Mia with a large cone of cookies and cream ice cream and Iain with a mug of black coffee.

They had been there for a short time, though long enough for Mia's face to become covered in ice cream, when she let out a yell, 'Look, Grandad, it's the dog we met on the beach. It's Milo.'

Iain looked in the direction she was pointing to see the ungainly dog she'd been playing with on the beach. But today, he wasn't with the woman who'd introduced herself as Libby. Today he was with a man who looked vaguely familiar.

Clearly recognising Mia, the dog pulled on his lead forcing his owner to make his way over to where Iain and Mia were seated.

'Milo appears to know you,' the man said, chuckling. 'I'm Adam.'

'Iain… and Mia,' Iain replied. 'We met Milo on the beach the other day. He was with Libby… your wife?'

'Partner. You must be the people who're renting on the boardwalk. Libby mentioned meeting you.' He offered his hand.

'Don't I know you?' Iain asked as he shook Adam's hand. Then he took a closer look. 'Adam… You're Adam Holland, aren't you? I love your books.'

Adam appeared embarrassed. 'Thanks.'

'Sorry. I guess you get a lot of that. I didn't know you lived in Bellbird Bay. Sorry, that's a pretty stupid comment, too. Excuse my bad manners. Can I buy you a coffee?' Iain was embarrassed and wanted to make amends. The woman – Libby – had been friendly and welcoming, and he had, if not been downright rude, embarrassed this man who was one of his favourite authors.

'I do get it a lot,' Adam said, 'and thanks to the coffee.' He took a seat, and Milo settled at his feet, after sniffing at Mia's, making her giggle with pleasure.

When he'd been served a mug of coffee, Adam said, 'To answer your question, I came here from Canberra before last Christmas to fulfil a promise to an old mate. I liked the place. I met Libby. And the rest's history as they say. I even got to like this creature,' he said with a chuckle, nudging the dog gently with his foot. 'You? There's obviously a story there, too. Are you on your own with your granddaughter, is your wife with you, family?'

Iain sighed. He didn't want to go into the whole sad story. But this was Adam Holland. He'd read all his books, and his political opinion pieces before that. He felt he knew the man. And Adam deserved an honest response. 'No wife. We split long ago. I'm here with Mia and her dad. Bryan lost his wife in a car accident, and I thought he – we – needed to get away from Sydney and all its memories. I took early retirement. I was an architect. Coming here is an attempt to make a fresh start.' Iain stopped, wondering if he'd said too much. Once he started, the words just seemed to roll off his tongue.

'I'm sorry about your daughter-in-law,' Adam said, his voice sombre. 'It was a death that brought me here, too. It's a good place to find refuge.'

The pair were silent for a few moments, until Mia said, 'I'm finished now, Grandad. When are we going home? I want to show Daddy my new uniform.'

'Sorry, am I holding you up?' Adam asked.

'Not at all. Mia's dad is at a job interview this afternoon. He may not be home yet, Mia. He's applied for a job in a local garden centre,' he said to Adam.

The Pandanus Garden Centre?'

'That's the one. You know it?'

'Everyone around here knows it and its owner. From what I've heard, Bev Cooper built up the place from scratch. It's quite something. There's a café, too. It's worth a visit, even if your son doesn't get a job there.'

'Thanks. I'll keep it in mind.' Though Iain couldn't imagine why he'd need to visit a garden centre, at least not till he'd bought a place of his own.

'Good to meet you,' Adam said as they got up to leave. 'Libby did mention meeting you and your granddaughter and having you around for a drink sometime. What are you doing for lunch on Sunday? Libby's daughter, her partner and her daughter are coming for a barbecue. Clancy's around your granddaughter's age and I guess Emma and Nick are close to your son's. What do you say?'

'Oh, I don't know.' Iain hesitated. It was kind of Adam. He remembered Libby's invitation, too. How would Bryan feel about meeting new people? But it was exactly what he needed. And it would be good for Mia to make a little friend, too. 'Well, if you're sure,' he said.

'I'm sure. Give me your number. I'll get Libby to call you to confirm.'

'Thanks.' Iain reached into his wallet and took out a card, one of his old business cards he still hadn't discarded. 'The mobile's still okay,' he said.

'Connor Grant Architects and Urban Planners,' Adam said, reading the card. 'I've heard of you. Didn't you win some award a few years ago?'

Iain knew exactly how Adam had felt when he told him he recognised him. 'We did.' Iain shrugged. 'It was in another lifetime.'

'Hmm. Well, expect a call from Libby and I look forward to seeing you all on Sunday.'

'Thanks again.' Iain and Mia made their way to Iain's car, and Adam and Milo set off in the direction of the boardwalk.

*

When Iain and Mia arrived home, Bryan was already there with the hint of a smile on his face.

'Hi, Daddy,' Mia called, rushing up to give Bryan a hug. 'We went to my new school, and I like my new teacher, and there's a big playground, and I love my uniform. Where is it, Grandad?'

'Here you are.' Iain handed Mia the parcel containing the two uniform dresses.

'Try to guess what colour they are, Daddy,' Mia said, then, before waiting for a reply, she dashed off to the bedroom.

'How did the interview go?' Iain asked Bryan when they were alone. 'From your expression it went well.'

'Yeah. The garden centre is much bigger than I expected, and Bev seems like she'd be a good person to work for. There's a café, too. We had coffee there.'

'And the job?'

'Yeah. I start on Tuesday.' He paused, looked down at his feet, then up to meet Iain's eyes. 'I can take Mia to school on Monday.'

'Sounds good. You think you'll like it? It's very different…'

'You said that already, Dad. I need different. It'll be outdoors. I think I'll like it. And I won't have to deal with people.'

Iain said nothing. He hadn't realised it was the people part of his former job which Bryan wanted to get away from.

At that moment, a flash of blue and green entered the room, and Mia twirled around between Iain and Bryan.

'Look, Daddy. Did you guess?'

'Looking good, princess.'

'Looks great, sweetheart,' Iain said.

'I'll wear this one on Monday,' she said. 'Will you take me to school, Daddy? I want to show you the playground and my classroom.' She wrapped her arms around Bryan and looked up into his face pleadingly.

'Of course I will, peanut. I wouldn't miss it.'

Mia grinned and disappeared again.

'I'm going to try harder, Dad. You've been good since…' He still couldn't bring himself to say Nadia's name. 'It was a good plan to come here, to give us all a fresh start. I know what it must have cost you to leave the practice, to leave the Middle Harbour house. I'm grateful. I really am. Although it may not always seem like it. It's been difficult for me.'

'I know, son. I'm your dad. That's what dads are for.'

'Mum…' Bryan began.

'Your mum has made her own life.' Iain couldn't keep the bitterness out of his voice. Since their divorce some twenty years earlier, just when the teenage Bryan needed her most, Roslyn Grant had decided marriage and a teenage son weren't for her. She'd flown off to the UK without a backward glance and had rarely been in touch since. It was only due to his solicitor and friend, Bob Roper, that he knew she had remarried – twice now – and was currently living in the south of France.

'She didn't even get in touch after the accident.'

'That's your mum.'

Roslyn hadn't always been like that. When they met, both in their early twenties, Iain had been dazzled by the vivacious redhead he met at a friend's party. She was studying art at East Sydney Tech and living in what was little more than a squat in the inner city.

They'd hit it off straight away, spending every spare minute together and, when they both graduated and found employment, they married and moved into a tiny flat in Glebe where they stayed until Bryan came along.

Iain could never pinpoint exactly when things began to go bad, when the distance between them grew until, one day, Roslyn decided she'd had enough. By that time, he had a successful architectural practice and they were living in what Iain considered to be their dream home overlooking Middle Harbour. Bryan was showing the usual teenage angst, but Iain had thought they were a happy family.

'Doesn't she even care?' Bryan's voice broke into Iain's thoughts.

'I'm sure she loves you.'

'She has a strange way of showing it. The odd present for me and Mia at Christmas and birthdays – if she remembers,' Bryan said bitterly. 'Does she know we've moved?'

'I asked Bob to advise her of our new arrangement.' Iain had only had occasional personal contact with his ex since she left, leaving most communication to be conducted through his solicitor. At first, it had been his way of coping with her loss. Then it seemed impossible to change the process, even if he wanted to, and he wasn't sure he did. The Roslyn who flitted around the world, moving from one man to the next as the fancy took her, wasn't the Roslyn he married. He preferred to remember her as she was, the good years they had together before she decided life with him was stifling her. The sporadic exchanges, sent from various spots around the world only served to remind him of how much she'd changed from the woman he fell in love with.

'Hmm.' Bryan sighed.

Iain sighed, too. He wished he could wave a magic wand and make everything right for his son, but all he could do was be here when Bryan needed him.

Nine

Had she done the right thing? The question plagued Bev all that night and into the next day, surfacing from time to time in odd moments. *Had she only offered the position to Bryan Grant because he looked like Phil? How would she cope with seeing him every day? Would it bring back pleasant memories or be like turning a knife in a wound which had never healed?* By the time she reached home on Saturday evening she was a quivering mess.

Wishing she hadn't promised to meet Ailsa and Martin at the surf club for dinner, Bev almost called to cancel. But she knew her best friend too well. Ailsa would want to know why, which might lead to Bev revealing the secret she'd kept hidden for years. Better to go, eat dinner and leave as soon as she could, pleading an early start on Sunday – not exactly a lie, but the garden centre didn't open any earlier than usual on a Sunday, though it did tend to be their busiest day. She'd much rather stay home and take care of the paperwork she'd received from the council regarding permission to hold the wedding in the centre.

Knowing she'd feel better after a shower, Bev headed to the ensuite, shedding her clothes in the bedroom and standing under the spray until it ran cold.

Half an hour later, dressed in a pair of black pants teamed with a white sweater which she realised was not dissimilar from the uniform she donned every morning, she pulled on her favourite blue jacket, grabbed her bag and headed out.

When she entered the surf club, the familiar atmosphere swirled around her, reminding her of all the evenings she'd spent here in her teenage years. Although the club had been renovated since then, not a lot had changed. There was still the horseshoe bar dividing the restaurant from the sports bar, the outdoor deck stretching all the way along one side and the sound of the poker machines almost drowning out the music.

Being Saturday night, the place was busy, the chatter of multiple conversations almost deafening. Bev stood at the top of the stairs and gazed around. She was trying to see where Ailsa and Martin were seated when a voice in her ear startled her.

'We're on the deck.'

'Will! I didn't know you were coming. Is Cleo here, too?'

'Of course. We can't discuss the wedding without the provider of food,' Will Rankin said. The veteran surfer, now surf instructor who was Martin's oldest friend, soon to be best man at the wedding, was casually attired as usual in a pair of jeans and a long-sleeved tee shirt with the logo of his surf school emblazoned on it. His long blond hair was tied back in an untidy bun.

Bev had known Will most of her life. He was like a second brother to her. He hadn't had an easy life, losing his wife and oldest son in the same year, but the former surfing champion had buckled down to raise his younger son to follow in his footsteps, was a keen supporter of local charities and a respected member of the community.

'I'm fetching beer for the guys and wine for the women. What will you have?'

'Wine for me, too, Will, thanks. White.'

'No problem.'

Bev weaved her way through the crush to the door which led out to the deck. Once there, she spied Ailsa and Martin sitting with Cleo at a table in the far corner under a free-standing heater. They were accompanied by three younger people, Bev recognised as Ailsa's son, Nate, Will's son, Owen, and Cleo's daughter, Hannah.

'Hi Bev, good to see you.' Ailsa rose to give Bev a hug. Martin and Cleo did the same.

'Hi, Auntie Bev,' Nate said with a wide grin, while Owen and Hannah smiled hello.

'Quite a party,' Bev said, as she slipped into the vacant seat next to Ailsa. 'You didn't say.'

'Sorry. It was only going to be Martin and me, then we thought if we were going to talk about the wedding, Will should be here with Cleo, then Nate… and somehow his whole household came too.'

Bev knew Nate shared a house with Owen and Hannah, so that explained things to some extent.

'We're going on to a party later, Auntie Bev,' Nate said, seeming to sense her confusion.

'Right.'

Will appeared with a tray of drinks and after a few sips of chardonnay, Bev began to relax. What wasn't to enjoy? She was here with her favourite people. They were her family, the only family she had, the only family she wanted.

'I ordered pizza,' Will said, taking his seat between Martin and Cleo. 'Hope it's okay with everyone. Saves us agonising over the menu.'

They all nodded and laughed. They knew the menu off by heart. It never changed. But Will was right about one thing. It would be easier to talk about wedding plans over slices of pizza, and the club pizzas were mouth-wateringly good.

'So…' Ailsa asked, '…where are we up to, Bev? Have you heard back from the council? Can we do it?'

'The short answer is yes. At least, we can seek permission. As I think I said, I've had the possibility of holding weddings at the centre in mind for some time. There are two steps. First there is your wedding – I know that's all you are bothered about. But I'm thinking longer term, too. I can do it in two bits. For your wedding, I can complete an application for a temporary event on private land. I think it should be fairly straightforward.'

'Oh, I hope so.' Ailsa gave Martin a loving glance and squeezed his hand.

'I can do it in the next couple of days. They need at least six weeks' notice, so we should be right there, too. We already have all the requirements re insurance and toilets.'

Ailsa beamed.

'What about the other?' Cleo asked.

'That's going to be more complicated. Though I don't see it should present a major problem either. I'll need to apply for a change of purpose license. I still have to go through all the requirements.'

'And the awning you mentioned?' Cleo asked.

'I still have to do the research on that, too. But I do plan to have it in place before your wedding.' She smiled at Ailsa and Martin. 'Nothing is going to spoil your big day.'

'Is there anything I can do to help?' Will asked.

'Or us, Auntie Bev?' Nate asked, nudging Owen.

'Not at this stage, thanks. But we'll no doubt need help with chairs and things on the day.'

'You can count on us,' Owen said.

Bev looked around the group, thinking how lucky she was to have such good friends.

When the pizzas were finished, the younger members of the group drifted off, and Martin and Will disappeared inside the club on the pretext of ordering more beers, leaving the three women alone.

'More beers indeed,' Ailsa said. 'I can see them from here. They're watching the footy on the big screen in the sports bar. Once Martin and Will get together…' she shook her head in mock annoyance.

Cleo laughed. 'You're lucky you don't have to put up with that,' Cleo said to Bev with a grin which faded when she saw the expression on Bev's face. 'Sorry, I didn't mean…'

'It's okay.' Bev stifled the impulse to share her disappointment and grief. She'd managed to suppress it for thirty-five years, why did it start recurring now? But she knew the reason… and maybe it was time to share her secret with her friends, maybe in sharing she'd be able to finally put the past to rest.

Ten

'Do I need to go? Mia would be fine with you.' Bryan gave a yawn and drained his coffee. 'I don't know these people.'

'I don't really know them either, but one of the reasons we came here is to make new friends. Both Libby and Adam seem like nice people, and I feel I know Adam from his books. It's kind of them to invite us to their home, to meet their family, thoughtful, too. Libby's daughter and her partner are close to your age, and her granddaughter is only a little younger than Mia. If we're going to live here, we need to become part of the community, and that means making friends with our neighbours.'

'Yeah, yeah. I've heard it all before, Dad, but I'm not ready to…'

Iain lost patience. Up till now, he'd given Bryan the benefit of the doubt, allowed him breathing space to handle his grief. But it was time he joined the human race again. Getting the job in the garden centre was the first step, taking Mia to school was another. Surely it wasn't expecting too much for him to agree to going to a barbecue? 'Nadia wouldn't want you to become a hermit,' he said.

Bryan flinched at the sound of Nadia's name, but Iain's words hit the mark.

'You're right, Dad,' he said, after a long pause. 'She'd tell me to get a life. I'll come with you.'

'Thanks, son.' Iain pulled Bryan into a warm hug. 'I know I'm pushing you, but it's for your own sake – and Mia's.'

'I know, Dad. I'll get dressed.'

*

Mia ran ahead, as Iain and Bryan made their way down the boardwalk, but she fell back, suddenly shy, when they reached Libby and Adam's gate.

There was already a group of people standing around on the deck, and a small girl was weaving in and out between the grownups' legs.

'Welcome,' Libby said, when she caught sight of them standing there. 'Come in.' She walked towards them, a glass in one hand, and opened the gate. 'You must be Bryan,' she said. 'Thanks for coming.' She ushered them in and introduced Bryan to Adam, then both Iain and Bryan to her daughter, Emma, and her partner, Nick. 'And this is Clancy,' she said, taking the hand of the little girl who was now standing by her side gazing at Mia. 'Mia will be going to your school, Clancy.'

The two girls stared at each other, then Clancy held out her hand to Mia who, after a wary glance at Iain and Bryan, allowed herself to be led away and into the house.

'They'll be fine inside till we're ready to eat,' Libby said. 'I have a basket of toys and a pile of books I keep here for Clancy. My guess is we won't hear a peep out of them. Milo is in there, too. He'll make sure they don't get up to mischief. Now what will you have to drink?'

Bryan seemed mystified by this barrage of words, but Iain said, 'A beer would be good, thanks. Bryan?'

'Yeah, thanks.'

Once drinks had been served, Iain found himself talking to Libby and Adam, while Emma and Nick made an effort to make Bryan feel welcome. When he saw his son participating in the conversation, Iain felt himself beginning to relax.

'It's not easy, is it?' Libby asked. 'We never stop worrying about them. I found that with Emma when her marriage broke up. Of course, I'm not suggesting there is any comparison with your son's loss…' Her voice trailed off.

'What Libby is trying to say is she understands your concern,' Adam put in, throwing an arm around Libby's shoulder.

She looked up at him with a smile. 'And I know what it's like to lose a loved one,' she said, her eyes going to the viewing platform on the other side of the boardwalk.

Iain's eyes followed hers, unsure what he was looking at.

'The bench over on the viewing platform is Libby's memorial to her husband. It's how we met.'

'Maybe it would help your son to have something similar, somewhere he could go to talk to her,' Libby suggested.

'Maybe.' Bur Iain felt uncomfortable. What sort of memorial could Bryan have here in Bellbird Bay – a place Nadia had never visited? *Had he been wrong to insist they move here, move away from all the memories? Would it have been better for Bryan to have stayed in Sydney?* But as soon as the thought crossed his mind, Iain dismissed it. No, in Sydney Bryan had trouble getting out of bed. In Bellbird Bay, he had already found himself a job and was here, at a barbecue and… Iain glanced across to where his son was engrossed in conversation with Nick and Emma, …was acting like a normal human being.

'You're renting up the boardwalk?' Adam asked.

'Yes, the blue and white house. It's very comfortable and a great spot.' He wondered why Adam grinned.

'Grace Winter's place. I stayed there for a bit when I arrived in Bellbird Bay. Have you met Grace?'

'No, I made all the arrangements through the realter. She's a friend of yours?'

'She is now, her and her partner, Ted. You'll meet them before long. Bellbird Bay is a small place, and those of us who live on the boardwalk tend to know each other. Libby and Grace work together at the library.'

'Ted?'

'He's a retired solicitor and local surfing hero. You'll see him portrayed on the mural at the surf club.'

'We haven't been there yet.'

'Oh, you must visit it,' Libby said. 'It's quite an institution here. The food's good and the view is superb.'

The conversation continued for some time then, at an almost imperceptible sign from Libby, she and Emma disappeared inside, and Iain gravitated towards the barbecue where Adam and Nick proceeded to load steaks and sausages onto the grill.

'Anything I can do?' he asked.

'I think we have it covered,' Adam replied. 'Just enjoy your beer.'

As he watched the meat being cooked, Iain learned Nick owned a boat building business along the coast and Emma had only recently moved in with him.

'I suggested Bryan and his daughter might like to come out sailing with us one weekend,' he said.

'What did he say?'

'He seemed keen, said he'd done a bit of sailing in Sydney.'

Iain let out the breath he'd been holding. In days gone by, before Nadia's death, the pair of them had been keen sailors, members of Middle Harbour Yacht Club. Bryan had been part of the crew touted to win the Sydney Short Ocean Racing Championship. But Nadia's death had put paid to his sailing along with everything else in Bryan's life. His agreeing to go sailing with Nick was a huge step forward.

No more was said about sailing right then, and they were joined by Emma and her mother who carried out plates and salads. Then Mia and Clancy came bounding out with Milo, and everything seemed to become chaotic.

On their walk home, Mia never stopped chattering about her new friend, Clancy, and the wonders of her new school. 'And,' she said, her voice rising with excitement, 'Clancy's going to join Nippers. They meet on the beach every Sunday morning in summer and do all sorts of fun things and wear pink uniforms. Can I join, too, Daddy?'

Bryan looked at Iain, a question in his eyes.

'I think that's a good idea, don't you, Bryan?' He remembered reading about Nippers in the local paper. There was some sort of information session coming up at the surf club. He supposed it was time he joined the club. Nippers were an Australian beach institution, the young lifesavers focussing on fun and surf awareness, learning about dangers such as rocks, animals, and surf conditions. He had fond memories of his own days as a nipper, growing up on Sydney's Northern Beaches. It would be wonderful for Mia.

'If you think so.' Bryan seemed about to withdraw into his silent mood again. But, when they arrived at the house, he surprised Iain by saying, 'Thanks, Dad. I'm glad you made me go. I liked Nick and Emma. It was good to meet people who didn't know… I think coming here was a good decision. Mia seems happy with it, too.'

'Thanks, Bryan.' Iain hugged his son, glad to have done something to please him. He knew it would take time, but it seemed Bryan was on the road to recovery.

Eleven

Done! Bev stretched her arms above her head and sighed, pleased to have finally finished the council form. She knew this was only the start, but at least it should cover Ailsa and Martin's wedding. She would worry about the others another time.

Now she deserved a glass of something stronger. She'd been drinking peppermint tea since she got home from the garden centre what seemed like hours ago. But when she checked the time, she realised it had been less than one hour since she'd sat down at the computer, determined to complete this.

It hadn't been easy. The parts about parking, toilet facilities, and bins had been fine. But when it came to noise and the music, she drew a blank and had to check with Ailsa to determine if she needed to provide a noise management plan – she did. Then there was the issue of serving alcohol. *The Pandanus Café* had never required a liquor license, but what was a wedding without alcohol for the toasts? So that meant the proper paperwork. It was all more complicated than she had anticipated. And, after stating she had an awning to cater for bad weather, she knew she had to arrange it sooner rather than later.

She was just taking her first sip from a glass of pinot noir when there was a knock at the door.

'Hi, Auntie Bev.' Nate and Hannah stood there grinning. 'Can we come in?'

Bev hugged the pair – Nate was like a son to her – then stood aside to let them enter, wondering why they were there. 'Is there anything wrong?' she asked, as they headed straight for the kitchen, even though their grins didn't indicate a problem.

'We want to help,' Hannah said, taking a seat while Nate leant against the benchtop. It was a familiar pose, one he'd often taken when he first came to Bellbird Bay.

'Help?' What did they mean?

'With the arrangements for the wedding,' Nate said. 'Han and I have been thinking and we came up with this idea.'

'Oh, yes. Wine?' Bev asked, picking up her glass and gesturing to the bottle on the benchtop.

'Thanks. Han?' Nate asked.

When Hannah nodded, he went to the cupboard for two glasses.

'Now…' Nate began, when all three were seated around the kitchen table, '…we've worked out a way we can take some of the load off your shoulders.'

Bev stifled a grin. He made it sound as if she was an old woman, but to these two twenty-somethings, perhaps she was. 'I'm listening,' she said.

'You'll want to serve alcohol at the wedding, and I can take responsibility for that – the ordering and serving. It's what I do,' he said, referring to his job behind the bar at the surf club. 'I can help with the application for a liquor license, too. And Han…' he turned to the girl who was gazing adoringly up at him.

Ailsa was right about these two, Bev thought.

'I've been researching party hire for an event we're hosting at school. I've made a good contact at a company which hires out chairs and sound equipment. I'm happy to take charge of that aspect,' Hannah said.

'That would be a big help.' Bev felt a sense of relief to have at least some of the preparations taken care of. Now she only had the awning and the second application to worry about. Only! It wasn't going to be easy. She hoped it would be worth it.

*

Next morning, Bev awoke with the feeling something was about to happen. It was only when she was standing in the shower that she remembered. Her new staff member was due to start today.

She had managed to put Bryan Grant and his likeness to Phil to the back of her mind all weekend. But she could no longer pretend. At half-seven, he'd be fronting up at the garden centre ready for work. But was *she* ready for *him*?

Dressed in her usual work outfit, Bev drank a cup of peppermint tea, but her stomach rebelled at the thought of food. Perhaps she'd get something at the café later. She often did this, so Cleo wouldn't be surprised.

The rising sun was creating a rosy glow in the sky when Bev drew into the Pandanus car park. As usual, she was first to arrive, though she didn't normally get here this early. Once in her office, curiosity got the better of her and she opened the computer to google Bryan Grant. What she found shocked her.

While Bryan had mentioned his wife's death and was clearly grieving, he hadn't said anything about how she died. Bev's hand went to her mouth. Her eyes widened in disbelief. The article she was reading described a car accident which was almost identical to the one in which Phil had lost his life. It was as if history was repeating itself, only this time it was the woman who died.

Bev quickly closed the computer. What was she thinking? There was nothing similar about the two deaths. Her memories were getting to her. It was as clear to Bev as if it had happened yesterday. She could visualise Phil, hurrying to meet her. The car which had swerved off the road. The loud thud as it hit him, tossing him into the air. He had no hope of survival. He was dead before he hit the ground. Even after all this time, she shivered at the memory.

Attempting to push all thought of Phil and the accident which took his life to the back of her mind, she turned her attention to the tasks which needed to be completed that day and was engrossed in them when there was a hesitant knock on her office door.

Looking up, she saw Bryan Grant. This morning he was dressed in a pair of well-pressed jeans with a long-sleeved grey tee-shirt. He looked wary, as if he'd like to run and hide.

'Good morning, Bryan. Welcome to Pandanus. Let me get you an apron. We all wear them.' She gestured to her own dark green one with the pandanus logo on the front. 'Come with me.'

She led him through to the shop, where other staff members were beginning to make a start to their day, gave him an apron and introduced him. There was a chorus of welcomes.

'You'll be working with Andrea today,' she said. 'She'll show you the ropes. Tomorrow, I'll team you with Dean who can explain the heavier work, then we'll set you up with your own roster of tasks. I hope you're going to like it here.'

'Thanks for the opportunity. I'll do my best.'

When she saw Bryan walk away with Andrea, Bev heaved a sigh of relief. Bryan was just another staff member. There was no need for her to spend time with him. But she knew she would. It was her habit to chat to all of her staff on a regular basis. They were part of the family she'd made for herself when her parents died, and her brother was on the other side of the world. They were what had kept her from falling into a depression.

What she needed was a strong mug of coffee. She headed to the café where Cleo was already set up for the day.

Ten minutes later, she and Cleo were seated at Bev's favourite table, Bev with a mug of macchiato and one of Cleo's delicious almond croissants. Cleo was drinking lemon and ginger tea.

'Thanks, Cleo. I needed this,' Bev said, as the first mouthful of caffeine hit her system. 'I feel better already.'

'And the day has barely begun.' Cleo smiled. 'Didn't your new guy start today?'

'Bryan. Yes. I've paired him with Andrea.'

'She'll see him right. Is something else bothering you?'

'It's personal.' Bev looked across the table at the concerned expression on Cleo's face and came to a decision. 'Bryan... he... he reminds me of someone... someone I used to know.'

'Oh!'

Bev knew she should give Cleo more information but saying what she already had almost choked her.

'Do you want to talk about it?'

'No. Yes. I don't know.'

'Anything you say to me will go no further.'

Bev realised Cleo might be the perfect person to share her secret with. Ailsa and Martin were too close. They'd want to know why she hadn't told them at the time. Ailsa would be annoyed she hadn't known about Phil, when they'd promised to share everything with each other. She couldn't bear to face her disappointment. 'Not now. Maybe after work?'

'I'll let Will know I'll be late home.'

'Thanks.' As her eyes met Cleo's, Bev knew she'd made the right decision. She couldn't keep this to herself any longer, and Cleo had lost a loved one, too. She might understand.

*

The garden centre and café were deserted by the time Bev returned to the café. Bryan had appeared at her office door again to tell her how much he'd enjoyed his first day, and Andrea had been full of praise for him.

'For someone who's never worked with plants before, he did pretty well,' she said. 'I think you made a good choice, Bev.'

Bev had made a noncommittal response, enough to satisfy Andrea who was currently more concerned with her coming baby than the garden centre these days. As it should be. Bev managed to suppress her own disappointment as she saw Andrea's baby bump grow larger as her pregnancy progressed. She was able to be the consummate professional here at work. It was only at home, when she was alone, that her memories sometimes returned to overwhelm her.

'Now,' Cleo said, placing two mugs of peppermint tea on the table along with a plate of Ruby Sullivan's delicious brownies.

Bev didn't know where to start. She took a sip of tea. 'It was all so long ago,' she began.

'Oh, Bev, I'm so sorry for what you've gone through.' Cleo said when Bev finished. 'And Bryan looks like him?'

'Exactly.' Bev took a bite from a brownie.

'So, let me get this straight. A guy walks into your office to apply for a job. He's the image of someone you were in love with over thirty years ago. He died, then you lost his baby. Why on earth did you give this guy a job?'

It was something Bev had been wondering about, too. Her only excuse was that he was the only applicant… or was it? She had felt sorry for him. But had his likeness to Phil encouraged her to offer him the job knowing she'd have to see him every day?

'I've been asking myself that,' Bev admitted. 'But it's done now. Thanks for listening. It's helped me to share.'

'You haven't told anyone till now?'

'I was too ashamed. I suppose I blamed myself. And my godmother didn't help. She told me to put it behind me. Then my father became sick, and I came back here to help care for him. Mother was becoming too frail to cope by herself.' Bev thought how her godmother, who had been so supportive during her pregnancy, had suddenly seemed to change, to become more distant. She hadn't seen the woman she called Aunt Bea since. They'd corresponded for a while, but Bea had aged rapidly and been in an aged care home for the past fifteen years. Perhaps she should have made more of an effort to keep in touch, but she'd taken the advice to put it behind her, and Bea was part of the time she wanted to forget. Until now.

Twelve

The house was so quiet Iain could hear the hum of the refrigerator. He looked around the empty kitchen. It was tidy now he had cleared away the breakfast dishes. The place seemed strange without Bryan's brooding presence and Mia's continual chatter. He wondered how Bryan was getting on at the garden centre. It was tempting to make a visit to check it out, but Iain knew Bryan would feel humiliated if he turned up unannounced, He could only hope all was well.

He didn't need to worry about Mia. She had come home yesterday, after her first day at Bellbird Bay Primary, full of excitement and with a list of all the new friends she'd made. The little girl had quickly adapted to her new surroundings and, although she still missed her mother, the move to Bellbird Bay had worked for her. When he dropped her off at school this morning, she had happily run off to join her new friends.

Now he was home again, and the day stretched emptily ahead of him. He checked his emails but there were only two, one from his solicitor confirming he'd followed Iain's instructions to put his house on the market. Iain breathed a sigh of relief. Now he was experiencing life in Bellbird Bay, he had no desire to ever return to Sydney. The other was from his former partner asking how he was settling into retirement. It was so different to what he was used to – arriving at the office to find emails galore, a full diary and a coffee provided by his personal assistant.

Well, he thought, at least he could have a coffee. After debating the alternatives of making one and drinking it by himself on the deck or going out, he decided to walk down to the café he'd seen on the esplanade. *The Bay Café* looked like a decent spot.

The café was almost empty when Iain arrived. He took a seat outside where he could enjoy the view of the ocean and watch the passers-by, ordered a macchiato with a slice of banana bread and began to relax. This was what he'd expected of Bellbird Bay – a small community, a slower pace of life.

Iain's coffee had arrived, and he was enjoying his first bite of banana bread when he was conscious of a shadow falling over him.

'Iain, mind if I join you?' Adam Holland asked.

'Of course not.' Iain was surprised to see the author here in the early morning. He didn't know much about how writers worked but thought Adam would have been busy writing.

'The coffee's good here,' Adam said taking a seat. 'I came here every morning for breakfast when I first arrived. Now I come for coffee when Libby's working. It sets me up for the day. What's your excuse?'

'I'm on my own. Bryan has started work at *The Pandanus Garden Centre* and Mia is in school. I feel at a bit of a loss. I'm not used to having nothing to do.' He grimaced.

'Must be difficult. But I expect you'll soon find things to occupy yourself. I've met a few guys like you who have come here to retire and found a new lease of life.'

'Hmm.' Iain couldn't imagine what he might find to occupy his time – other than house hunting – but appreciated Adam's encouraging words. 'What about you?' he asked. 'I really enjoyed your last Phil Hanlon thriller. Is there another one in the works?'

'Not exactly.' Adam chuckled. 'I'm writing a new series set in a coastal town not unlike Bellbird Bay. Book one in the series will be released later in the year. I'm hoping it'll find a market with my existing readers.'

'Sounds interesting. And did I read something about a television series?'

Adam looked embarrassed. 'Later in the year, too. But enough about me. How are you finding Bellbird Bay?'

'I like what I've seen of the town. A sleepy coastal town is what I wanted for Bryan, a refuge from the memories of what happened to his wife. I know it'll take time, but I feel he's making a start with this job.'

'He'll be right with Bev Cooper,' Adam said. 'She's lived here all her life and has an excellent reputation for being fair – if a bit blunt at times. Has he experience with plants?'

'No. He was a sports reporter in Sydney, but I think doing manual work, being in the open air, will help him. I hope so.'

'And your granddaughter?'

'She seems to be recovering more quickly. She loved meeting Clancy on Sunday and is settling into school better than I could have hoped for.'

'Good.'

Adam's coffee arrived and the conversation ceased as the pair drank their coffees.

'There are some good walks around, if you're so inclined,' Adam said when he had drained his mug. 'Then, of course, there's swimming and surfing. You said you intend to look around for something more permanent?'

'That's the plan.'

'It might be worth having a chat with Grace, your landlady. Now she and Ted are settled as a couple, she might be interested in selling. If you like where you are, that is. I found it ideal, and Libby and I love living on the boardwalk. It's so convenient.'

'That's a thought.' Iain hadn't considered that possibility. But he hadn't met his landlady and didn't feel he could front up to her home uninvited.

Seeing his concern, Adam laughed. 'I'd be willing to bet you'll bump into her sooner rather than later. Bellbird Bay is like that, and she and Ted live only a few doors away from you. They're a lovely couple. Ted is another guy who came here to retire. Now he paints in pastels, landscapes mostly. The local gallery has examples of his work. It's worth a visit.'

'Thanks.' Iain mentally added the art gallery to the places he should visit. He'd be interested to see some local artworks. In Sydney, he'd been a member of the Art Gallery of New South Wales for years, enjoying the benefits of free access to exhibitions. It was one of the things he'd miss.

When the pair parted, Adam to head back up the boardwalk, Iain decided to walk in the other direction. As he left the esplanade behind, he found himself on a concrete path, in which patterns of surfboards and fish were embedded. As he walked along, he came across several tables made from thick roughly hewn slabs of timber with matching benches providing perfect rest areas. He stopped at one to sit and enjoy the view.

It was a peaceful spot and pleasant in the warmth of the sun. He closed his eyes for a moment, only to be awakened by the shrill of his phone. Startled by the noise disrupting the peace, he checked the screen to see his ex-wife's number. What did Roslyn want? Iain hadn't heard from her for months, didn't even know where she was.

He pressed to accept the call. 'Ros?'

'Iain. Where are you – and where are Bryan and Mia? I arrived in Sydney to see them to discover the house deserted and a *For Sale* sign on the front lawn. I contacted your office to be told you'd left. Why didn't you tell me?' Ros's voice held the peevish tone he'd become accustomed to over the years, the tone of an unhappy woman.

Iain sighed. The fact Ros was back in Australia, back in Sydney, was a sure sign her current romance was on the skids. She'd be off again before long, but in the meantime would no doubt be a thorn in his side.

'I had to get Bryan away, Ros. He had sunk into a depression, wouldn't eat, wouldn't go anywhere. It was all I could do to force him to get up and shower. It wasn't good for Mia to see her dad like that.'

'So where are you and what are you doing?'

'I've retired.' Iain held the phone away from his ear at her cackle of laughter. 'We've moved north, to a small town where hopefully our son can start a new life; where we can *all* start a new life,' he said when Ros fell silent again.

'You're selling the house?'

Iain remembered when he'd designed their house overlooking the harbour. Those had been heady times in the early days of their marriage, a marriage Iain had thought would last for ever. Marriage and children were what he wanted out of life, that and his architectural practice. But Ros had other ideas. She wanted to travel, to see the world. In hindsight, he wondered if he'd pushed her into having a child, the child he loved, but she had often treated as a burden which kept her in one spot, prevented her from seeing the exotic places she longed for. Well, she'd seen them now, and was no happier.

'It seemed the sensible thing to do. I aim to look around here.' When she left, Ros had been happy to let Iain buy her out of their home. Now it was his to do with as he pleased. 'Where are you staying? How long are you in Sydney for?'

'I'm not sure. I thought…' Her voice trailed away. Had Ros intended to stay in the Middle Harbour house while she was in the city? She hadn't lived there for over twenty years.

There was silence while Ros clearly digested his words.

'You say you've retired? You're too young to retire.'

'What about you?' Iain decided to turn the tables. 'What brings you back to Australia, to Sydney?'

'I'd have thought it was obvious. I've come to see my son and granddaughter.'

Iain almost laughed at this. Ros had made no effort to spend time with either of them, only sending birthday gifts when she remembered. He doubted if Mia would recognise her.

'I have some business to conduct in the city. I'll be in touch. I don't suppose…' There was a pregnant pause.

Iain knew what she was thinking. He knew his ex-wife so well. 'It's not possible for you to stay in the Middle Harbour house,' he said. 'The keys are with the realtor, and he has sole access. I'm hoping it'll sell soon.'

By the time the conversation was over, Iain's peace was shattered. He needed something to take his mind off Ros and her claim to want to see Bryan and Mia. Though he doubted she'd turn up here unannounced, the prospect made him uneasy. Remembering Adam's mentioning the art gallery, Iain googled the place on his phone, then made his way back into town.

The sign, *The Bay Gallery*, was engraved in gold lettering above the door of the small gallery. Iain stopped and peered into the window where there was a display of several prints depicting a local beach scene and one large floral painting. He pushed open the door to see a tall, slim, silver-haired man who appeared to be in his early sixties, a pair of old-fashioned half-moon spectacles perched on his nose.

'Good morning.' The man came towards him. 'Can I help you? I'm John Baldwin. I haven't seen you around here before. Are you visiting Bellbird Bay?'

'I'm new in town but planning to stay.' Iain gazed around, impressed by the display and strangely comforted by the ambiance of the gallery. 'I'd just like to browse if it's okay with you. You have a lovely gallery. Iain Grant,' he added, realising he hadn't introduced himself.

The two men shook hands.

'Take all the time you want. I'll be here if you have any questions.'

'Thanks.'

Iain slowly made his way around the gallery. It seemed to him the various paintings and etchings on display were the work of local artists, though he recognised the name of the photographer whose work had prime position on one wall. Martin Cooper was world-renowned for his daring shots in the world's hot spots and exotic locations. These were different, all showing what appeared to be local beaches and surfers.

Iain was examining them when John appeared at his side. 'Martin's another of our local artists,' he said. 'Since he returned to Bellbird Bay, he's produced several new portfolios of work. We're fortunate to be able to show them in my small gallery. Brilliant, aren't they?'

'Indeed.'

As they were speaking, a young woman rushed in. 'Sorry, John, I got caught up. Isla... Sorry,' she said, seeing Iain.

'Mel, my assistant,' John introduced her. 'Mel, this is Iain Grant who is new to the town.'

'Grant...' Mel gazed at Iain for a moment. 'You must be Mum's new tenant. Welcome to Bellbird Bay. She was saying she hadn't met you yet. Wait till I tell her I have.' She gave him a grin, before disappearing through a door in the back wall.

'It's a small town.' John raised both hands. 'So, you're living in Grace Winter's place. The pastels in the window are by Ted Crawford who is her partner. You're not an artist yourself, are you?' John peered at Iain hopefully.

'No... I... I have done a bit of pen and ink drawing at one time,' he found himself saying. Where had that come from? It was years since he'd indulged in sketching old buildings in Sydney. He'd been a student at the time. But now, standing in this gallery, artworks all around, John's gaze on him, Iain remembered how rewarding it had been. He recalled Adam's words again. Perhaps this could be a way to fill his time.

Thirteen

The last two weeks had flown past, and Bev was becoming used to seeing Bryan around the garden centre. She now realised the likeness she'd first noticed was only superficial. Bryan's hair was lighter than Phil's had been – it had a reddish tinge rather than the chestnut she remembered. There was something else familiar about the young man, something she couldn't put her finger on. But she had been too busy to take time to ponder on it.

It had been a good appointment. He was an excellent worker, easily fitting in to the routine and, while lacking in conversation, seemed to be getting along well with the other staff members. For the past few days, he and one of the other guys had been clearing out the area she'd designated as the wedding site. They had moved the pots which had been stored there to their new location and today were engaged in sweeping out the area. Already it was looking good.

Bev hadn't heard back from the council regarding her application, but Will Rankin, who had recently been elected to the local council, assured her the application to hold a temporary event on private land shouldn't be a problem, while warning her she might run into a few more hurdles with her next application.

But today, the application was the least of her worries. She'd arranged for Colin Jarrett of *Bay Blinds and Awnings* to come to measure up and give her a quote. She'd spent the weekend researching and investigating different types of awnings and providers, before deciding he was the one most likely to provide what she was looking for.

To Bev's relief, the meeting with Colin went well. He assured her he'd be able to provide the type of covering she envisaged and promised to email through a quote. Heaving a sigh of relief at having one more item ticked off her ever-growing to-do list, Bev was gazing at the details of the more complex council application process, confused by the host of requirements and zoning restrictions, when there was a knock at her office door.

'Bryan.' Despite herself, Bev's heart leapt at the sight of the young man. He'd been working hard all day and his hair was tousled, his face streaked with sweat.

'Ms Cooper, Bev. Can I have a word?'

'Of course.'

Bryan shuffled his feet. 'I don't mean to pry, but Dean said you're planning to hold weddings in the area we've been clearing.'

'That's right.' She should have known the staff would gossip.

'He also said you might need the services of a planning consultant.'

'Right again.' How on earth did Dean know that... and what did it have to do with Bryan Grant?

'I thought... my dad might be able to help.'

'Your dad?' Bev felt foolish repeating Bryan's words. She knew he and his dad were new in town; she didn't know much about them. 'Is he a town planner?'

'Not exactly.' Bryan shuffled his feet again, seeming unable to meet her eyes. 'Before we came to Bellbird Bay, he was an architect... an architect and urban planner. He and his partner were behind a lot of the new developments on the outskirts of Sydney and the Central Coast, Connor Grant Architects and Urban Planners.' There was a hint of pride in his voice.

'Really?' Bev was immediately interested. Even she had heard of the company which had won a prestigious award in New South Wales. But would someone who normally worked on large-scale projects be interested in her small business?

'I think... since we came here... he's at a bit of a loose end,' Bryan said, 'especially now Mia's started school and I'm working here.'

Bev was about to refuse, when her eyes fell again on the council website with the regulations she'd been trying to make sense of. If Bryan's dad was willing to help, it might be a good idea.

*

Iain had had a good day. After his visit to *The Bay Gallery* the previous week, he'd furnished himself with the wherewithal to attempt some simple pen and ink drawings. Today, he'd walked up the boardwalk to the headland, where he'd noticed an old two-storey weatherboard house. Positioning himself opposite the gate, with the necessary materials and enough water to last him a few hours, he'd settled down to attempt to transfer the image of the house onto paper.

Now, back home again after picking Mia up from school and settling her down with milk and biscuits and a favourite jigsaw, he looked through the drawings he'd produced and smiled to himself. While not perfect, they proved he hadn't lost the skill he'd developed as a teenager and in his early twenties – before the more serious business of earning a living took over.

Filled with a sense of satisfaction, Iain set his drawings aside and started to cook the spaghetti Bolognese he planned for dinner. While his repertoire had grown over the years and he was proud of his cooking, this was a family favourite.

Dinner was almost ready when Bryan walked in. Iain had noticed a difference in his son since he'd started working at the garden centre. It was barely perceptible, but to Iain who saw him every day, the difference was there.

Today, Bryan, who rarely opened a conversation, came into the kitchen and leant against the bench. 'Dad, I spoke to Bev Cooper about you, today.'

'About me?' Iain turned from the stove where he'd been stirring the sauce.

'She's working on this application to the council – planning to set up a wedding venue. We were clearing the area today. Anyway, I heard she was having challenges with it. It really needs someone with planning experience. So, I thought of you. You used to do that all the time. I told her you could help.'

Iain was torn between annoyance his son had offered his services and delight that, finally, Bryan was taking some initiative and sounding more like he used to.

'You could, couldn't you?'

Iain hesitated. Loath though he was to dent Bryan's new-found enthusiasm, he had put all that behind him when he made the decision to retire and come to Bellbird Bay. 'I don't know, son,' he said after a long pause. 'Every council has different requirements – and we're in a different state, too.'

'But you could at least look at it?' Bryan pleaded, a sullen expression coming into his eyes.

'I could... and I will,' he said, unwilling to disappoint his son. Bryan had suffered enough recently. Surely it couldn't be too hard to look at what this woman was trying to do?

'Thanks, Dad.'

To Iain's surprise, Bryan gave him a quick hug before disappearing to shower and change for dinner. Well, if that's all it took to turn Bryan's mood around, maybe he should agree with his suggestions more often. But, he remembered, this was the first time since for ever that Bryan had suggested anything.

There was no opportunity for further discussion of the issue over dinner, during which Mia kept up a continuous stream of chatter about what she and her new friends had been doing at school, and how her teacher was planning a class trip to the botanic gardens. But afterwards, once Mia was in bed, Iain poured two glasses of wine and took them into the living area where Bryan was sitting in front of the television flipping through the channels.

'Tell me more about what you've let me in for,' he said, handing Bryan a glass.

'It's just what I said,' Bryan replied peevishly. 'She wants to organise weddings in the garden centre and needs to get permission from the council. We've cleared an area and there was a guy there today measuring for some sort of covering. But she seems stumped by the paperwork.'

'Right.' Iain knew how confusing council requirements could be and, despite what he'd said to Bryan, they didn't differ too much from place to place. 'Is she going to contact me, or should I call her?'

Iain could see from Bryan's expression that he hadn't thought so far ahead. He sighed. 'Why don't I drop into the garden centre tomorrow and have a chat with her? There's a café there, isn't there? I can have a coffee there, too.'

'O…kay.'

Iain could see Bryan wasn't too keen on Iain coming to his place of employment. 'Would you prefer me to call her?'

Bryan exhaled, clearly relieved. 'I think that would be better.'

Having got that out of the way, Iain took a sip of wine and leant back in his chair. 'I walked up to the headland today and did some drawings.'

'Drawings? You're designing a house?'

Iain chuckled. 'No, drawing in pen and ink. It's something I used to enjoy but I got out of the habit, too intent on the design side of things. It was good to get back to basics.'

'Hmm. Saw something in the local paper today,' Bryan said, changing the subject. 'One of the guys had a copy and I read it in my lunch break.'

'Oh, yes?' Iain had been meaning to catch up on the local news. It was something he knew he should do.

'There was an article about a triathlon in October.'

Iain glanced at his son. Before… Bryan had always been very concerned with fitness, but lately he'd let his regular regime go. Only since coming to Bellbird Bay, had he started to ride his bike again, and then, only to and from the garden centre. He bit his tongue and waited.

'I thought I might give it a go. What do you think, Dad?'

'I think it's a great idea.'

'I'd need to get back in training.' Bryan looked at Iain, a spark of the old Bryan in his eyes. 'I'll check it out tomorrow.'

When Bryan headed off to bed, Iain poured himself another glass of wine and took it out to the deck from where he could see the moon and the stars and could hear the roar of the ocean. He smiled to himself. It seemed Bryan was finally emerging from his grief and beginning to live. He had his son back.

Fourteen

The phone rang just as Bev walked into the office. She'd been busy all morning, sorting out a new order which had arrived, and hadn't even had time for her usual morning coffee with Cleo. She checked her watch before picking up the phone, aware she'd arranged to meet Ailsa for lunch in *The Pandanus Café* and it was close to twelve-thirty.

'Hello, *The Pandanus Garden Centre*, Bev Cooper speaking.'

There was a pause, then a well-modulated, educated, male voice spoke.

'Ms Cooper, my name's Iain Grant. I'm Bryan's father. He mentioned you were in need of assistance with a planning application.'

'Oh!' Bev hadn't quite decided if she did want his assistance. She didn't realised Bryan might have already spoken to his dad.

'If he was mistaken…' the voice trailed off, as if embarrassed.

'No… I do need help, but he said you are retired. I don't want to impose.' Bev imagined an elderly man, tall and stooping, perhaps with a goatee beard. But his voice sounded younger than she'd expected.

'Not a problem.' He chuckled. There was something attractive about his chuckle, as if he was inviting her to join in his amusement. 'I took early retirement… came up here in an attempt to help Bryan get over his wife's death. Some days I'm at a loss for what to do with myself. I'd welcome the opportunity to be of some use. Bryan said something about a wedding venue?'

'Yes.' Bev bit her lip. It wouldn't do any harm to at least talk to the man. After all, he'd taken the trouble to call… and if he could help…

'It's very kind of you to offer. I plan to set up an area as a wedding site and I'm trying to get my head around the council's requirements for an application to add a function facility to the garden centre. I've managed to complete one for a family wedding in October. It's the more commercial one that's stumping me.'

'Well, I don't have any experience with Bellbird Bay council but over the years I've found most councils have pretty similar regulations. I'm happy to take a look.'

Bev only hesitated for a moment, before replying, 'Perhaps we could meet for coffee? We have a café here.'

'Bryan said. Sounds like a plan. When would suit you? It would have to be in school hours. I have a granddaughter…'

'Of course.' Bev thought quickly. Better to get it over with. 'How about tomorrow… around ten?'

'I look forward to it.'

Bev stared at the phone when the call finished. What had she let herself in for?

*

'Sorry I'm late.' Bev slid into the seat opposite Ailsa. 'Today's salad and a pot of green tea, please,' she said to the waitress who immediately appeared at her elbow.

'No problem.' Ailsa took a sip of her tea and searched her friend's face. 'Problem?'

'Not really. No. I don't think so.' Bev stared down at her clenched hands and unclenched them.

'You sound as if there is, or as if you think there might be.' Ailsa sounded concerned. 'It's not about the wedding, is it? It can still go ahead?'

'No.' Bev exhaled. 'Your wedding's fine. I've sent in the application which Will assures me will go through without any trouble. Nate and Hannah have offered to take care of the chairs, music and the grog, and I've ordered an awning made of plexiglass panels which should let in the light but keep out the rain. Colin Jarett assures me it is both stylish and functional and can be installed in plenty of time.'

'Then what?'

'Thanks,' Bev said, as her tea and salad was served. 'It's the other part, the commercial application, and...' she paused.

'And?' Ailsa appeared mystified.

'My new staff member – Bryan Grant – his dad has offered to help me with it, and I don't know...' She pulled on her ponytail.

'Why would *he* be able to help?'

'He was an architect in Sydney, architect and urban planner. He and Bryan came to Bellbird Bay recently. The council website suggested I should get a planning consultant to help with the application.'

'Well, he sounds like the answer to your prayers. What's the problem?'

'I don't know.' Bev sighed. 'I just feel a bit odd about it. Bryan mentioned his dad to me yesterday, then the guy rings me today.'

'So?'

Bev sighed again. 'I guess it's a good idea, but... I don't know,' she repeated.

'What did you say?'

'I said it was kind of him and agreed to meet him tomorrow... here... for coffee.'

'Well, then. There's not much can happen here with Cleo to look after you.'

'Why do you need looking after?' Cleo joined them and had clearly heard Ailsa's last remark.

Ailsa repeated what Bev had told her, finishing with, 'It sounds like a good plan to me.'

'To me, too,' Cleo said, placing her mug of peppermint tea on the table. 'I'm glad I've caught both of you. I wanted to discuss the menu for the wedding. I'm anticipating nibbles to hand around while the guests are having drinks and the photographs are being taken, then there's the meal.'

The next half hour was taken up with Ailsa and Cleo discussing food, while Bev worried about the meeting with Iain Grant next day. *What had possessed her to agree? But, if not him, who could she turn to for the help she knew she needed?* She let their conversation flow over her, only paying attention again when Cleo asked, 'Who's going to take the photos?'

It was a good point. Martin was the best photographer around, but it was *his* wedding and he couldn't take photos of himself.

'We're working on it,' Ailsa said. 'Martin has some ideas but hasn't shared them with me yet. He can be very secretive at times.' She looked across at Bev who nodded, remembering how, when they were growing up together, her twin had often frustrated her by refusing to let her into his secrets, though she'd always managed to find out eventually.

'I should get back to work,' Bev said, rising. 'Thanks for your advice – both of you.'

'I'll keep my eye out tomorrow,' Cleo said with a grin. 'Make sure your guest doesn't make any wrong moves.'

Bev grimaced at her before leaving, but a tiny part of her was glad she had such good friends. While Ailsa and Cleo might mock her at times, they always had her best interests at heart. She was the one who had trouble letting others into her inner circle.

*

Next morning, Bev awoke early as usual. She wanted to ensure she was ahead with her daily checklist before she met with Bryan's dad. She had dreamt about Phil last night, a happy dream in which he was still alive, they were both young and had their whole lives ahead of them. It had been hard to wake and find it had all been a dream.

The first few hours of the day went quickly as Bev counselled a teary staff member who had been verbally abused by a customer and organised the holiday roster for those who wanted leave over the busy Christmas period. By the time ten o'clock came around, she felt as if she'd already done a day's work. Tidying her hair and glancing in the mirror to ensure she looked reasonably respectable, she picked up a folder and her iPad and made her way towards the café.

The tall rangy man with close-cropped grey hair wearing a loose royal blue shirt over a pair of white capris, his feet thrust into a pair of brown Birkenstocks, wasn't what Bev had expected. To her relief, he looked nothing like his son which she now realised was what she had been afraid of – meeting an older version of the man she'd once been in love with.

He rose to greet her. 'You must be Ms Cooper.'

'Bev. And you are…'

'Iain Grant, Bryan's dad.' He held out his hand.

Bev shook it, noting his firm handshake. She always thought you could tell a lot about a man from his handshake. Iain Grant's was strong, brief, and was accompanied by a smile, good eye contact and friendly body language, all of which indicated to Bev he was genuinely interested in what he had come to discuss.

'Thanks for coming.'

'This is quite an operation you have here,' he said admiringly.

'Thanks,' Bev said again and smiled, relaxing. Maybe this wasn't going to be too bad. 'What will you have to drink?' she asked, seeing Cleo coming towards them. She should have known Cleo would want to see him for herself.

'Black coffee for me.'

Bev could see Cleo raise her eyebrows. 'One black and a pot of lemon and ginger tea, Cleo,' she said. 'This is Cleo who manages the café,' she said to Iain, then to Cleo, 'Cleo, this is Iain Grant who has offered to help me with the council application.'

Cleo smiled and nodded, then gave Bev a sly wink behind Iain's back, before disappearing into the kitchen.

'First I'd like to thank you for giving Bryan a chance,' Iain said. 'He's gone through a bad time. He's enjoying working here and is beginning to put it behind him – as much as he can. I fear he'll never completely recover from his loss.'

'He's a good worker. I'm glad if we've been able to play some part in his recovery. There are some losses that never heal.' As Bev knew to her cost.

Their coffees arrived along with a plate containing a couple of Ruby Sullivan's brownies, and Bev thanked Cleo with a smile.

Opening her iPad, Bev explained what she intended to do, then sat back and allowed Iain to examine the details of the application process.

She had almost finished her pot of tea, when he raised his head again.

'Looks pretty straightforward,' he said. 'I'll make an appointment to talk with the relevant people in the council and if you could show me the area you have in mind before I leave?'

'Sure. Bryan said you've done this sort of thing before?'

'Usually on a bigger scale, but yes. I do have a bit of experience dealing with town councils. The trick is to discover their hot buttons and make sure to cross all the t's and dot all the i's. This one shouldn't be too difficult.' He drained his coffee which must now be cold.

Bev rose and led the way into the garden centre and to the area she'd designated for weddings.

'There will be plexiglass roofing and an archway,' she explained, waving an arm in the air. 'My brother and his partner are marrying here in October. I've already completed the application for a temporary event on private land. It should be a good test of the facilities.'

'You'll be using the café for dining?'

'Yes. We already have a commercial kitchen. My brother's future stepson is organising a liquor license. He works as a barman.'

'It's a good spot,' Iain said, his eyes scanning the cleared area. 'What about customers in the garden centre and café?'

'Oh, we won't be holding weddings here during business hours. I thought evenings only. Will that be a problem?'

'I shouldn't think so. If I can take your folder with me, I'll check out the council website, see who I can talk with. Then I may need to meet with you again. Will that be all right?'

Bev nodded, suddenly realising she hadn't actually agreed to Iain helping her. He had just assumed he would. But he seemed like a nice man, and he was the father of one of her staff members. And, she thought, as she watched him walk away, he seemed confident he could do what was needed. It was a relief to be able to hand over the application to him. She suppressed the thought that he was attractive, too; the first man she'd found attractive in over thirty-five years.

Fifteen

Iain laid Bev's folder on the passenger seat and stared into space. What had he let himself in for? Compared to the plans he was accustomed to dealing with, this was a piece of cake. Paul would laugh if he knew. But there had been something about Bev Cooper that made him want to help. Something about the way she spoke about loss told him she understood how Bryan must be feeling, told him she had suffered loss herself, might even still be suffering.

The garden centre itself was impressive. Iain was surprised at the size of it. Bev Cooper had done well to establish such an extensive operation in Bellbird Bay. And from what he'd seen, it was a flourishing business. Bev herself had been a surprise. He wasn't sure what he'd expected, but the tall, elegant blonde wearing a dark green apron bearing a pandanus logo, her blonde hair pulled back in an untidy ponytail, took his breath away. Given what she'd established here, she must be close to his own age, but gave the impression of a much younger woman, one who was efficient and driven but who also had a vulnerable side to her. It amazed him he'd managed to sense all that from their brief contact, but, over the years, he'd become adept at reading people. It had served him well in his architectural practice, though not so well in his personal life.

As he drove home, Iain thought over his past. After Ros left, he had been too traumatised to consider another relationship and he had the teenage Bryan to look after. But, a few years after Bryan married, he gave in to Paul's persuasion to take the plunge and join an online dating agency.

He'd been hesitant at first, merely lurking on the site. Eventually he had made contact with several likely ladies and begun dating again, but although he met some nice women, women he would like to have as friends, there was no sign of the spark he knew had to be there if there was going to be any future to a relationship. All of that had come to an end with Nadia's untimely death. The need to provide support for Bryan and Mia put all thought of forming a relationship out of his mind. He had more important matters to worry about. And now he was in Bellbird Bay, away from any possible matches.

He wasn't sure what made him think of this now, but there had been something about Bev Cooper which had raised his antenna. He wondered if she was married or in a relationship.

*

Mia had gone to visit Libby and Adam, something she often did after school, having formed a bond with their dog, Milo, so Iain was alone when Bryan walked in.

'Saw you at the garden centre, Dad. I was too busy to stop and say hi. How did you get on with Bev? She's pretty cool for an old bird, isn't she?'

Iain almost choked. *Old bird?* That wasn't how he'd describe the woman he'd spent much of the morning with. But he guessed to Bryan she might be. He probably counted his dad as an old guy, too. Iain remembered how he'd thought of his own parents when they were his age. But surely they'd seemed older then than he did now?

'She's a nice lady, Bryan. There's no need to be disrespectful.'

Bryan chuckled – something he'd never have done a few weeks earlier. 'She's better than some of those women you met on that dating site.' Before Iain could reply, he walked out, and Iain soon heard the shower running.

What did Bryan know of the women he'd met? Iain had never brought them to meet his family. Had Bryan been checking out his computer or his phone? He flinched at the thought of his son checking up on his dating habits, not that there was much to see. But it was a reminder he should cancel his membership.

'Where's Mia?' Bryan appeared on the deck where Iain was enjoying a beer before starting to cook dinner.

'At Adam and Libby's. Want a beer?'

'Thanks, Dad. Not now. I might walk up to fetch her.'

'Suit yourself. Don't take too long. Dinner will be ready in around half an hour.'

With a contented smile on his face he watched his son go, walking away to the house of people he barely knew without any hesitation. It gladdened his heart.

Iain finished his beer. He gazed out at the ocean, calm tonight after a few wild days. Several people were walking along the beach, a few surfers hoping for a swell and a trio of hardy swimmers making the best of the fading light and risking the rip, the surf lifesavers having already packed up for the day. It was all so different from the busy harbour scene he'd been accustomed to in the city. The serenity was evident everywhere he went in Bellbird Bay. Even in the busy garden centre, there had been the same sense of peace he could feel here by the ocean. He could feel himself slowing down, becoming more at one with himself and the environment. And he could sense the same happening with Bryan.

*

'I was talking with this guy today, Dad. Nate McNeil is some sort of relative of Bev's – he dropped in with some forms for her. He told me more about the triathlon. Seems it's an annual event run by the surf carnival committee. His mate's dad runs the committee and the surf school – a guy called Will Rankin. He said people come from all over to take part. It sounds like a big deal. Don't know how I never heard of it.' He dragged a hand through his hair.

Iain and his son were seated on the deck enjoying a beer after dinner and after Mia was in bed. He liked this time of day when, now Bryan had come out of his shell of grief, they could talk about their day and make plans for the future.

'So you're serious about taking part?' Iain asked.

'Sure am. Nate said he and his mate train on the main beach every morning, then they run up to the headland and back. They take their bikes out on the weekend. I thought I might join them, if you're happy to look after Mia. It'll only be till the event's over.'

'Happy to, if you're sure it's something you want to do.'

'The exercise… it's like the work in the garden centre… it stops me thinking too much,' Bryan said.

Iain said nothing, merely patting his son's hand. How could he understand? He'd never been in Bryan's position, never suffered the death of the woman he loved. When Ros left him, it had been a blow, but they had been drifting apart. They had married in haste – some would say lust – not realising how different their goals and values were. It had almost been a relief when she'd finally left.

'I got a text from Mum,' Bryan said, as if he'd read Iain's mind. 'She wanted to know why you'd decided to leave Sydney and sell the house.'

'What did you tell her?'

'I didn't. I haven't replied. You know Mum. She always had some agenda. I'm guessing her latest romance fell through and she suddenly remembered she has a son and granddaughter. Mia barely knows her and it's not fair for Mum to appear in her life for a few weeks then to disappear again when something better turns up.' He gazed moodily into his beer. 'Does she know where we are?'

'Not as far as I'm aware.' But Iain couldn't be sure. Paul might have told her. Ros had always been able to wind men around her little finger, and even his former business partner wasn't immune to her charms.

'Hmph. Well, I'd better turn in.' Bryan drained his beer and crushed the can. 'Early start tomorrow. I'm meeting Nate and his mate on the beach. I'll be back for breakfast. Night, Dad.'

Alone again, Iain pondered the conversation. He thought he'd managed to put Ros off, but it seemed she'd contacted Bryan. *What did she want from them? Was she only interested in seeing her granddaughter or did she have something else in mind?*

Sixteen

Bev gave a sigh of relief as she stood under the shower and washed away the dust and dirt that always accumulated during a day at the garden centre. It had been a strange sort of day. First there had been the meeting with Iain Grant which had unsettled her. It wasn't the man himself, but the way he'd assumed she'd agreed to his assistance. Well, she had now, but there was a niggle in the back of her mind that wouldn't go away.

Still, he seemed to know what he was doing, said he was familiar with dealing with councils.

Then there was the weird call from Will Rankin. She'd known Will all her life. He and Martin were great mates, always had been till Martin left town. And now her brother was back, they seemed to have picked up where they left off – and Ailsa's son, Nate, and Will's son, Owen, were now best mates too.

Will had always been there for her. Whereas her twin had left Bellbird Bay as soon as he finished school, Will had stayed, married and started his surf school. Widowed several years earlier, he and Cleo were now in a relationship. Will had become a pillar of the community, supporter of several charities as well as being a member of the council.

He hadn't given much detail in his call, only said he'd drop round this evening after seven, as he had something to say to her.

Bev dried herself off, slipped on the cut-off jeans and tee-shirt she always wore and pulled her hair back into its customary ponytail, wondering as she did so when she'd be too old for this hairstyle. She remembered her mother who, starting in her mid-fifties and till the day she died, had worn her hair short and tortured into a rigid series of waves.

Too tired to cook, she made herself a cheese and ham sandwich, taking it out to the deck with a mug of peppermint tea and pulling on a sweater. Although the days were becoming warmer as they moved closer to spring, there was still a chill in the air in the early morning and evening.

This was her favourite time of day. She loved watching how the sky changed colour as the sun dropped below the horizon and listening to the sound of the seabirds as they flew overhead on their way to their resting spots.

Tonight, the sea was calm and peaceful, reminding Bev of evenings long ago when she, Martin and Will would sneak out on their bikes to go fishing on the beach. They rarely caught anything with their homemade rods, but they had hours of fun. That was before Martin and Will discovered girls and became surfing legends. She sighed. So much had happened since then.

It had turned dark, and Bev was about to take her plate and mug inside when she caught sight of Will coming up the boardwalk. 'Thought you'd be driving,' she said.

'I had a meeting at the surf club and decided I needed the exercise,' he said with a laugh.

Bev laughed too. Will was one of the fittest people she knew. He surfed every day and Cleo had confided he had a gym set up at home.

'I was about to take these inside.' She nodded at the plate and mug. 'Come in. It's getting too cold to sit out here. Would you like a glass of wine?'

'Thanks. I've always envied you this spot.' Will gazed out at the view Bev had been admiring earlier.

'So,' she said, when they were both nursing glasses of cabernet sauvignon and seated in the warm living room, 'what do you want to talk to me about. Not bad news, I hope.'

'Good and bad. First the good. I got the heads up your application for the temporary event is going through without a problem.'

Bev heaved a sigh of relief. Ailsa and Martin's wedding could go ahead. 'I've spoken with a planning consultant about the other,' she said. 'But I expect it'll be some time before it's ready to submit. Iain Grant is new to town. He's renting Grace Winter's place a few doors up. He was an architect in Sydney and his son works for me.'

'That's where the problem lies.'

Bev stared at Will. How could it be a problem when the application had still to be submitted. Then she remembered. 'He said he was going to speak to someone at the council.'

'Seems he's already done that. I heard on the grapevine some Sydney guy had been asking questions about wedding venues.'

'So?' Bev couldn't see why that was a problem.

'You'll have heard talk of Milton Harris, the city guy who bought the hotel on the outskirts of town?'

'The one where you and Cleo…?' Bev chuckled at the memory of how Ailsa had set the pair up, pretending to feel sick.

'That's the one. He has the idea of turning it into a deluxe wedding venue and doesn't take kindly to the idea of competition from you.'

Bev's eyes widened. 'But… we'd be no competition for something like that. I'm only planning to do it on a small scale.' Then it occurred to her. 'How does he know what I'm planning?'

Will shrugged. 'Small town. Friends on the council. There's talk he'll stand himself at the next local election.

Bev's heart dropped. 'Damn! Can he stop us going ahead?'

'Not at this stage, but it'd pay you to be careful. He doesn't have a good reputation. It's not a good idea to get in his way. People who cross him have…' Will left the rest to Bev's imagination.

'Thanks for the heads up.' Bev bit her lip. There wasn't much she could do, not until the application had actually been submitted. She wondered how long Iain Grant would take.

'Having a newcomer working on it doesn't help either,' Will said.

'But this Harris guy's a newcomer.'

'Yeah, but he's been throwing money around like it's going out of fashion. Made a few enemies, but friends with the people who matter. As I said, just be careful.'

'Okay, but I hope you can put in a good word for me when the time comes.' Bev fumed inwardly. Despite her own misgivings about Iain Grant's help, the thought of others taking the same attitude made her blood boil.

*

The rest of the week passed without incident and with no further contact from Iain Grant. Bev was beginning to wonder if he'd changed his mind or found it too difficult, when her phone rang just as she arrived home late afternoon on Sunday. Bev didn't recognise the number but picked it up anyway.

'Hello, Bev Cooper.'

'Ms Cooper, Bev. Iain Grant here.'

Bev didn't speak – couldn't speak – surprised by the burst of relief she felt at the sound of his voice.

'I talked with a couple of people at the council offices and I've been working on your application. I wonder if we can meet again so I can show you where I'm up to?'

'Of course.' She felt a hint of anticipation. It was actually happening. Despite Will's warning, she had a good feeling about this and, to her surprise, she was eager to see Iain Grant again, too. Without stopping to analyse this feeling, she said, 'I'll be home this evening and live just down the boardwalk. Why don't you come down after dinner and you can show me over a glass of wine?'

Did she really just say that?

Bev barely heard his agreement or her own bumbling directions to her house. What had possessed her to invite him here? It would have been better to have kept the arrangement professional, to have met at the garden centre again. She looked around the living room which was her private domain and felt as if she was about to be invaded.

Seventeen

'You're looking very pleased with yourself.' Bryan opened the fridge, pulled out a beer and offered one to Iain. 'Who were you speaking to?' He gestured to Iain's phone.

Iain shook his head and didn't immediately reply. Bev's invitation had taken him by surprise and sent an unexpected thrill through him. 'Your boss,' he said at last. 'She's invited me for a drink… to discuss the application I've been working on.'

Bryan raised his eyebrows. 'Doesn't sound like her. She has the reputation of being a very private person. Must like you, Dad.' He chuckled.

Iain wasn't sure about that. Bev Cooper gave him the impression of being a woman who liked to keep things businesslike, and to keep her business and personal life separate. He couldn't fathom why she'd invited him to her home rather than arranging to meet at the garden centre like before. But, despite the reason, he was glad to have the opportunity to see her in different surroundings, surprised to learn she lived so close.

'What's for dinner, Grandad?' Mia appeared as if by magic. He had spent the afternoon with her on the beach where they'd been joined by Adam and Libby with Clancy. The two girls had enjoyed playing in the sand together and running in and out of the shallow water with Milo. Libby explained that Clancy's mother and her partner had gone to Brisbane for the weekend and left the little girl with them.

They hadn't arrived back much before Bryan, and Iain hadn't given any thought to dinner. 'Why don't we have fish and chips?' he asked, remembering seeing a fish and chip shop on the esplanade. 'We can eat them at one of the picnic tables by the beach.'

'Yay!' Mia said. 'Clancy says they do that all the time.'

Iain doubted it but was glad his suggestion met with Mia's approval.

'Good one, Dad. No washing up,' Bryan said with a grin, the old Bryan appearing again, to Iain's delight.

Before long, they were heading down the boardwalk. As he passed the house Bev had described as hers, Iain stole a quick glance over the white fence which surrounded the garden and deck. It was no surprise to see how the plants were flourishing, a testament to their owner and her green fingers and a perfect advertisement for her business. It made him ashamed of his lack of care of the garden where he was living.

Thinking of the garden reminded him of Will Rankin's suggestion his landlady might be willing to sell. He'd had a few offers on the Sydney house, one of which he was considering accepting. Was the house here on the boardwalk in Bellbird Bay where he wanted to spend the rest of his days, and how long would Bryan and Mia be content to stay here and to live with him?

Mia was happy here, had settled in well and made friends, but how long would Bryan be satisfied with working at the garden centre? Now he was coming out of his abyss of grief, would he want to return to his former life as a sports journalist? And if Bryan and Mia returned to the city, would Iain want to stay here in Bellbird Bay? He was pretty sure he would.

The fish and chips were a success, Mia delighted by the seagulls which surrounded them as soon as they began to eat and, despite Iain and Bryan's warnings, managed to share her meal with them. It was a tired but happy little girl who accompanied them back up the boardwalk, begging for a story from a Dr Seuss book she'd borrowed from her friend, Clancy.

'You'll be right?' Iain asked Bryan as he printed out the copy of the application he wanted to share with Bev.

'Dad, I'm not sixteen anymore – and I didn't need your supervision then, either. I know I was out of it for a while after Nadia…' his voice broke as he spoke his wife's name for the first time since her death, '… but I'm getting my shit back together. I didn't understand at the time why you wanted to get us away from the city, away from the memories. I just wanted to wallow in my grief. But it was the best thing you could have done. If we were in Sydney, I'd probably still be sitting staring at the wall or lying in my room with the door closed.' He grimaced.

'You really like it here?'

'I do. I've met some good people at work, and the guy who's running the triathlon – he's all right, too. I met his son Owen yesterday. He designs and makes surf boards. I might look at getting myself one when the triathlon's over.'

Iain grinned. Maybe he'd been worrying needlessly. Maybe Bryan would be happy with his new life here.

*

It was a few minutes past seven when Iain pushed open the gate to Bev's house. It was similar in design to the one he was renting but had been painted white and the garden was a riot of colour. An outside light illuminated the deck on which there was a large table and some very comfortable-looking chairs. He stepped onto the deck and knocked on the glass door.

Bev appeared almost immediately, looking exactly the way she had in the café apart from the fact she was no longer wearing the green pandanus apron. Instead, she was dressed in cut-off jeans and a white tee-shirt emblazoned with a large sunflower, her faded blonde hair pulled back into the same untidy ponytail. She looked about sixteen until Iain got closer and could see the tiny lines around her eyes and mouth which she hadn't made any attempt to hide with makeup.

'Come in,' she said, a tremor in her voice. *Was she nervous? Of him or about the application?*

A few minutes later he was seated in a large living room, not unlike his own. But this one was furnished with soft sofas in shades of cream and green. There were two large bookcases filled with books which Iain would love to have examined, and a low coffee table held a healthy pot plant, a bowl of nuts and stuffed olives, and a couple of coffee table books he recognised as containing photographs by the world-renowned photographer, Martin Cooper. He'd attended an exhibition of his works in Sydney several years ago and been blown away by the unusual angles of his shots taken in various exotic locations around the world. He picked up one of the books.

He was still holding the book when Bev reappeared carrying two glasses of white wine.

'Oh, you've found my brother's books,' she said, handing him a glass.

'Your…?' Iain hadn't made the connection, but now it was obvious. Bev Cooper… Martin Cooper.

'Twin brother. Martin left as soon as school was over. Only came back a few years ago. Now he's marrying my best friend. Theirs is the wedding I've already put in an application for.'

'Is that what gave you the idea?'

'Actually, no. It had been on my mind before they decided to marry. I guess it provided the impetus I needed to put things in motion. Now, what have you got for me?' she asked, immediately reverting to the businesslike manner he remembered from their earlier meeting.

Iain took the papers he'd brought and spread them out on the coffee table. 'I just need your approval and signature in a couple of spots and they're ready to go. Is something wrong?' he asked, seeing her forehead crease.

'No, not really.' Bev took a sip of wine. 'Well, maybe. I had a visit from Will Rankin last night.'

Will Rankin, the guy Bryan spoke about, the one organising the triathlon. What did he have to do with this? He must have looked puzzled, because Bev spoke again.

'Will's an old family friend. We all grew up together, Will, Martin and me. He's on the council now and hears things.'

Iain waited.

Bev twisted her hands in her lap.

Iain couldn't help noticing her hands and fingers. They were long and elegant, surprising for someone who grubbed about in the earth every day. He wondered how they would feel… He brought his attention back to what she was saying.

'He told me there could be some opposition to my proposal. There's a businessman – Milton Harris – he owns a hotel on the outskirts of Bellbird Bay. He's expanding into weddings, too, and may see me as competition, though my small operation can hardly be construed as that.' She fell silent.

Iain practically rubbed his hands together. There was nothing he enjoyed more than a conflict about a development proposal. He'd weathered a few in his time and usually come out on top. He hadn't expected to find one in this sleepy town. It made the prospect much more interesting.

'What do you know about him?' he asked, trying to hide his enthusiasm.

'Not a lot. He's a newcomer to Bellbird Bay, arrived here a few years ago, bought the old hotel and renovated it to make it look like something out of a Hollywood movie. I haven't been there, but Will and Cleo have. It tends to cater for the upmarket tourist trade. I'd imagine they'd be the target for his weddings, too. You know the sort of thing – *share your vows in a luxury coastal setting*. Not my scene at all.'

No, looking at Bev, her legs drawn up under her, strands of hair falling around her face, Iain couldn't imagine her in the scene she described. She'd be much more at home in a garden or on the beach.

'Does he have much of a following, contacts in the council for example?'

'I'm not sure. He does seem to throw his money around, and I guess there are some who are easily impressed.'

'Or bought?'

'I don't think... But Will did warn me about him, told me it's not wise to cross him. Will says he has council ambitions, too. There's a local election next year.'

'Hmm. Any idea where he came from... before he arrived in Bellbird Bay? People like him usually have a history.'

'No idea.' Bev frowned.

'Well, I'll dig around, see what I can find out. I have contacts, too.' Iain guessed the internet might yield a few answers, failing that, Paul was usually a good source – or would know someone who was. If this Harris guy had a history, it shouldn't be too difficult to ferret it out.

'Thanks. So you think it'll be all right?'

'Should be. It might take a bit of time. When did you intend to get started?'

'Not till after Christmas. It's our busiest time in the centre. But I'd hoped to be able to start advertising before then.' She bit her lip.

'I'll see what I can do.' Iain didn't know why, but there was something about Bev Cooper that raised his desire to do anything he could to help – to be her knight in shining armour. He almost laughed out loud at the image of him riding into battle, lance in hand to face this guy, to the sound of a cheering crowd.

Bev leant back in her seat, seemingly satisfied.

'If that's all?' Iain began to gather the papers together into a neat pile. 'I'll leave these with you to read at your leisure. Sign the parts I've marked if you're happy with it, and I can get it to the appropriate section of council. Then we wait.'

'Thanks.' Bev smiled and rose to shake Iain's hand. 'I appreciate your doing this.'

Iain made his farewells and headed back up the boardwalk, reflecting as he did so how in only two meetings, Bev Cooper had made more of an impression on him than any of the women he'd met online.

Eighteen

Iain Grant was there again, sitting at the same table as before, on the three previous occasions he'd appeared in *The Pandanus Café*, his tall rangy frame seeming to take up more space than was warranted.

Bev wasn't sure whether to be pleased or annoyed, but irritation was her uppermost emotion. She was still going over the application. At first, she'd dismissed Cleo's suggestion he was there to see her, but now Bev wasn't so sure. Didn't the man have anywhere else to go?

When he'd left her house a week ago, it had been her understanding she'd be the one to contact him when she was ready, when the application was signed. Then he'd been in the café when she went for her morning break on Tuesday, again on Wednesday and now it was Friday, and he was here again.

On the two previous occasions, she'd merely nodded to him and taken her coffee back to the office where she could drink it in peace, without feeling his eyes on her. They were unique, his eyes, brown with a ring of gold around the iris. She'd noticed them when he was going over the application with her. She'd noticed other things about him, too. His big hands as he set out the documents, the way his mouth curled up in a smile, the way he… She stopped herself. What was she doing?

'Everything all right?' Cleo's voice broke into her thoughts.

'Yes, fine.'

'Your usual? Taking it back to your office again?' Cleo asked with a smile and nod to where Iain Grant was drinking coffee and reading a paper.

'Yes. No.' Bev made up her mind. Today, she'd join him, ask him what he thought he was doing, why he was stalking her. 'I'll take it here,' she said with a tight smile.

'Hello.' Iain looked up from his paper with a grin as Bev joined him.

'You seem to be making a habit of coming here,' she said, as Cleo appeared with her coffee and a slice of banana bread, a knowing grin on her face.

'I like it here, and I knew you'd join me one day.'

Bev couldn't hide her smile at Iain's admission he'd planned this meeting. Why was he doing this when he could easily have phoned her? 'I've been studying the application. It all looks fine. I just have to sign it.' Maybe then he'd leave her alone.

'About that. I thought… we could have dinner together… to celebrate.'

A shiver of something inexplicable ran down Bev's back. For a moment she was lost for words, then she stuttered, 'I… I can drop it in to you.'

'Of course you can, but I'd really like to have dinner with you. I don't know many people in Bellbird Bay, and I think Bryan's getting a bit sick of my company every night – now he's recovering. I hear there's a good Italian restaurant on the esplanade. What do you say?'

Bev still hesitated, but *The Firenze* was a favourite eating place of hers. A family restaurant that had been in Bellbird Bay for as long as she could remember. She knew Gino, who now managed it for his parents, along with his wife who had come to the town as a backpacker some years earlier and been won over by the young man's charm and exotic good looks. 'That sounds lovely,' she said.

*

Bev gazed at the contents of her wardrobe in despair, wishing she'd never accepted Iain Grant's invitation. But the lure of a meal at her favourite restaurant had been too strong to resist, and she'd seen Cleo hovering in the background, clearly listening in and willing her to accept.

But now, as she sorted through the collection of jeans, shorts, tee-shirts and shirts, she could see nothing suitable for what could only be construed as a date. There was the lemon shirt dress she'd worn to Martin's photographic exhibition. Perhaps that would do. Her bed was strewn with various outfits when there was a knock at the front door. Relieved to have the decision delayed, Bev closed the door on her bedroom and went to answer it.

'Ailsa, I wasn't expecting to see you tonight,' Bev said, seeing her best friend on the doorstep.

'Martin has a meeting at the surf club, so I thought I'd drop in and get you to help me choose a format for our wedding ceremony. Martin says he doesn't care, as long as we end up as husband and wife, but I'd like it to be special but informal. I did the big church wedding last time...' She fell silent, as if remembering. 'You don't mind, do you?' She breezed in past Bev, straight through to the kitchen. 'I brought this to help us.' She flourished a bottle of wine.

'I'm not disturbing you, am I?' she asked as, without speaking, Bev reached into the cupboard for two glasses.

'No, I'm glad of the interruption. I was just...' She stopped mid-sentence.

Ailsa raised her eyebrows.

'I was trying to decide what to wear. I've agreed to go to dinner with Iain Grant and I don't think my usual jeans and a shirt would be appropriate.'

Ailsa burst out laughing.

Feigning annoyance, Bev said, 'It's not funny, Ailsa.'

'Sorry, Bev. I'm delighted to hear there's someone who's managed to get through the barrier you seem to put up where men are concerned. I think this may be the first time...'

'Yeah, yeah. He's been helping me with the application to the council, we've met a few times and...' Bev thought of how she'd imagined he was stalking her, of how she felt in his company. 'We're going to *The Firenze*,' she said, opening the wine, pouring two glasses and handing one to Ailsa, while avoiding her eyes.

'And you want to make a good impression?' Ailsa nodded. 'You need to visit Greta.' She nodded again.

'Greta?' Bev considered. She knew Greta well. The woman who owned *Birds of a Feather*, the fashion boutique on the esplanade, had been a couple of years below her at school, one of the girls who had hung around Martin. Bev had never frequented her shop, always considering it too fashionable for her needs. 'I don't think… I do have one dress.'

'Of course you must. I always go there. Not all her stock is over the top. I bet you can find something to suit you, something you'll feel comfortable in. A dress… or a pair of those wide-legged pants that are becoming popular,' she added, clearly seeing Bev grimace. 'When is this dinner date?'

Flinching at the word *date*, Bev said, 'Friday.'

'Good. Why don't I meet you when you finish tomorrow, and we can go together?'

Bev could see she wasn't going to be able to avoid this, so decided to agree. After all, it might not be too bad to buy something more… feminine… than her usual attire. She did own a couple of dresses, including the lemon one, but they'd been stuck at the back of her wardrobe for years and had seen better days. For some reason she wasn't willing to examine too closely, she wanted to look her best for Iain Grant who must be accustomed to squiring elegant women around in Sydney.

'Now that's settled, I need your opinion,' Ailsa said, pulling her iPad from her bag and firing it up.

Seated together at the kitchen table, Ailsa opened the website of the celebrant she planned to use and scrolled through various options.

While it brought back memories Bev preferred to forget, she knew she would have to become used to things like this if her new project was to succeed. She pushed the past firmly to the back of her mind and concentrated on what Ailsa was showing her.

'I think I like this one,' Bev said, after they'd scrolled through several different types of vows. 'It's simple wording and seems more like you and Martin. Which one do *you* prefer?'

'I'm torn between that one and this.' Ailsa scrolled back to an earlier page which described a ceremony which included a loving cup where the bride and groom drank from the same cup. 'It sounds so romantic.'

'Oh, I must have missed that one. Yes, I see what you mean,' Bev said, looking at the illustrations of the double-handed bowl and the description of it being an ancient Scottish tradition. 'Maybe you could ask her to combine the two. There must be Scottish blood in the family somewhere.'

'In my dad's family,' Ailsa said in a small voice. 'He'd have loved it.'

They were both silent, remembering Ailsa's dad who passed away not long after she and Martin got together.

'Okay, that's what we'll do. I wonder where we can find one of these loving cups.'

'It says here,' Bev read further, 'many couples drink from regular glasses.'

'I suppose. But I do like the sound of a special one.'

'Mmm.' Bev didn't say any more but vowed to try her best to find one for the happy couple. They were both special to her, her family.

'Thanks, Bev. You made it easier to decide. Now I have to run it past Martin, but he did say he'd be happy with whatever we chose. Now, I should be going. Martin's meeting should be finished, and I guess he and Will will be sinking a few beers in the club if I don't turn up soon. See you tomorrow,' she reminded Bev as she rose to leave.

*

Bev stood outside the fashion boutique feeling out of place in her workday outfit of cut-off jeans and a tee-shirt with the slogan *Life is Good*, she'd quickly dragged on that morning. The window display of gaudy outfits did nothing to allay her concern that this wasn't the place for her.

'Here you are.' Ailsa rushed up to give her a kiss on the cheek. 'I was worried you'd chicken out.'

Ailsa knew her so well. But Bev knew her friend had her best interests at heart, even if she sometimes misread the situation. Had she misread this one? Did she imagine Bev and Iain Grant were a couple? Surely not? Iain Grant was just a newcomer to town who wanted to make friends. He had helped her with a troublesome task and invited her to dinner. So why was she about to look for an outfit in a shop she'd always avoided?

Bev had to admit Ailsa had been right. Greta welcomed Bev as if she was a valued customer and was wise enough to avoid showing her any of the brightly coloured outfits on the racks. Instead, she brought out several cotton dresses and a pair of wide pants in a cream linen which Greta called palazzo pants, and with which Bev instantly fell in love. Minutes later, carrying a bag containing the pants, a loose white silk blouse and a cream pashmina, Bev and Ailsa left the shop.

'Coffee, I think,' Ailsa said, 'or would you prefer wine? I'm meeting Martin at the surf club for dinner. Why don't you join us?'

Buoyed up with her purchase, the prospect of a glass of wine was attractive, so Bev agreed, and they walked across to the club together.

Martin was chatting to Ailsa's son, Nate, who was working behind the bar.

'Hi, Mum. Auntie Bev,' Nate said, while Martin kissed both women on the cheek. 'White wine coming up.' Nate grinned and reached for the wine bottle, while the two women placed their food orders.

'Been shopping?' Martin asked, gesturing to the *Birds of a Feather* bag, when they had found a seat on the deck.

'Bev has a hot date,' Ailsa said with a grin and a wink.

Martin's eyes widened. 'Bev?'

'Not really.' She blushed, inwardly cursing Ailsa. 'I'm only having dinner with Iain Grant.'

'Oh, the architect guy who's renting Grace Winter's place? He has a son who's in training for the triathlon.'

'Oh? Bryan works at the garden centre.'

'Yeah, so he said.'

'You know Bryan?'

'Met him the other morning. He's training with Nate and Owen. Seems like a nice guy.'

'He is.'

'And his dad?'

'He's a nice guy, too. He's been helping me with the application to the council.'

Their meals arrived at that point, so Bev was saved from saying more, but she caught Martin's surprised glance and knew she'd be in for an interrogation sometime soon.

During their meal, the conversation revolved around the plans for the wedding. Martin had been happy to agree with Ailsa and Bev's decision regarding the ceremony and applauded the idea of sharing a loving cup, suggesting the drink be champagne which they could drink out of a champagne flute. Ailsa was able to report the celebrant was happy to combine the two ceremonies for them, so all was well.

Bev left as soon as the meal was over, citing the need for an early start next day. She was pleased with her shopping but, as she walked up the boardwalk, swinging her shopping bag, she wondered why she had allowed Ailsa to persuade her into such an extravagant purchase for dinner with a man she hardly knew.

Nineteen

Iain was feeling good. The application for Bev Cooper had been completed and, after a few attempts, he'd finally managed to persuade her to join him for coffee at *The Pandanus Café* and to agree to have dinner with him. He wasn't sure why it was such a big deal, but he had the impression she didn't normally go on dates. He couldn't imagine why. As a single woman in a small town, surely she was accustomed to being invited out. But perhaps, the unobtainable vibes he'd sensed, put others off. He didn't give up easily, and there was something about Bev Cooper that made him want to know her better.

Also, he was increasingly pleased with his sketches and had decided to take a few in to show John Baldwin at *The Bay Gallery*. He wasn't sure they were up to his standard, but it was worth asking.

He was humming to himself and making breakfast when Bryan came back from his morning swim and run.

'You sound happy, Dad,' Bryan said.

'I am. It's a lovely day, and I plan to take my drawings in to the guy at the gallery this morning; see what he thinks.' He decided to say nothing about his date with Bryan's boss; his son would find out soon enough.

'I think they're pretty good. Sorry I didn't inherit the artistic gene. I think Mia might have it,' he said, ruffling his daughter's hair.

'Have what?' she turned to gaze at her dad.

'Grandad is an artist. I think you may become one, too.'

'I will,' she said confidently. 'Miss Hodge says my drawings are really good.' She preened.

'They are indeed,' Iain said. 'Your talents lie in a different direction,' he said to Bryan. 'Your writing…'

'No, Dad.' Bryan raised both hands. 'That part of my life is over. I'm content with what I'm doing now.'

Iain wanted to tell him being content wasn't enough, he should be following his passion. It used to be sports writing, but what if that passion had left him? What would his future be? He bit his tongue.

After dropping Mia off at school and watching her run off to join her friends, Iain headed towards the gallery, disappointed to find it closed. The sign on the door indicated there was still an hour till opening time. Spotting a café nearby, and smiling at its name, Iain decided to fill the time with another cup of coffee.

Entering *The Greedy Gecko*, he carefully set the folder containing his sketches on the table, ordered and took out his phone to check his emails, something he hadn't taken time to do earlier. He clicked his tongue when he saw there was one from Ros. What did his ex-wife want now? He opened it.

Iain,

I'm not sure what your problem is, why you're avoiding me – and why you seem to be encouraging our son to do the same. Bryan hasn't responded to my last message either. I only want what's best for him and Mia, and I want to understand why you're selling the Sydney house. We had a lot of good years there. I'm sad to see it go. I remember you saying you loved it too much to ever sell it. What changed?

I've managed to find out from Paul that you are presently living in the tiny town on Queensland's Sunshine Coast where we spent a few holidays when Bryan was little – not your usual scene. I expect you'll soon get bored and rush back to the city.

Anyway, I'm at a loose end and have a few days up my sleeve, so I plan to visit you to see my son and granddaughter. Don't worry, I don't expect you to put me up. I've booked into what seems to be the only decent hotel in the place. I'll be there on Saturday week.

Be in touch when I arrive.

Ros

As Iain read the email, his eyes widened in disbelief. As he'd suspected, Paul had caved in to her pleading, no doubt combined with mock tears at the loss of her son and granddaughter. But to think she had taken it upon herself to book accommodation, to make plans to come here. The only decent hotel. No doubt it was the one owned by Milton Harris, the guy who threatened to block the application he'd been working on. Damn him! Damn Ros! Why did she have to decide to visit now? Why did she have to decide to visit at all?

*

'Hello there, you're back. Do you have something to show me?' John Baldwin removed his old-fashioned half-moon spectacles and pinched the bridge of his nose before replacing them. 'Can you take over here, Mel?' he asked the young woman at his side, her long dark brown hair tied back from a pretty face.

'Of course.' She smiled at Iain.

'Come through,' John said. He led Iain into an office at the back of the gallery, took a seat and signalled to Iain to do the same. 'So, you took my advice,' he said with a smile.

'I did. I'm not sure what I've produced is up to the standard you require, but I thought I'd ask your opinion.' He opened the folder and handed it over, wondering if this was a mistake, if he had overrated his ability and his work.

The young woman appeared again while John Baldwin was examining Iain's sketches. She was carrying two mugs. 'I thought you might like coffee,' she said, handing one mug to Iain and placing the other on John Baldwin's desk.

'Thanks, Mel,' he said distractedly, not taking his eyes from the sketches.

'Thanks.' Even though he had just had a coffee, Iain was grateful to have something to do with his hands. Why was it taking so long? If they were no good, why didn't Baldwin just say so?

Finally, John Baldwin removed his spectacles again and looked across at Iain. 'These are very good,' he said. 'I'd be happy to display them in the gallery. I'd like to take those on consignment and if they go well, which I expect they will, I'd be happy to take any others you produce.'

'Really?' Iain could hardly believe his ears. The gallery owner liked them. He hadn't lost his touch. After all those years of spec drawings, of making plans for homes and offices, he could still turn out decent pieces of work that might sell. 'Thanks so much.'

'Thank *you*. It's a pleasure to add those to my stock. They will look good alongside the usual watercolours and Martin Cooper's photographs. Tourists are always looking for something a bit different. These will fit the bill. I'll have Mel draw up our usual agreement then, if you're happy with it, we can put them on display.'

'Thanks,' Iain said again, feeling euphoric. He didn't care much about the agreement. It wasn't about the money. He was just glad Baldwin considered his work good enough to add to his collection.

*

When Iain picked Mia up from school, she was full of chatter, excited about the fact Nippers was due to start on Sunday, having discovered many of those in her class were also going to be involved.

Once she was settled with a glass of milk and her current favourite snack – a rice cake liberally spread with Nutella – Iain opened his laptop to see the agreement Baldwin's assistant had promised to send through. It was there, along with the email from Ros he'd read earlier, plus one from his former partner.

Iain opened Paul's first, anticipating what it would say. He was right. It was an apology for revealing his whereabouts to Ros, with the excuse she'd caught him at the office, they'd gone for a drink, and she'd wheedled it out of him. Iain sighed. He knew how persuasive Ros could be when she put her mind to it. He'd often been the target of her sweet talk, until it no longer had any effect. Then he'd seen the other side of her, the less pleasant side which came to the fore when she was thwarted. In a way, he'd been glad when she finally left to pursue what were to her more attractive options – in other words men who could still be taken in by her wiles.

Now, it seemed she was on her own again and wanted to play happy families, recapturing the roles of mother and grandmother she eschewed for so long. Iain stared at her email, but there was no need to respond. Tempted as he was to reply and tell her to stay away, he knew it would be of no use. Once Ros made up her mind, nothing could change it. All he could do was hope her visit didn't prove too disruptive, and that it would be short.

It wasn't till Mia was in bed that Iain had the chance to talk with Bryan, to tell him about his mother's email and proposed visit.

'Mum's coming here?' Bryan dragged a hand through his hair. 'How does she know where we are?'

'Paul told her,' Iain said shortly, cursing his former partner for what must be at least the tenth time that day.

'How long for?'

'She didn't say. I know she's your mother, Bryan, but…'

'She left us. She didn't want us in her life. Mia barely knows her. When Nadia… she didn't… How can she…?' He slammed his fist on the table, stood up and left.

Iain stared after him in despair. Bryan had been doing so well. It was true Ros hadn't shown much sympathy when Nadia died, too enamoured with her current fellow to come to the funeral. And she'd only met Mia a couple of times. The little girl probably didn't remember her, wouldn't know who she was if it wasn't for the photographs Nadia used to show her. Iain wondered where these photos were now. He hadn't seen them since Bryan came to live with him. He guessed they were in storage with all the other paraphernalia of his son's former life.

Iain shrugged off the feeling of hopelessness threatening to engulf him and settled down to compose a reply to Paul and read the agreement from *The Bay Gallery*. Then he'd see if Bryan was willing to talk to him. He needed to tell him he'd invited his boss out to dinner.

Twenty

To her surprise, Bev found herself looking forward to having dinner with Iain Grant. She'd liked what she saw of the tall grey-haired man, and he was Bryan's dad. That alone might have swayed her thinking and convinced her to accept his dinner invitation, even if he hadn't mentioned her favourite restaurant. Also, she was curious about Bryan's likeness to Phil and wondered if there was any family connection.

Some days, she regretted not having made contact with Phil's family, but they knew nothing about her. She'd gone to his funeral, fully intending to introduce herself. But, as she sat in a pew at the back of the church through the formal funeral service, her eyes red and swollen with weeping, her hand protecting the small bump that would become their child, and watched his parents grieve for their son, she knew she couldn't approach them that day. It would have to be later.

But later never came. Next day, the Canberra papers were filled with stories of the young cadet who'd led an exemplary life and been taken too soon. There were stories about his father's military service, the family's hopes for their son, the son who was the epitome of the upright product of the military family, his public school and the defence academy. It made Bev feel she had no right, no claim on him. It would have been different if he'd lived, but there was no going back. It was the eulogy, more than anything else that had encouraged her to seek refuge with her godmother in Sydney.

At the time, she had thoughts of perhaps contacting them when her baby was born, in the hope the arrival of a grandchild would overcome her shame. But that wasn't to be, either. Over the years, she'd tried to keep abreast of the family through the media. Both Phil's parents were now dead, and he'd been an only child. She knew nothing about his extended family, so it was possible Iain or his wife were related in some way. It would explain the striking resemblance.

Although she saw Bryan every day and was becoming accustomed to the sight of his tall figure around the garden centre, there were still times when a glimpse of him made Bev's heart leap into her throat, when she couldn't subdue the memory of that other young man, taken too soon. Today, she'd caught him eyeing her speculatively and wondered if Iain had told him about their dinner date.

Bev was almost ready to leave when her phone rang.

'Ailsa.'

'Just calling to make sure you haven't chickened out.'

Her friend knew her so well.

'No, I'm dressed and ready to go. He'll be picking me up shortly.'

'I've never understood why you never formed a relationship. I know you always claim you could never find a man who'd put up with you, but... If I didn't know you better, I'd think...'

'I need to go now,' Bev cut Ailsa off, trembling with panic. In all the years they'd known each other, Ailsa had never questioned Bev's solitary lifestyle, never probed why she'd left uni so suddenly, accepted the explanation about her parents. Why did she have to bring it up now?

She was still feeling shaky when she heard a knock on the glass door leading out to the deck and heard Iain call, 'Hello.'

Forcing a smile, she grabbed her bag, threw the pashmina over her shoulders and headed out without bothering to check herself in the mirror. 'Hello,' she said.

On the way down the boardwalk, their conversation consisted of comments about the weather and the beauty of the sky as the sun dropped below the horizon. The changing colours of the evening sky was something Bev never took for granted, one of the joys of living here on the boardwalk with the ocean as her backyard. Tonight, the colours were particularly beautiful, the sun seeming to dance on the edge of the water, bright, vibrant colours like an artist's palette painting the sky with purple, pink and orange.

They stopped to admire the spectacle, Iain's hand reaching for Bev's as the last rays of the sun disappeared.

When they reached the restaurant, Bev cautiously extricated her hand and walked in with Iain to be greeted familiarly by the waiter.

'You come here a lot?' Iain asked, as they were shown to a table.

'Not as often as I'd like. It's a favourite of mine. I love Italian food.'

'It was a good choice, then.'

Once seated, Iain picked up a menu. 'What would you recommend?' he asked.

Bev didn't hesitate. 'The garlic bread's a must. It's unleavened and delicious – unless you don't like garlic?' She raised one eyebrow feeling more comfortable now she was in familiar territory. The feeling of his hand in his had shaken her.

'No, I'm fine with garlic.' He grinned, a cheeky glint in his eyes.

Bev shivered despite the warmth of the restaurant. 'Well, for starters I usually order the cannelloni then either the spaghetti carbonara or a pizza. Their pizzas are out of this world.'

'Sounds good. Cannelloni for two it is followed by spaghetti carbonara. Do you have any preference for wine?'

'No, you choose.'

Once the order was settled, Bev glanced around the restaurant which, being Friday, was almost full and becoming noisy as a large group appeared to be celebrating a family birthday.

'I've signed the application,' she said. 'Shall I submit it, or would it be better if you did?'

'Best I do it. Then they can see you followed their advice to use a planner. Also, I'm curious to get more of an insight into the workings of the council here, given Will Rankin's warning.'

'Okay. I'll get it to you.'

There was a pause, then Iain said, 'I had some good news today. *The Bay Gallery* is going to display some of my sketches.'

'I didn't know you were an artist, too. Though I suppose I shouldn't be surprised. An architect needs to have artistic skill.'

'It's something I used to do a lot, but not recently. It's been good to recapture an old skill. Keeps me out of trouble.' He chuckled, his eyes crinkling.

'What have you been sketching?'

'Oh, just a few local scenes mostly from the headland. It's amazing how the view changes from minute to minute.'

'The headland? Have you come across the woman who lives there in *Headland View*?'

'No, should I have? Why do you ask?'

'No reason. But… Ruby Sullivan who lives in the old house up there is quite a character. She usually manages to meet any newcomers to the area and…' she bit her lip, wondering whether to say more, '… she's famous for making what many take to be predictions.'

Iain grinned. 'You're not serious?'

'Very. She also makes the delicious cakes you've been eating at our café.'

'That sounds more believable. I'll be sure to let you know if I come across her.' He chuckled again.

Bev wished she hadn't said anything. Now the poor man would be looking for Ruby next time he went up there.

'How is Bryan going at the garden centre?' he asked, once their meals had arrived. 'I notice a difference in him at home. He seems to be more settled. It's been a difficult time for him.'

'He's doing well. He's a good worker, and for someone with no previous experience with gardening or plants, he seems to have an aptitude for it. I understand he was a journalist before coming here.'

'Before his wife died. Yes. He was the top sports reporter in one of the Sydney dailies. Nadia's death knocked him for six. It's why we upped sticks and came to Bellbird Bay. Mia, my granddaughter, has settled in well, too. She's made friends at school and is joining Nippers.'

'Oh, she'll love it. I remember when Martin and I joined, Will, too. Those were some of the best times we had growing up here. I didn't continue, but the guys did and became surfing heroes.'

'I heard about Will, but not your brother.'

'Will was the one who stayed to become a champion. Martin's love of photography took him to Sydney, then overseas.'

'And his wedding will be your first in the garden centre?'

'Yes, hopefully the first of many if…' Bev's forehead creased, remembering what Will had said about opposition to her plan.

'I'm sure it'll be fine. I've fought bigger battles than this.' Iain recounted several of his experiences with anti-development groups in the city in which he'd managed to win over their opposition.

The rest of the evening passed pleasantly for Bev, but there was no opportunity for her to discover anything about Iain or his wife's families, though he did say his ex-wife intended to pay them a visit. He didn't appear pleased at the prospect, making Bev wonder why their marriage had fallen apart and interested to meet the woman who was Bryan's mother.

To Bev's relief, Iain made no attempt to take her hand again as they made their way back up the boardwalk, stopping at her gate.

'Thank you. I've enjoyed this evening,' she said with a smile.

'I have, too.' Iain hesitated for a moment before giving her a kiss on the cheek. 'Perhaps we can do it again?' he said, then he was off striding up the boardwalk as if regretting what had barely been a touch of his lips.

Twenty-one

Sunday morning was a hive of activity as Mia prepared for her first session at Nippers. She was so excited she could barely sit still to eat breakfast, desperate to don the new pink rashie and cap and go to the beach. She'd completed her pool proficiency at The Bellbird Bay Aquatic Centre on the other side of town a week earlier and was eager to start what she thought of as *the real thing*.

'Clancy will be there too, and Chloe, and Tayla, and Marianne,' she said, counting off her new friends on the fingers of one hand.

Iain was relieved when they finally reached the beach, and they were able to hand Mia over to the surf lifesavers who were instructing the group of excited young children. He was surprised to see Bryan chatting to one of the two young men.

'It's Owen Rankin,' Bryan said, when he re-joined Iain. 'He's one of the guys I'm training with.'

Iain gave the young man a closer look. He resembled the photo Iain had seen of Will Rankin in the local paper. Hadn't Bryan said Owen was his son?

'He was the local surf champion three years running,' Bryan said with a note of respect. Only one other guy has done that, He's featured on a mural in the surf club.'

Iain gave his son a puzzled look. Bryan had never shown any interest in surfing before now. 'You want to give it a try?' he asked.

'Wouldn't mind. Maybe when the tri is over. Owen's dad runs the surf school. If we're going to be living here, it makes sense for me to learn. Can't let Mia have all the fun.'

'You're happy here? You don't think you'll want to go back to the city?'

'No, Dad. And, yes, I do like it here. I like the air. It's different up here. And no one knows me, I can become a new person, not…' His mouth turned down.

Iain patted Bryan's shoulder. 'How about a coffee?' he asked. 'Looks as if Mia's fully occupied.' He gestured to where Mia and the other small, pink-covered bodies were seated on the sand listening intently to what was being said.

'Okay, Dad.'

By the time Iain returned with takeaway coffees from the café on the esplanade, the children were running into the ocean, a heaving mass of pink in the waves. The pair took up a stance in the shade from where they could watch the activity on the beach and be available if Mia needed them.

'Thanks, Dad,' Bryan said after a long silence.

Iain gave him a puzzled look.

'For bringing us here. I feel I can breathe again. It was the right thing to do. But what about you? Don't you miss your old life?'

Iain was surprised. It was unlike Bryan to consider what it had been like for him to leave his home and work, to upend his life to start again here in Bellbird Bay. He thought for a moment before replying, 'I made the choice because I was worried about you. I couldn't bear to see you in such a state. It was a risk. It might not have worked but it did. It's so good to see how living here has brought you back to me.' His voice broke. 'You – you and Mia – you mean the world to me. I'd have done anything to see you happy again. Your life can never be the same. I knew that. But… to see you making a new life for yourself… it means a lot.'

Bryan smiled and placed his hand on Iain's shoulder.

They stood in silence again until an older man, who had been standing nearby watching the action on the beach turned towards them. 'You have a youngster here?' he asked with a smile.

'My granddaughter. Mia,' Iain replied. 'You?'

The man shook his head. 'Mine are too old and too young for Nippers. Zack's aiming for the championships next year – he's helping out over there – and Isla is still a toddler. Ted Crawford,' he said, offering his hand.

'Iain Grant, and this is my son, Bryan, Mia's dad.' Iain shook his hand while Bryan nodded. Ted Crawford, he'd heard the name somewhere. The penny dropped. 'Ted Crawford, you're the artist whose water colours are on display at *The Bay Gallery*,' he exclaimed.

Bryan who had appeared lost in thought, now said, 'Aren't you the guy on the surf club mural, the one who was three times surf champion?'

'Guilty on both counts,' Ted chuckled. 'And you're my wife's new tenants. We've been hoping to meet you. I know Grace will be delighted I've bumped into you. Do you surf?'

Iain shook his head. 'Neither of us, but Bryan's keen to learn. He mentioned a surf school.'

'Will Rankin. Can't go wrong there. Will's a great guy and a champion surfer. You're working at *The Pandanus Garden Centre*, aren't you, Bryan? Your boss there is a good friend of Will's. She and her brother hung around with him when they were young. I was a bit older than them, of course, but everyone knew the terrible trio, as we used to call them.' He chuckled. 'Now we've met, Grace will chide me if I don't invite you to meet her, too. You must join us for a drink. How about this evening?'

'There's Mia…'

'No problem. Bring her along. Around five?'

'Thanks.'

'We're four houses up from you.' He grinned.

'That was kind of him,' Iain said, when Ted had wandered off.

'You go, Dad. Mia and me…'

'He invited us all, Bryan. It would be rude to stay home.' Iain was disappointed in his son, just as he'd imagined he was making an improvement. 'We won't need to stay long.'

'Okay,' Bryan said reluctantly. 'What is it about this place. Everyone is so darned friendly.'

'It's a small town. It's what people are like.' Growing up in Sydney, Bryan hadn't been exposed to the small-town friendliness he had experienced himself when he visited his grandparents in country New South Wales. How he'd loved those visits which had suddenly ceased when he was only eleven and his grandparents had died one after the other.

All of a sudden, it seemed, the group further down the beach began to disperse and Mia rushed towards them. The hour had gone quickly.

'It was so much fun, Daddy,' Mia said, throwing her towel at Bryan, then haring off again to join up with three other girls, one of whom Iain recognised as Clancy.

'I thought I saw you,' Adam Holland appeared at their side. 'Clancy insisted Libby and I come along to watch. She's over there.' He pointed to where a group of older women were gathered. 'Nick's helping out in the water with the kids. He grew up here and has his SLS Bronze Medallion. Emma's helping on the beach.'

'Do you surf, too?' Iain asked. It seemed everyone who lived here did.

'Not me. I'm a newcomer to all this. You?'

Iain shook his head. 'You're the second person to ask us that. Guess most people here do.'

'It's almost compulsory, but so far, I've managed to avoid it. I stick to swimming.'

At that moment, Libby joined them and, after exchanging greetings the two sauntered off.

'See,' Iain said, when Bryan grimaced. 'It doesn't hurt to be polite. People just want to be friends – and we all need friends.'

*

'Who are these people we're going to see, Grandad?' Mia asked as they walked up the boardwalk to Grace and Ted's house.

'Grace is the lady who owns the house we're living in,' Iain said, remembering again how Adam Holland had suggested she might be willing to sell. It was looking more and more likely Bryan and Mia would be staying here with him, and it was a sound house in a good location. He needed to raise it with Bryan to get his thoughts on the idea

'Does she have a dog?' Mia asked, hopping back and forth on the worn wooden boards. 'Like Milo.'

'I don't know.' Iain thought it possible. He knew how Mia had become attached to Libby's dog and had been meaning to ask Bryan about getting one for Mia on her birthday. But it would depend on having their landlady's permission – unless they bought the house. So many things to consider – and there was Ros's impending visit the following weekend to survive.

When they pushed open the white gate, Ted appeared in the doorway, followed by a woman with a kindly expression whose silver hair fell in waves around her face. A tortoiseshell cat wound its way between their legs to stand staring at them.

'Oh, look!' Mia ran towards the cat who turned over to lie on its back. She crouched down to pet it.

'Tiger will love you for ever if you do that,' Grace laughed. 'Hello, you must be Iain and Bryan.' She smiled at the two men. 'I'm very pleased to meet you at last. And this is…?'

'I'm Mia. I love your cat.' Mia had lost her shyness as soon as the animal appeared.

'It's such a lovely night, I thought we could stay out here on the deck,' Grace said, gesturing to where two comfortable-looking benches and a couple of chairs surrounded a table on which there were several platters containing biscuits, cheese and other nibbles.

While Ted went inside to fetch drinks – beer, wine and juice – Grace told Iain and Bryan a little about herself. It seemed she had moved to Bellbird Bay from country New South Wales – not far from where Iain's grandparents had lived – after the death of her husband. She had two daughters, one of whom lived here on the coast with Ted's son, the other in Sydney. It was a lot to take in all at once. Iain was glad when Ted reappeared with the drinks and the conversation turned to other matters.

Ted was interested to hear about Iain's architectural background, and they exchanged anecdotes about the challenges of running a business in the city. Even though Ted had been a solicitor in Brisbane, and Iain an architect in Sydney, they discovered many similarities. Meanwhile, Iain was pleased to see Grace keeping Bryan occupied by chatting about various activities in Bellbird Bay and arranging for him to meet her daughter and Ted's son who were close to his age. Mia was oblivious to the adult conversation as she played with the cat.

When they rose to leave, Iain was pleased to see Bryan looking happier.

'Grace said I'd like Aaron and Mel,' he said, when they were on their way down the boardwalk. 'She didn't go into details, but I got the impression they've both had a hard time. It might be okay to meet some other people life hasn't been kind to, though…'

'They may not have suffered the same loss you have,' Iain said, 'but life doesn't always go smoothly. It can sometimes help to realise others can have problems, too. I met Grace's daughter, Mel, at the gallery. She's John Baldwin's assistant.'

'Wow! It's such a small town. I think I'm getting used to it. I know what I said this morning, but I enjoyed meeting Grace and Ted.'

'And Tiger,' Mia added, skipping along beside them. 'I liked Tiger.'

'And Tiger,' Bryan agreed.

When they'd eaten, and Mia was tucked up in bed, Iain and Bryan took their coffees out to the deck. It was a beautiful evening, the silence only broken by the waves lapping on the shore and the distant sound of voices from further down the boardwalk.

'What would you think of my talking to Grace about buying this place?' Iain asked Bryan. 'I don't think we could find anything better in Bellbird Bay and I already feel attached to it.'

'Good idea, Dad. But would you want Mia and me living with you for ever? You have your own life to lead, too.'

'You're my family. Where else would you go?'

'Dunno.' Bryan gazed into space, making Iain wonder if he'd brought up the subject too soon, if Bryan wasn't ready to think of the future, a future in which there was no Nadia.

'Mia likes it here,' he said at last. 'It would be good for her to feel secure.'

Twenty-two

As the early morning light peeped through the planation shutters on her bedroom window, Bev stretched her arms above her head and was about to leap out of bed when she remembered. She was taking the day off. It had been so long since she'd had a day all to herself, and the past few weeks had been so hectic with the day-to-day running of the garden centre combined with her plans to establish a wedding venue, she'd been run ragged. Over dinner the previous evening, Martin and Ailsa had ganged up on her and persuaded her to take the day off.

'We can drop in to make sure everything is running okay,' Ailsa said. 'It'll be like old times.' She had nudged Martin, forcing Bev to remember how she'd persuaded the pair to work together in the garden centre when she'd had an accident. She wasn't entirely sure but had always suspected it was what brought them together.

Now the whole day stretched before her, enticingly empty. Closing her eyes, she curled up in bed, her mind going back to her dinner with Iain Grant three days earlier. She'd enjoyed the evening more than she anticipated. He was a nice man, and it was the first time she'd had dinner with an attractive man since she couldn't remember when.

When she returned to Bellbird Bay to help her mother care for her father, she'd been shellshocked, too traumatised to consider seeing anyone, even if the invitations had been there, which they weren't. She didn't blame the local men; dating was the furthest thing from her mind. Then she'd started the garden centre… and it had become her life. Phil was the only man she'd ever loved, ever thought she'd love.

She'd never imagined finding another man attractive. Then she'd met Bryan Grant who'd stirred up memories of Phil… then she'd met his father.

Bev knew it wasn't the likelihood of a connection to Phil that kindled the spark she'd experienced when Iain took her hand, when his lips touched her cheek. It was Iain himself. After over thirty-five years, she was finally attracted to another man. But his son's likeness to Phil was still something she wanted to investigate.

She rose, took a leisurely shower and filled a bowl with muesli topped with blueberries and yoghurt, before taking it and a mug of peppermint tea out to the deck. It felt very odd to be sitting here while everyone else was starting their day. For a second she wondered what was happening at the garden centre, then she dismissed the thought, knowing Ailsa, Martin and her staff would cope, and remembering Ailsa's direction to forget all about it 'for just one day'. That's what she'd do.

But breakfast over, Bev saw the council application lying on her desk and decided to walk up the boardwalk to deliver it to Iain Grant.

It was mid-morning, and she didn't expect him to be home, so it was no surprise to find the house locked up. With a sigh of relief tinged with disappointment, she slid the envelope containing the signed application under his door before deciding to continue up the boardwalk towards the headland.

It was a glorious morning, and Bev was relishing the joy of being alive. She could feel the hint of spring in the air, a taste of the summer to come as she made her way up the steep slope past the row of old beach shacks which had been there as long as she could remember. Most, like hers, had been renovated and now bore little resemblance to their original state but were still a reminder of the small fishing village Bellbird Bay had once been.

Enjoying her own company, Bev was surprised to see a figure seated at the top of the boardwalk, leaning against a Norfolk pine. As she drew closer, she saw it was Iain Grant. Remembering he'd mentioned he had been sketching up here, she silently cursed. What if he thought she was stalking him. She stopped in her tracks and was about to turn back, when he spotted her.

'Bev!' Iain put aside what he had been working on and rose to greet her. 'Not working today?' He smiled, his eyes crinkling, and Bev felt her stomach churn.

'No. I'm taking a day off. I… I didn't expect to find you here,' she said. 'I popped the signed application under your door.'

'Thanks. Join me in a coffee?' He held up a flask. 'I have a spare mug.'

Bev hesitated, but after her climb, the sound of coffee was tempting. 'Thanks.'

She joined him on the grass and accepted the coffee, taking a long gulp. It was good. She glanced at the sketch Iain was making of Ruby's house. It was good, too. 'I like what you've done,' she said. 'You've captured the essence of Ruby's place. No wonder John Baldwin is keen to display your work. I'm sorry if I disturbed you.'

'Not at all. I'm almost done here. I've been sitting in the same position for too long. I'm not as flexible as I used to be.' He gave a mock groan, making Bev chuckle. He looked pretty fit to her. 'You've lived here all your life, you said. You must know everyone in Bellbird Bay.'

'Almost.'

'What about the woman who lives in this house? You mentioned something about her when we had dinner.'

'Ruby? Everyone knows Ruby Sullivan.' Bev tried to remember what she'd said, probably warned him about her strange ways.

'I met her this morning.'

'And?'

'You were right. She says some odd things.'

Bev waited, but Iain didn't elaborate.

'I hope she didn't spook you.'

Iain shook his head, but Bev thought she saw a strange expression flicker in his eyes. Then it was gone.

'Did you aways live in Sydney?' she asked, eager to discover any connection with Canberra and Phil's family.

'All my life. I grew up on the Northern Beaches, met Ros there. Never saw any reason to move… till now.'

'Oh.' Bev was disappointed, but it didn't mean there wasn't a distant connection.

'Shall we walk down together?' Iain was gathering up his things, preparing to leave.

'Okay.' There was no reason to refuse. Bev could hardly say she wanted to stay there. And she was enjoying his company.

They walked together in companionable silence till they reached the house where Iain was staying, then they stopped, standing awkwardly together.

*

What a serendipity, Iain thought. He'd been thinking about Bev Cooper when she appeared as if by magic. It had been a stroke of genius to take along a mug in addition to the cup on top of the flask which enabled him to offer her coffee. He hadn't been entirely honest about his encounter with the woman she called Ruby Sullivan. He had just set up for the day when this strange apparition wearing an old straw hat laden with flowers had ridden up on a green bicycle and stopped right in front of him. He'd known right away who it was – the woman Bev had warned him about. But he hadn't been prepared for what she said. Gazing at him with eyes which seemed to peer right through him she'd announced, 'You are close to finding your true partner in life. Be open to possibilities and don't allow misunderstandings to divert you from your true path.'

It had sent a shiver down his spine. Then she had disappeared and the sun, which had been hiding behind a cloud had emerged, and all was normal again. But the woman's words were still there in the back of his mind. What had she meant? Was there any truth in what could be construed as a prediction – or a warning?

Now, as he stood at his gate, a thrill ran through Iain as he stared at Bev. Her lightly tanned face was devoid of makeup apart from a slight colour on her lips, so different from Ros and the women he'd met on the dating site. All of them seemed to feel the need to pile on the war paint. Bev was a woman happy in her own skin, natural. Even her hair was merely tied back in an untidy ponytail, the light breeze blowing strands across her cheeks. Was she the one Ruby had referred to? And what sort of misunderstandings could possibly occur?

He knew he had to say something before Bev disappeared down the boardwalk. 'Why don't you join me for lunch?' he asked. 'It won't be much, but I have some good cheeses and a loaf of Vollkorn bread I bought from the German bakery on the esplanade, plus there should be some fruit.' He gazed at her hopefully.

Bev hesitated indecisively for a few moments, then with a nod she said, 'Thanks, that sounds good,' and followed him inside.

'Excuse the mess... two men and a child,' Iain said apologetically, shifting a bundle of papers from the kitchen bench and seeing the breakfast dishes still in the sink. He raked a hand through his hair, unsure where to begin. He hadn't anticipated having a guest to lunch. 'I...' he stammered.

'It's okay. I have a twin brother. I grew up with Martin. I know what men can be like.' She chuckled.

Iain joined in. 'Well,' he looked around the kitchen, 'take a seat while I put this stuff away.' He gestured to the satchel containing his sketch pad and pens. 'I'll be with you in a tick.'

Instead of being seated, Bev was standing at the kitchen sink when Iain returned. The breakfast dishes had been washed and were neatly stacked on the draining board.

'You shouldn't have,' he said, embarrassed at having been caught in such disarray.

'It's nothing.' She waved away his thanks. 'Where's this lunch you promised me?'

'Coming up.'

Before long, they were seated outside on the deck, the light breeze fanning them as they tucked into the bread and cheese Iain had promised along with two bottles of One Fifty Lashes beer he had found in the fridge.

'This is nice. Thanks for inviting me.' Bev leant back in her chair. 'It always interests me to see another of these houses. I never visited when Grace lived here... or Adam. I like what's been done to improve it. Do you intend staying here for long?'

Iain thought before replying then said, 'I'm thinking of offering to buy it... if Grace is agreeable. There doesn't seem to be much point in looking around. I doubt I could find anything better... and I don't want to build again.'

'Mmm, you could do worse. We're a great little community here on the boardwalk. You've met Adam and Libby, too, haven't you? Eddie?'

'Adam and Libby yes. Who is Eddie?'

'She lives next door to Adam and Libby. You're bound to run into her.'

'Mmm.' Iain didn't need to meet another woman. The one he was with was enough for him. He wanted to find out more about her. 'Tell me about your garden centre. What made you start it? Have you always been interested in plants?'

Bev paused for a moment before replying, as if trying to decide how much to reveal. 'Not really. I did intend to become a teacher. Ailsa and I met at uni in Canberra. But I didn't finish my degree. My parents became sick, and I came back home. Dad had let the garden go, so I began to spend time in it. I found I enjoyed getting my hands dirty,' she grinned, 'and it was satisfying to see things grow. It also helped me to…' she seemed to search for words, '…find a sense of peace, I think.' She gazed out towards the ocean, lost in thought.

Iain felt there was more to it than Bev was willing to reveal, but said nothing, deciding to pursue it at another time, when they knew each other better. He had the distinct feeling there was something she wasn't telling him, something important to her, perhaps even the reason she had never married. Or had she? Could she be widowed or have an ex-husband tucked away somewhere? 'You never married?' he asked.

'No,' Bev said shortly, her tone one which brooked no further questions.

'Well, as I discovered, marriage isn't always the happy-ever-after it's touted to be in books and movies, though some people seem to manage it.' He gave a sigh, remembering his own fated marriage, though he and Ros had enjoyed some good years together Thinking of Ros reminded him. She'd be here the following weekend.

'Something wrong?'

'No, just remembering my own marriage and my ex-wife. Sorry, you don't want to hear about my sad past. You were telling me about starting the garden centre. I interrupted you.'

'There's not much more to tell. When Dad died, I found I had more time on my hands. Then, when the local garden centre came up for sale, Mum encouraged me to take a look at it. It was pretty run down, but I could see the potential and knew I'd enjoy building it up into something I could make my life's work. That's how *The Pandanus Garden Centre* began. As time went on, I was able to expand, hence the café.'

'And now into a wedding venue?'

'Yes, hopefully.'

'I intend it make sure it goes through. I've asked Paul, my friend and former partner to look into Milton Harris. I'm willing to bet this isn't his first venture into the hotel and wedding venue business. Guys like him tend to keep moving on as they are caught out in dirty dealings. You said he'd been throwing money around?'

'So Will said.'

'I need to meet this Will. I keep hearing his name mentioned. Sounds like an okay guy. A bit of a local hero?'

'He is. He hasn't had a good run – his wife and older son died one after the other and he became a single dad to his other son. Owen has turned out well. And now Will and Cleo are together. Now, that's a happy-ever-after story – like Martin and Ailsa.' She paused for a moment. 'There are quite a few of those in Bellbird Bay. Must be something in the air.' She laughed awkwardly.

'When do you think your friend will come up with information about Milton Harris?' she asked, adroitly changing the subject.

'Shouldn't take too long. He has a lot of contacts. He was… is… more involved with commercial development than I was – hotels motels, shopping centres and the like. If there's anything to find, Paul will ferret it out.'

'Good. Thanks for lunch. I should be going.' Bev rose to leave.

Iain rose too, wondering how he could delay her departure. He was just beginning to get to know this elusive woman. 'You said you have the day off. How do you intend to spend the rest of it?'

Bev appeared stunned by the question and didn't answer immediately. When she did, it was to say, 'I hadn't really thought about it. Do some much-needed housecleaning, I expect.'

'Seems a waste of such a lovely day.' He thought quickly. 'I hear the botanic gardens are worth a visit. Why don't you accompany me? I'm sure I could benefit from your superior knowledge.'

Again, Bev paused before replying.

What was it about the woman that she didn't seem able to give a straight answer – or was his company so boring she needed time to compose an excuse?

Giving him a rueful smile, she finally replied, 'Why not? It's ages since I've been there. There never seems to be time. I should probably go home and freshen up first.' She looked down at what she was wearing, and for the first time, Iain took note of the three-quarter denim pants and the tee-shirt bearing the logo *Life is Good*.

'You look fine to me,' he said, while thinking, more than fine. She looked good enough to… He took a deep breath. Their friendship certainty hadn't reached that stage yet, though he hoped it would.

Twenty-three

Bev wasn't quite sure exactly how it happened, but here she was driving to the botanic gardens with Iain Grant. It had been a surprise to meet him at the top of the boardwalk, pleasant to talk with him, even to join him for lunch. But this was a step too far. Why hadn't she refused, found some inescapable reason to go home? It was only three days since they'd had dinner together, since... She remembered the spark she'd felt, and her gut clenched. She wasn't going to get involved with him, she couldn't. Everyone she cared about had died, except her twin brother, and for years she'd lived in constant fear he'd die too. His lifestyle, spent photographing in war zones and risking his life to find the best shot, didn't augur well for his safety. It was why she'd never allowed herself to get close to anyone, apart from Ailsa who had been her best friend at uni.

'Everything okay?' She felt Iain glance at her.

'Sure, just thinking.' She'd been doing a lot of that recently, ever since Bryan Grant appeared in her office, she realised.

By the time they'd wandered around the gardens, and she'd familiarised herself with the place, providing information on various plants in response to Iain's questions, and noted the changes since her last visit, Bev had discovered more about Iain Grant and what made him tick without revealing more about herself. When they found themselves outside a glassed-in building with a few tables outside and a sign which read Acacia Cottage, they stopped.

'This is new,' Bev said, looking around at the nearby Japanese garden, the roofed pavilion overlooking a koi pond, and the raked stone garden to the side. 'I read about it. Bellbird Bay has a sister agreement with a city in Japan.'

'Shall we go in? I must admit to feeling a tad peckish.'

'Always happy to check out the competition, though I hardly think a café out here is competition for us. But I can tell Cleo about it.'

Although there were a few tables and chairs outside, the pair entered the almost empty café and chose a table with a view of the special garden. After their order of coffee for Iain and green tea for Bev, along with two slices of lemon cheesecake had been served, Iain said, 'Well, what's the verdict?'

'Mmm,' Bev said, taking a bite of cheesecake. 'It's good, but not a patch on Ruby's baking. The blackboard menu looks interesting. I wonder what their lunch trade is like.'

'It does look good,' Iain agreed, 'but I can't imagine anyone coming all this way just for lunch. My guess is it's mostly drop-in trade from people whose main purpose is to see the gardens.'

'Mmm,' Bev said again. 'And I guess they do more trade during the holiday season. It would be attractive to the tourists who've had their fill of the beach scene.'

She fell silent. What were they doing chattering on about the café when she wanted to find out more about Iain's family – and his wife's; to find out if they were related, even distantly, to Phil's family.

But Iain continued to chat, asking her about her life here and what it was like growing up in Bellbird Bay, and there was no opportunity to grill him about his family. Finally, he looked at his watch. 'I'm sorry,' he said. 'I need to get back. I have to pick up Mia.'

Bev gave him a puzzled look. She'd all but forgotten about his granddaughter.

'I normally pick her up from school, but she was going to Libby Walker's with Clancy today. The pair have become good friends, and Mia is devoted to Libby's dog. But I need to get her home and make dinner.' He gave a rueful grin. 'I'm sorry.'

'Nothing to be sorry about. Of course you need to get your granddaughter.' Bev felt the usual pang at the thought of the grandchildren she'd never have, then managed a smile. 'Bryan often talks about her. I'd love to meet her sometime.' The words were out of her mouth before she realised it. What had she said? What would Iain think?

During the drive back, Bev was surprised to realise how much she'd enjoyed Iain's company again. It wasn't how she'd envisaged spending her day off, but it had been good to find out a little more about him.

This time, there was no kiss on the cheek. Iain allowed her to get out of the car, merely saying, 'I'll be in touch. I'd like to see you again – and we'll arrange something about Mia,' before he drove off.

*

Bev was finishing her solitary dinner of leftover pizza, when there was a knock on the door, and Martin and Ailsa walked in. Although pleased to see them, Bev sometimes wished they didn't treat her house as if they lived there, even if they had done for several months when Ailsa first arrived in Bellbird Bay, and a broken Martin returned from his travels.

'We're here to report on our day,' Ailsa said, taking a seat beside Bev while Martin went to the fridge to help himself to a couple of beers.

'No problems?'

'None, unless you count Colin Jarett and his men arriving to fit the special roofing.' She grinned. 'Oh, Bev, it looks so good.'

'Colin was there today?' Damn! He'd said he'd be there sometime this week. But she thought he'd call first. She'd wanted to be there when it was put up to ensure it was exactly what she wanted. Now it had been done while she was wasting her time with Iain Grant. Though it wasn't entirely wasted time, she thought, as a warm glow told her how pleasant it had been to spend the day with him.

'Arrived as we were setting up,' Martin said, joining them and handing a beer to Ailsa. 'Bev?' he asked.

Bev shook her head. She'd already had a glass of wine with her meal. 'How does it look… really?'

'Perfect. The panels are clear so the sun can shine through, and it will keep out any rain. It was exciting to see it go up. It won't be long now,' Ailsa said, nudging Martin. 'What did you do today? I hope you managed to relax and spoil yourself.'

Bev felt herself redden.

'What?' Ailsa asked.

'I went for a walk... to the headland... and I met...'

'Not Ruby Sullivan?' Martin chuckled.

'No. I met Iain Grant.'

'Oh, the guy who's been helping you with your application to the council.'

'And...' Ailsa was more perceptive than Martin and could guess there was more to it.

'We spent the day together.'

'Wow!' Ailsa put down her beer and gazed at Bev. Making her blush even more.

'I know who he is.' Martin rubbed his chin. 'John Baldwin has some of his pen and ink drawings on display in the gallery. They're damned good. I didn't know you were on friendly terms with him. What gives, sis?'

'Bev went to dinner with him on Friday,' Ailsa told him. 'I guess it went well. Hmm?' She grinned at Bev.

'It's not what you think,' Bev began. But what was it? For the first time in what seemed like forever, she'd spent time with an attractive, eligible man who seemed to enjoy her company. 'Anyway, how are the wedding plans going?'

'Pretty good. We just have to finalise the invitation list.' She looked across at Martin, who appeared unconcerned.

'It's all up to Ailsa,' he said. 'As long as you and Will are there, I don't care.'

'That's not quite true,' Ailsa objected. 'What about your American friend and...'

Bev held up her hands. She could see this was a well-worn argument. 'That's enough, guys. Have you decided about the ceremony? Is there anything I need to do?'

'Don't think so,' Ailsa said, 'unless you can find an original loving cup. I know you suggested a champagne flute,' she said to Martin, 'but it would be nice to have the real thing.'

As Bev watched her two favourite people spar affectionately, something niggled at the back of her mind. Where had she seen something recently? She remembered the photo of the loving cup she and Ailsa had seen on the internet, but it wasn't that. It was more recent. She was sure she'd seen a cup with two handles.

'We need to find you a dress,' Ailsa said, giving Bev a searching look. 'I think a trip to Brisbane is called for.'

Bev flinched. 'When am I going to find time for that?' she asked. 'You keep saying it's going to be an informal ceremony. Can't I wear the outfit you made me buy at Greta's?'

Ailsa appeared stunned. 'Absolutely not. It's a wedding, Bev, *our* wedding, and, informal or not I want it to be special. I've persuaded Martin and Will to wear white dinner jackets.' She glanced at him lovingly.

'With fancy bow ties and cummerbunds. It's becoming bigger than Ben Hur,' Martin complained, though Bev could tell he was secretly amused. 'Next thing, you'll be wanting someone to scatter rose petals as you walk towards the arbour.'

'What a good idea,' Ailsa exclaimed. 'I wonder if Libby's granddaughter… Only joking,' she said quickly, seeing the expression on his face.

But Bev could see the idea had taken root. Libby's little granddaughter was only five and would look very cute with a basket of petals. She tucked the idea away, planning to speak with Ailsa about it later. She might have been denied her own wedding, but she intended to make this one between her twin brother and her best friend a day to remember.

Twenty-four

The week seemed to have flown by, and Friday arrived before Iain was ready for it, before he was prepared to face Ros again. He'd managed to fit in another lunch with Bev, and dinner last night had been even better than on the previous occasion. This time, they'd gone to the surf club where she'd introduced him to Martin, her twin brother, and Will Rankin. It was good to meet two men he'd only heard about, but he sensed Bev had been reluctant to make the introductions. There had been no sign of Martin's bride-to-be or Will's partner, Cleo, who he had already met at the café.

'When does she arrive?' Bryan asked when he was on his second cup of coffee. 'I suppose she'll be expecting us to have dinner with her?'

'No idea and yes. I assume she intends us to be available all weekend.' Iain grimaced. He'd much rather be free to spend more time with Bev. He was just beginning to break through the barriers she seemed to have built around herself and getting to know the vulnerable woman inside. He didn't know what had happened to her in the past but realised something must have occurred to make her the way she was. It seemed every time he got close to her, she closed up and became distant again.

'Mia and I are tied up on Saturday,' Bryan said.

'We're going on a big boat,' Mia said excitedly.

'What?' Iain laid down his cup. 'You knew your mother was coming this weekend. How could you make other arrangements?'

Bryan had the grace to look guilty. 'It's Nick Armstrong,' he said.

'He spoke to me last Sunday at Nippers and suggested it. Emma and Clancy will be there, too. Mia's been looking forward to it.'

Iain was lost for words. Much as he disliked the idea of Ros arriving in Bellbird Bay, she was coming ostensibly to see her son and granddaughter. Now neither of them would be available for the whole of Saturday. Knowing his ex, she would most likely think Iain had arranged it to frustrate her. 'I wish you hadn't,' he said weakly.

'Too late now. I need to get off. Have a good day at school, sweetheart.' Bryan dropped a kiss on Mia's forehead and ruffled her hair. 'See you later, Dad. Let me know if you hear when she's arrived.'

Iain heard the door slide closed behind him and saw Bryan leap onto his bike and cycle off down the boardwalk.

'Will I like Grandma?' Mia asked. 'I don't remember her, but she sends me presents.'

'She's your grandma, and she loves you,' Iain said, realising he hadn't answered her question and not knowing if what he had said was true. What sort of loving grandmother would stay away for years, only to reappear when it suited her? 'Now let's get you ready for school.'

Half an hour later, Iain and Mia arrived at the schoolyard and, with a wave of her hand, Mia ran off, leaving Iain gazing after her and wondering exactly why Ros was coming to see them.

Back home, he headed to the room he'd designated as his office and opened his emails. To his relief, there was one from Paul in response to his enquiry about Milton Harris. It seemed he'd been right. After several comments about Iain's new relaxed lifestyle, he wrote,

Regarding your enquiry about a Milton Harris. You are right to be concerned. His reputation stinks. While always staying on the right side of the law, he's known for sailing close to the wind with his developments and throwing his money around to get what he wants. I don't envy your friend if he – she? – manages to get on his wrong side. What on earth have you got yourself into? I thought you were retired. But I know from experience how you like a fight. Just be careful. This guy has powerful friends, too, and isn't afraid of playing rough.

He continued with some local news, before signing off. Iain stared at his friend's words with mixed emotions. Uppermost was concern for Bev, but there was an underlying sense of excitement at the prospect of a good fight, albeit one of words and development proposals. Paul had attached a couple of articles which Iain now read before printing them out, pleased he now had an excuse to visit *The Pandanus Café* and see Bev, even if the news he had to convey wasn't necessarily good.

He scrolled down the remaining contents of his inbox, only opening one from his realtor which was to inform him contracts had now been exchanged on the Middle Harbour house. Iain breathed a sigh of relief. But he realised he had still to talk with Grace Winter to see if she was willing to sell this one to them. After only a short time here, it was already feeling like home, so he hoped fervently her answer would be *yes*.

Iain felt his heart lift as he drove into the car park of the garden centre, contemplating again what an amazing enterprise Bev had created here.

'Iain!'

He was enjoying a coffee accompanied by one of the delicious cakes the café served – a slice of strawberry cheesecake today – when Bev walked, in stopping at his table. 'Thought I'd catch you. I have news,' he said.

Bev's face lit up. 'Give me a minute.' She disappeared into the kitchen to reappear carrying a mug of tea and precariously balancing a plate with a croissant. 'Didn't have any breakfast,' she explained, taking the seat opposite. 'Have you heard about the application?'

'Sorry, not yet,' Iain said, to see her face fall with disappointment. 'But I have heard from my former partner. He found out some stuff about your friend, Milton Harris.' He passed over the sheets he'd printed out.

'No friend of mine,' Bev said taking a gulp of coffee and a bite of the croissant, then picking up the papers, her eyes quickly reading them. 'So,' she said, 'it's as you thought. He's a crook, but just hasn't been caught.'

'Not exactly. He's managed to stay on the right side of the law, but he may know a few who don't. Your friend, Will, was right. He may prove to be a challenge. I met him, by the way – Will Rankin – and your brother. He looks like you.'

'Martin? I guess so, but in a male sort of way. What do we do about Harris?'

'Nothing at the moment. We need to wait, let him make the first move – or not. We may be worrying unnecessarily, but…' he rubbed his chin, '…given his previous form, I'm guessing it won't be long before we hear he's submitted an objection to your plan.'

'Then what?'

'If we play our cards right, we can make a counter proposal.'

'You're enjoying this,' Bev accused.

Iain shifted in his chair, 'Not exactly, but I do like the adrenaline rush I get from a good property dispute.'

Bev's eyes widened. 'You're mad,' she said, but there was a note of respect in her voice. 'I'm glad you're in my corner. I'd hate to get on your wrong side.'

Bev had left to go back to work, having agreed to have dinner with him the following week when he hoped Ros would have left, and he was enjoying a second cup of the coffee which was much better than he could make at home when his phone pinged with a message. Ros's plane had landed.

While the message gave no further indication of how long she intended to stay, it did say, as he expected, she was booked into the hotel he knew was owned by Milton Harris, and suggested they join her there for dinner that evening. Iain grimaced at the prospect of spending an evening in the upmarket hotel, which would no doubt be completely unsuitable for the sort of family meal Mia would enjoy. But it might give him the opportunity to check out the man who promised to disrupt Bev's plans.

*

'How do I look, Grandad?' Mia twirled into the room, dressed in one of the new dresses they'd bought in a shop on the esplanade. It was in her favourite blue and green, and barely distinguishable from her school uniform, but she had insisted on it.

'You look lovely,' Iain said with a smile, hoping Ros would make some comment on the outfit. Mia loved to be the centre of attention, and any grandmother would be thrilled to have her. Why did he doubt Ros's intentions?

'Perfect, honey,' Bryan said, appearing in the doorway. He drew his fingers around the inside of the collar of the shirt Iain had suggested he wear as being appropriate to the occasion. 'Are you sure about this?' he asked, pulling on the tie which hung loosely from the neck.

'Your mother likes to make a fuss,' Iain said, glancing down at the dress shirt and tie he was wearing for the first time since leaving Sydney. 'And if I know the restaurant, it's expected there, too.'

'Hmm.' Bryan knotted his tie with a grimace.

'You look nice, Daddy,' Mia said.

'Thanks, sweetheart. This had better be good,' he added to Iain.

Iain whistled when they reached the hotel. On the outskirts of town, it was surrounded by a large car park. The entrance was brightly lit, but the restaurant's lights were dimmer, clearly designed for romantic encounters. Iain's gut shrivelled. Then he saw Ros. Her solitary figure rose from a seat in the foyer to greet them. From this distance he could see she hadn't changed, her hair still the shade of blonde he remembered, her figure as trim as ever, her outfit looking as if it had come from one of the designer boutiques she'd always favoured. It was only when they drew closer, he noticed her makeup was heavier than he remembered and did nothing to disguise the network of small lines around her eyes and mouth.

'So this is Mia,' she said to the little girl who was clinging to her dad's hand and trying to hide behind him. 'I'm your grandma.'

'Say hello,' Iain prompted, since Bryan seemed to have lost his voice.

'Hello… Grandma,' Mia whispered.

'And Bryan,' Ros continued. 'It's been a long time. You look…'

'It's been almost six years,' Bryan said. 'A lot has happened.'

'I was sorry to hear about Nadia.'

Iain could feel Bryan stiffen at the sound of his wife's name on his mother's lips.

'Good to see you, too, Ros,' Iain said, reminding her he was here, too. 'Maybe we should go into the restaurant?'

Ros seemed to hesitate, then, 'Of course. I booked a table. Have you met the owner of the hotel, Iain? He's quite the gentleman.' She simpered and gave a small wave to the dark-haired man who was sitting at the table they were passing. He nodded in return.

What was going on here?

The dinner went better than Iain had expected. Mia was happy, digging into a bowl of sweet potato wedges, although she had wrinkled her nose at the picture book Ros had chosen as a gift for her, more suited to a four-year-old. Now Mia had graduated to what she proudly called *chapter books.*

The conversation flowed reasonably smoothly, the only awkward moment being when Ros asked what Bryan was doing and expressed her shock when she learned he was working in a garden centre.

'Surely you could find something more suited to you?' she asked, her lips tightening disapprovingly.

'This does suit me,' Bryan replied. 'Ask Dad. He's become friends with the owner of the centre.'

At this, it was Iain's turn to be the focus of Ros's displeasure. It amused him to see the changing expressions in her eyes as she digested what Bryan had said.

'You mean…?' she asked.

'She's a nice woman.' Iain decided to play along. There might not be anything between him and Bev – not yet, anyway – but it amused him to stoke Ros's suspicions.

Before she could respond, a voice said, 'Won't you introduce me, Roslyn?'

Looking up, Iain saw Milton Harris standing at Ros's shoulder.

Immediately, Ros's expression changed to one of delight. 'Milton! This is my son, Bryan and granddaughter, Mia… and my ex, Iain Grant.'

Something flickered in Milton Harris's eyes and was gone before Iain could identify it. 'I believe I might have heard the name,' he said, extending a hand.

Much as it went against the grain, Iain shook the man's hand.

'Your mother's quite a woman,' Milton said to Bryan, who almost choked. Ignoring his reaction, Milton turned to Ros. 'I hope to see more of you while you're in Bellbird Bay,' he said.

Ros preened and smiled in the way Iain had come to recognise over the years they were together. It was a smile he'd hoped never to see again, a smile indicating she had found a new conquest. Though, this time, he thought, she might have met her match.

By the time they left the restaurant, it was past Mia's bedtime, and Iain carried the tired little girl to the car, leaving Bryan to say his farewells to his mother.

'I hope you told her about your outing tomorrow,' he said, when Bryan joined them in the car. He glanced at his son. 'You didn't, did you?'

Bryan shrugged. 'It didn't come up.'

Iain wanted to give his son a piece of his mind, remind him of his responsibilities, but mindful of Mia in the back seat, he said nothing, merely fumed silently all the way home.

Twenty-five

Next morning, Iain had barely waved away an excited Mia and Bryan when there was a knock on the front door. 'What did you forget?' he asked, before seeing who was standing there.

'Not expecting to see me?' Ros asked with a chuckle. This morning she was dressed more casually than the previous evening, but he was sure the white three-quarter pants teamed with the navy and white striped top and rope-soled espadrilles had cost a bomb. 'I've come to see Bryan and Mia. Milt has invited the three of us out on his yacht and...'

'They're not here.' Iain couldn't believe the pleasure it gave him to say the words, despite his admonishment to Bryan.

'Not here? It's only eight o'clock.'

'They've already gone sailing... with a friend of Bryan's.'

'But...' Ros tapped her foot.

Iain almost felt sorry for her... almost but not quite. He was curious how she had managed to wheedle an invitation from Milton Harris to go sailing on such a short acquaintance, but Ros had always had a way with her. He of all people should know that.

He didn't have to wonder for long. 'Milt and I had a nightcap together after you all left last night. He's on his own – poor man – and wanted company.'

'And you were happy to oblige?'

'Whatever do you mean?' Ros affected to be offended, but Iain could see she was really flattered to have been singled out by what must be one of the most affluent residents in Bellbird Bay.

'Well,' she huffed. 'I guess I'll have to give their apologies. I'll drop by again when we get back. Perhaps you'll find it in yourself to provide dinner since last night was my treat.'

Perhaps I'll treat you to McDonald's, Iain thought. He was glad to see her go, suspecting the shadow in the BMW into which she stepped belonged to Milton Harris.

With the prospect of having the day to himself, Iain decided to take his sketching gear to the viewing platform he'd noticed on the boardwalk and try his hand at capturing the line of cottages which lined the path.

He'd been there for some time, lost in his own little world with only the sound of the waves and the seabirds for company when he was aware of a different sound and footsteps approaching.

'What are you doing?' a little voice said.

Iain paused in his attempt to capture the way the homes fitted together to give the impression they were somehow linked. Looking up he saw Clancy watching him. She was accompanied by Milo, the dog which Mia was so fond of.

'Clancy!' Libby Walker was coming out of the nearby gate. 'I told you to stay inside the fence.'

'I wanted to see what he was doing, Grandma. He's not writing like Adam does. He's drawing the houses. And Milo was with me.'

'So I see. Sorry,' she said to Iain. 'I hope she wasn't bothering you.'

'Not at all.'

Libby came across to peer over his shoulder. 'Wow, you've really captured the ambiance of our little community here on the boardwalk. I didn't know you were an artist, too.'

Iain smiled deprecatingly, pleased she liked his work.

'Grace and Ted are here. We were about to have coffee. Do you have time to join us?'

'Thanks, I'd love to.' Iain realised this might be the opportunity he'd been waiting for, the chance to sound out Grace about the house.

Once inside, Clancy disappeared with Milo, and Libby brought coffee and scones out to the deck where the others were seated. At first the conversation was general, then Libby said, 'Have you spoken to Grace about the house yet?'

Iain reddened. 'Not yet. I haven't had a chance to…' He saw Grace raise an eyebrow in Libby's direction.

'I told Iain he should talk to you about buying the house he's renting from you. I seem to recall you mentioning something about selling it in the New Year.'

'You're right. There doesn't seem to be any point in keeping it now Ted and I…' Grace glanced lovingly at her partner, who squeezed her hand. 'Are you interested in buying it?'

'I certainly am.' *Could it be this easy?*

'I'm not sure of the market, but I'll get a valuation. There's no need to involve a realtor. If you're happy with it, Ted can draw up the paperwork, can't you, honey?' She looked at Ted, who nodded with a smile.

'Sounds good to me.' It was a relief to get it over with, to know he could soon be the owner of the house he'd come to love.

It was still only mid-morning when he left Libby's, so, instead of going back to the house, which would now feel more like home than ever, Iain decided to continue his sketching – this time on the esplanade where he was able to focus on a different aspect of the town.

After some time, he began to feel hungry. Packing up his sketching gear, he was about to go back up the boardwalk, when he changed his mind. Rather than return to an empty house, he felt the need to have company, or at least to be surrounded by people, and decided to have lunch in the surf club.

When he pushed open the door, he was greeted by the sound of a loud cheer coming from upstairs. 'It's the old surfing crowd,' the girl on the desk said when he signed in. 'It's Will Rankin's birthday and they're celebrating.'

'Oh, if it's a private party…'

'Not at all.' She chuckled. 'They had a meeting in one of the rooms and are toasting him at the bar. I expect most of the guys will be leaving soon. We're still open to everyone else.'

'Okay.' But Iain was hesitant about climbing the stairs.

However, when he reached the top, there were only a few men drinking at the bar, among whom he recognised Martin Cooper, Ted Crawford, and Will Rankin himself. There were also a couple of younger men he'd seen before at Nippers the previous Sunday. Iain knew one of them was Will's son, Owen, and suspected the other was Bryan's other training companion, Bev's future nephew, Nate. He was about to make his way to the far end of the bar when Will caught sight of him.

'Iain, come and join us. It's my shout.'

Reluctant to join what seemed like a tightly knit group, Iain hesitated, then seeing the group begin to disperse, accepted Will's invitation. 'Happy birthday,' he said, raising the glass of beer which he'd been handed as soon as he reached the bar.

'Thanks. You know Martin and Ted, don't you?' Will gestured to his two companions. 'And these two...' he pointed to the pair of younger men who were the only others who remained of the original group, '...are my son, Owen, and Ailsa's son, Nate.'

Even if he hadn't already known, it was easy to tell which was which. Owen was clearly Will's son, his features and hair identical to those of his father. He drained his glass. 'We're off now, Dad,' he said. 'See you this evening.'

'Martin, Ted, and I were about to have lunch,' Will said. 'Why don't you eat with us? We have a table organised out on the deck.'

It was too tempting to refuse. Iain knew he'd welcome the opportunity to get to know the three men better. 'Only if you let me buy the next round,' he said with a grin.

During the meal of the club's famous burgers with chips, washed down with more beer, the men chatted about the history of the club and their own surfing stories. Iain already knew both Ted and Will had been local surfing champions while Martin had passed up his chances by leaving town as soon as he finished school. Now it appeared there was still a friendly rivalry between him and Will, even though they were best mates.

'I hear your son's keen to take part in the triathlon,' Will said. 'Owen tells me he's training with him and Nate.'

'So it seems.' Iain took a gulp of beer. 'I'm pleased to see him develop an interest again. It's been a difficult few months for him.'

'Bev said he'd had a hard time,' Martin said. 'Not that she's been gossiping about you both,' he was quick to add. 'She was telling Ailsa and me what a good worker he is and how you've been helping her with the application to council.'

'About that...' Will began. 'There could be some problems there.'

'So she said.' Iain sighed. 'Milton Harris. I met the guy last night.'

'You did?' Will appeared surprised.

'My ex is in town. We had dinner at his hotel and… it seems she and he…' He raised his eyes skyward.

'Oh, oh. Did you speak to him?'

'Only long enough to say hello. I have managed to find out a bit about him; had my former partner do some digging.'

'And?'

'He stays just inside the law, but isn't to be trifled with, though I can't really see how what Bev is proposing poses any threat to his operation.'

'I've come across guys like him before,' Ted put in, 'when I was practicing law in Brisbane. He's a narcissist, thinks everything's about him. I've heard what Bev wants to do at the garden centre. It's a good idea, no competition to anyone. But Harris no doubt imagines Bev is only doing this to spite him. If you're helping her, you may have your work cut out. But I wish you well. He doesn't need to throw a spanner into what Bev wants to set up.'

'I'm not unfamiliar with his type, either,' Iain said with a grin. 'It's just the sort of skirmish I relish.'

'Good man,' Ted said. 'If you need any help on the legal angle…'

'Thanks.' Iain was glad to have met this group of men, men he could relate to, men he could trust, men who could become good friends.

Twenty-six

Bev only gave a fleeting thought to Iain Grant on Saturday morning, and it was to wonder how he was coping with the arrival of his ex. She was kept busy with the number of locals who'd decided to replenish their gardens that day. Bryan didn't work weekends, having requested to have both days off to spend time with his daughter, a request Bev didn't have the heart to refuse. But it meant she was one staff member down on what tended to be the busiest days of the week.

As the day went on, in her spare moments, of which there weren't many, she imagined he and Iain would be spending the day with Mia and his mother, perhaps on the beach or in one of the other many attractions the town and the surrounding area had to offer. Iain hadn't seemed keen about his ex's visit, but it was none of her business, she reminded herself. He was merely the father of one of her staff, someone who was helping her out. So why did her mind keep going back to the time when their hands met, the touch of his lips on her cheek, and to how much she enjoyed his company? She couldn't allow herself to get close to him, to risk being hurt again. But…

By the time she closed up for the day, Bev realised Iain had been on her mind more than she cared to admit. She wondered what Ros was like, why she was coming to Bellbird Bay, if she had a hidden agenda, if she wanted to reignite their marriage, if…

Stop it, she told herself as she got ready for the birthday bash Cleo was throwing for Will, slipping on the outfit she'd worn to dinner with Iain and reliving again the feelings he'd evoked and which she was trying to forget.

*

When Bev walked into the surf club where they were to celebrate Will's birthday, the others were already there, sitting at a long table in the restaurant close to one of the windows overlooking the beach. It was dark outside, but the spotlight at the end of the deck lit up the ocean which shimmered in its glow.

'Happy birthday, Will.' Bev leant down to give him a kiss on the cheek and to present him with the gift she'd brought. Knowing how much he'd enjoyed the Adam Holland book Owen had bought him, she'd managed to obtain a signed copy of the latest one from the author.

'Wow! Can I borrow it when you've finished, Dad?' Owen asked when the book was unwrapped and held up for all to see.

'Get your own,' Will said with a laugh. 'This is my copy and it's a special one. Thanks, Bev.'

'A glass of champagne?' Martin asked, as Bev took her seat between Ailsa and Grace. They were a group of ten – Will, Cleo, Martin, Ailsa, Grace, Ted, Owen, Nate, and Cleo's daughter, Hannah, who shared a house with the two boys and was Nate's girlfriend.

'To Will,' Martin said, standing and raising his glass when all the other glasses had been filled. 'May the year ahead be filled with happiness, and may you continue to knock them dead in the surf for many years to come.'

'To Will,' they all chorused, then, 'Speech!' as Owen and Nate thumped the table with their fists.

Will stood. 'I don't know what to say,' he said. 'This club's been like a second home to me – until this lovely lady…' he gestured to Cleo with his glass, '…came into my life and gave me a reason to live when this one…' he gestured to Owen, '…left me for pastures new.'

Everyone chuckled.

'But tonight, to be here with my family and closest friends, celebrating another year, is something special. Thank you to all of you for helping me celebrate.' Seemingly overcome, Will sat down to a chorus of *Happy Birthday*.

'How're things?' Ailsa whispered to Bev when everyone was busy eating the wagyu steak which had been served with baked potato, sautéed mushrooms and asparagus, and enjoying the Pepperjack Barossa Shiraz which complemented the meal perfectly.

Bev didn't reply but continued eating.

'Iain Grant. Are you seeing him again?' Ailsa persisted.

Bev took a sip of wine. 'Not now, Ailsa.'

'Then when? No one's paying any attention to us.'

Bev stole a glance at the rest of the group. The younger members were arguing over something that had happened that morning, the three men were talking about the forthcoming triathlon, and Grace seemed to be lost in thought. Ailsa was right.

'So?'

'He mentioned something about meeting his granddaughter, but… his ex is here this weekend. I don't know for how long. It may be difficult.'

'And how do you feel about him?' Ailsa persisted.

To Bev's relief, she was saved from replying by Grace asking, 'How are the wedding arrangements going?' and the remainder of the meal was taken up with discussion of Ailsa and Martin's big day and the changes Bev was making in the garden centre.

'I hear we're going to have more Pandanus weddings in the future,' Grace said, as their plates were being removed.

'If all goes well with the council,' Bev replied. *Pandanus Weddings.* She liked the sound of it. Until now, it hadn't occurred to her to give a name to what she was planning. Though it might inflame Milton Harris even more. She must run it past Iain when next they spoke.

When the evening was over, they all rose to leave. For the younger members of the group, their evening was just about to start; Bev heard them mention a party they wanted to attend. But, like the three other couples, she was ready to call it a night. She walked up the boardwalk with Ted and Grace, farewelling them with hugs when they reached her gate.

But Bev didn't immediately enter the house. Ailsa's questions had disturbed her. What *were* her feelings about Iain Grant? She gazed out at the ocean as if she could find the answer there. She didn't understand the feelings she was developing for him, feelings she'd never expected to experience again, so firmly had she kept her emotions in check. And it had worked – until now.

Twenty-seven

The dinner with Ros the previous evening had been awkward. She hadn't hidden her annoyance at Bryan's decision to spend the day with his new friends, especially as Mia couldn't stop talking about what fun she had had and how she and Clancy had seen dolphins and whales. And Bryan had fallen into one of the silent moods Iain thought he'd seen the last of.

Iain was serving dessert – Mia's favourite Golden Gaytime bites – when Ros said, 'Well, since today was a disaster, we can at least spend tomorrow together. I thought we could...'

Before she could finish, Mia said, 'Are you going to come to watch me at Nippers, Grandma?'

Ros stared at her, eyes wide with shock. 'No, dear. I thought we could do something together, you, me and your dad.'

Mia shook her head. 'No, Grandma. It's Sunday. I have Nippers, and I've only just started. You need to come to watch me. Granddad will be there, too.'

While he was amused at how Mia had managed to thwart Ros's plans, Iain did feel some sympathy for her. 'Mia's right, Ros. Nippers on Sunday morning is obligatory. Then we can go to the surf club for coffee and maybe lunch. I'm afraid if you want to spend time with your son and granddaughter, you'll need to fit in with their schedule. You can't just arrive and expect everyone to fall in with your plans.' He fell silent, knowing that was exactly what Ros did expect, it was what she'd always expected and, to his shame, he'd often given in to her, taking the path of least resistance. But no longer.

Ros appeared to consider this for a moment before saying, 'So, what time does this event begin?'

'We have to be at the beach at eight o'clock,' Mia said. 'I get to wear my special pink rashie and cap and...'

'That's enough, Mia. I don't think your grandma is interested,' Bryan said, a vein beside his eye twitching. 'If you've finished dinner, we need to run your bath. Say goodnight to your granddad and grandma.'

With a glance at Bryan out of the corner of her eye, Mia slid from her chair. 'Goodnight, Grandad,' she said, giving Iain a hug. 'Goodnight, Grandma.' She took a step towards Ros, then stopped before leaving the room.

'Well!' Ros said, when she and Iain were alone. 'I didn't expect that.'

'What *did* you expect, Ros?' Iain asked in a tired voice. 'You disappear from Bryan's life, only dropping back in when it suits you. You don't come to his wife's funeral. Mia is six, and I could count the number of times you've seen her on one hand. The child doesn't know you. You can't expect to appear in her life and be greeted like her long-lost grandmother. It doesn't work that way. Why did you come to Bellbird Bay? Why did you seek us out now? It doesn't gel when you say you wanted to see Bryan and Mia. You haven't made any effort to see them for years. Where were you when they needed you, when they needed their family around them?' He ran out of words and breath and took a gulp of wine, glad there was some left.

'Do you mind if I smoke?' Ros reached for her bag.

'Not in here.' Iain hated cigarettes. He didn't remember Ros smoking. She must have taken it up since they last saw each other. It was so long ago, he couldn't remember when it had been. Perhaps just after Mia was born.

Out on the deck, Iain stood, leaning against the rail while Ros took a seat on one of the cane chairs Grace had provided.

'I'm sorry Iain,' she said, blowing a cloud of smoke into the air and pushing back a stray curl, bringing back the memory of how, when they first met, Iain had loved to run his fingers through her curls. 'I seem to be doing this all wrong. I did come because I wanted to see Bryan and Mia, but...'

Ian waited. He knew there had to be a *but*. With Ros, there always was.

'I'm sick, Iain,' she said at last. 'These have got to me.' She waved her cigarette in the air. 'I go in for surgery in Sydney next week… on Wednesday. Surgery then chemo, then… who knows? It's why I wanted to see Bryan and Mia… before it's too late.' She drew on her cigarette.

'Shouldn't you…?' He gestured to the cigarette.

'Too late, but you're right.' She pinched it out and dropped it on the deck.

Iain resisted the temptation to pick it up. Ros's news was a blow. While he was no longer in love with her – hadn't been for years – he had been once, they'd had some good years together… and she was Bryan's mother.

'I'm sorry, Ros,' he said. He meant it. Whatever differences they might have had, she didn't deserve this. 'Bryan…'

Ros shook her head. 'I don't want him to know, not yet, not until…' She took out her cigarettes again, then slid them back into her bag.

'And Milton Harris?' He had to ask.

Ros chuckled. 'It's good to know I can still attract the interest of an attractive man. He told me he has big plans for Bellbird Bay. You could learn a lot from someone like him.'

Iain snorted. 'Did he say anything about me?'

'No, why would he?'

'No reason.' Iain remembered the expression which had flickered in Harris's eyes when he was introduced. Harris knew who he was, knew about his connection with Bev, knew about the application to council. The only question was, what did he intend to do about it?

'I should go. I tire easily these days.'

'Can I give you a ride?'

'No, I'll call a taxi.'

'And we'll see you tomorrow… at the beach?'

'Wouldn't miss it for the world,' she said, her sarcastic tone sounding more like the old Ros.

*

Now it was Sunday morning, and Mia was again bubbling with excitement. 'Is Grandma going to be there to see me?' she asked, her mouth rimmed with milk.

'She is,' Iain said.

Bryan looked at his dad. 'Are you sure, Dad? She didn't seem too keen.'

'She'll be there.' It took all Iain's willpower to keep Ros's illness to himself. But he had to honour her wishes. 'She said so.'

'Right.' Bryan didn't look convinced. It was no surprise. His mother had let him down so often in the past, failing to attend his school play, his graduation, and finally, his wife's funeral.

'Let's get this show on the road.' Iain picked up the breakfast dishes as Mia giggled.

'It's not a show, Grandad,' she said. 'Nippers is serious stuff. We learn all about keeping safe, and when we get bigger, we can become real surf lifesavers.'

'Sorry, Mia. You're right. It's very important.'

When they reached the beach, things were a little chaotic as Mia greeted her friends. But they soon settled down when Owen and a couple of other young men took charge.

Iain looked around, but there was no sign of Ros. He cursed under his breath. She'd promised.

He was fetching coffee for himself and Bryan when a taxi drew up, and Ros emerged. She was wearing a smart linen dress, probably another designer label, and as heavily made up as before. This time, Iain wondered if the makeup was covering up the ravages her illness had wreaked on her face and felt more charitable towards her. 'Coffee?' he asked, holding out one of the paper cups.

Ros shook her head. 'Can't face it these days,' she said, grimacing.

Iain handed one of the coffees to Bryan, who said, 'I'm going down onto the beach, Dad,' completely ignoring his mother. Iain wanted to say something to him, but Ros put a hand on his arm.

'Let him be. I guess I deserve that,' Ros said, 'Now where is Mia?'

Iain pointed to the beach where the group of pink-clad youngsters seemed to be lining up for a race.

'They all look alike,' Ros said, peering down at them. 'Which one is she?'

'The one on the end,' Iain said with a chuckle. 'The one who looks determined to win.'

'Hmm. She gets that from you. Is there somewhere to sit?' She looked around.

'There's a bench over there.' Iain led her to one of the benches strategically placed along the esplanade and which gave a good view of the beach. As he settled Ros in the seat, he glanced across to road to where a familiar figure was standing watching them.

Twenty-eight

Curious to see what Iain's ex-wife was like and knowing his granddaughter took part in Nippers, Bev had given way to the impulse to go to the beach. Despite the crowds thronging the garden centre, she threw off her apron and, telling Julie, her second in charge, she had to go out for a short time, she got into the van bearing the pandanus logo and drove across town to the esplanade.

Once there and parked, she sat staring into space. *What on earth was she doing? What was it about Iain Grant that had her acting like a stalker?* Tempted to restart the engine and return to the garden centre, the desire to see the former Mrs Grant was too strong. She got out of the car and walked along the esplanade on the opposite side to the beach, just in time to see Iain help a well-dressed woman with blonde hair to a seat on a bench.

That must be her, and by the way Iain was solicitously helping her sit, he wasn't as upset about her visit as he'd pretended to be. Bev's heart sank. She shouldn't have come. She'd been right to avoid any sort of relationship. She was about to turn tail and leave when Iain caught sight of her.

'Bev!' He was crossing the road to meet her.

'What are you doing here? I thought you'd be working today.'

'I was. I am. I only came down to...' she searched for a reason, '...to buy a paper.' It was a weak excuse but the best she could come up with.

'O...kay.'

Bev could tell he didn't believe her but what else could she say. *I wanted to see your ex-wife, to see what she was like?*

'Do you have time to join us for coffee?'

'No, sorry. I must…' She gestured to where, thankfully, *The Bay Café* had a supply of Sunday papers sitting on the counter. Her face now red with embarrassment, Bev moved away from Iain and towards the café. 'Enjoy the rest of your weekend.'

'I'll see you…'

Bev didn't wait for him to finish his sentence but hurried into the café to purchase a paper, seeing Iain standing outside looking puzzled for a few moments before re-joining his ex by the beach. She breathed a sigh of relief when she saw he was no longer looking in her direction.

Feeling flustered when she got back to the garden centre, Bev almost tripped over a pile of bags of mulch.

'Are you okay?' Julie asked. 'Cleo was looking for you.'

'Oh.' Seeing the crowd was thinning and after checking Julie was able to cope, Bev headed for the café. A caffeine hit was exactly what she needed, not with Iain and his ex-wife, with Cleo in her own café where there was no man to distract her.

'Are you okay?' Cleo asked, the second person to ask that in as many minutes.

'I'm fine or will be after one of your coffees. Julie said you were looking for me.'

'It's nothing urgent. Last night I was working out a possible menu for the wedding and I wanted to run it past you before I talked to Ailsa. If it's not a good time…'

'No, it's fine.' Thinking about the wedding would help her get things back into perspective. It would focus her attention on something other than herself – and Iain Grant.

Cleo had outdone herself. Bev was blown away by what she was proposing – nibbles to be passed around during drinks while the photographs were being taken, then a tasting feast comprising six unique dishes starting with seared scallops and ending with a chocolate mousse. 'Ailsa said she wanted to keep it simple,' she said. 'Do you think this is too much?'

'I think it's perfect. I'll be seeing Ailsa and Martin tonight. Would you like me to take this to show her?'

'Would you? That would be great. I wasn't sure…'

'I'm sure she'll love it.'

'There's plenty of time to make any changes she wants. Sorry, I must dash,' Cleo said, seeing one of her staff waving to her from the kitchen.

Bev finished her coffee and picked up the menu sheets Cleo had left with her. Her mood had risen, the discussion about Ailsa and Martin's wedding managing to clear her mind of what she'd seen at the beach. Iain had every right to spend time with his ex-wife, to get back together with her if that's what was happening. Bev had no claims on him, or he on her, she reasoned.

*

Iain stared after Bev as she entered the café and picked up a paper. He could have sworn it was the first thing that came into her mind when he asked why she was here on the esplanade on a Sunday morning, instead of at the garden centre. Then he shrugged and walked back across the road to where Ros was seated.

He joined her on the bench, his mind going around in circles as he tried to work out what had brought Bev here. It was too egotistical to imagine she was here to see him, to see Ros, but what other reason could there be? He didn't buy her excuse she was here to purchase a paper. She probably had one delivered like most others in Bellbird Bay.

She *had* bought a paper, but had been overeager to get away from him, not even allowing him to finish his sentence. He'd wanted to make arrangements to see her again, to make good his promise to introduce her to Mia. Now, he'd have to call her or go to the garden centre, perhaps tomorrow.

'There she is now.' Ros's voice broke into his thoughts and, looking down to the beach he could see Mia running out of the ocean, a wide grin on her face. She was loving it. 'She's such a livewire. I've missed so much.' Ros's voice was subdued.

There wasn't much he could say. Ros had made her choice, and it had taken her illness for her to realise she had a family. 'It's not too late,' he said.

'I hope not.' Ros's eyes glazed over. 'I hope not,' she repeated. Then she seemed to rally. 'I'll be leaving for Sydney tomorrow,' she said. 'Milton has offered to take me in his private plane. It was too good an opportunity to refuse.' She gave a sly grin. 'He probably thinks he's onto a good thing. He doesn't know I'm checking into St Vincent's on Wednesday.' Her expression became more serious.

Iain covered her hand with his. 'You're sure you don't want Bryan to know?'

'I'm sure. I don't want his pity. I'd rather have his anger, but maybe… once I'm in recovery…'

'I'll tell him then. I'm sure he'll change his tune when he knows.'

'Maybe.' Ros sighed. 'I haven't been a good mother to him, or a good wife to you. I was too intent on getting what I wanted out of life.'

'But you enjoyed it… all those years of travelling around, of…'

'Of having a different man in each place?' She huffed out a laugh. 'I did, Iain. I was never meant to become the sort of wife you wanted, the mother Bryan deserved. You were both better off without me. I'm surprised you never remarried. I thought you'd have found someone else by now.'

Iain felt himself redden.

'You have? In Bellbird Bay? You're a good man, Iain. I hope she's worthy of you.'

'It's not… Bev's not…'

'Bev? Isn't that the name of Bryan's boss at the garden centre?'

Iain couldn't recall Bev's name being mentioned, but it must have been. He didn't reply.

Twenty-nine

Bev couldn't believe her eyes. Rows of plants had been destroyed. All the vegetable seedlings she'd carefully nurtured, and the pots of colour which were so popular – all thrown to the ground and trampled, the soil strewn everywhere.

She was gazing at the devastation, wondering how it happened, when Bryan appeared, ready for work.

'What happened?' he asked, his eyes taking in the mess. 'What can I do?'

Bev was so numb, it took her a moment to reply. 'I guess we should call the police,' she said. She wondered if this was Milton Harris's way of sending her a message, of trying to make her withdraw her application. 'Luckily the damage is limited to the two rows farthest from the entrance. Maybe we can rope it off somehow, till they've been.'

'I'll see to it.' Bryan disappeared in the direction of the workshop.

Bev continued to stare at the damaged plants.

'Bev?' She felt a gentle hand on her arm and looked round.

'I heard what had happened,' Cleo said. 'Who could have done this?'

Bev attempted to pull herself together. 'I have my suspicions, but it's up to the police, I'll call them now.'

'Then come to the café. You look as if you need coffee.'

'Later.' Bev waved Cleo away. 'I need to...' She went into her office, called the police, then sat staring into space. She needed to talk to someone about this, someone who knew what Milton Harris was capable of. She picked up the phone again.

*

Iain was running late. Dinner last might with Ros had been fraught as he kept his knowledge of her illness from Bryan who appeared surprised at the change in Iain's attitude to her. He hadn't slept well. He might not love Ros any longer, but he hated to think of her undergoing major surgery in Sydney all by herself, even though she'd assured him it was what she wanted, declining his offer to be at her bedside. He was in the midst of hurrying Mia out of the house and into the car when his phone rang.

He was about to ignore it when he saw Bev's number. 'Bev, sorry I can't talk now. Can I call you back?'

Bev's voice was filled with anger. 'My plants, Iain. The bastard has destroyed my plants.'

Iain almost dropped the phone. Whatever he had been expecting, it wasn't this. 'Hold on. I have to drop Mia at school, and I'll be right over. Have you called the police?'

'Just did.'

'See you soon.'

'What's wrong, Grandad?'

Iain stared at Mia as if he didn't recognise her for a moment, then replied, 'Something has happened at the garden centre where your daddy works. Let's get you to school.'

This morning, Iain tuned out to Mia's chatter about what was to happen at school that day and Nippers the day before. He was focussed on how much damage had been inflicted on Bev's precious plants. Like Bev, he was sure it was the work of Milton Harris. It was unlikely the man had wreaked the damage himself. He was too wily for that. But Iain had no doubt he was behind it.

Iain waved Mia off as usual and half an hour later he pulled into the car park at the garden centre and parked beside a police car. Two police officers were leaving as he entered the centre. There was no sign of Bev in the shop or the office, so he made his way into the centre proper.

Seeing her at the far side, he hurried over to find her staring at a mess of broken pots, plants and soil. It looked as if someone – or several people – had thrown them to the ground then jumped all over them.

'Bev!' Without thinking he pulled her into a hug.

She sank into him, then pulled away. 'Thanks for coming,' she said.

'I saw the police leaving. What did they say?'

'They said it must be the work of a group of teenagers,' she said bitterly.

'Fat lot they know.'

'I suppose it could be kids…'

'No!' Iain shook his head. 'Look what I received on the way here.' He pulled out his phone to show Bev the text from his contact at council. It was to inform him that Milton Harris had submitted an objection to her application. 'This is his doing. No doubt about it. The actual destruction may have been done by a group of teenagers, but I'm willing to bet he put them up to it, though I doubt we'll ever be able to prove it.' He sighed. 'Can I help you sweep this up? Can any of them be saved?'

'I doubt it. But you don't need to do anything. My staff will handle it.'

'Want me to do it now, Bev? Hello, Dad, what are you doing here?' Bryan said, appearing behind them.

'Bev called me,' Iain said.

'Thanks, Bryan,' Bev said. 'Can you take a couple of photos on your phone? I'm not sure whether my insurance will cover it, but photos might help. Then can you and Dean check if anything is worth saving and bin the rest. I hate to see such a waste, but we need to get this part of the centre ready for our customers again. When you've done, can you check what might be ready for sale in the greenhouse, and maybe spread out the others? I don't want there to be any empty spots.'

'What about you?' Iain asked Bev. 'How are you holding up?'

'I'll be fine,' she said, but Iain could see her swaying. She was suffering from shock.

'Have you had tea or coffee?'

'Cleo said…' Bev seemed disoriented.

'Come with me.' Iain took Bev by the elbow and steered her towards the café. Once there, he placed her in a chair and went into the kitchen. 'Bev is in shock. She needs…'

'Hot, sweet tea coming up. Coffee for you?' Cleo said.

'Thanks.'

Bev was still staring into space when the tea arrived. She clutched the cup with both hands. After a few sips, she looked across at Iain. 'Thanks. I don't know what came over me. I was fine when the police were here. It just suddenly hit me. What sort of man would do this?'

'The sort of man who is determined to get his own way, who will stop at nothing to get what he wants. Do you have a security system here? Cameras?' Iain wondered why he hadn't thought of this before.

Bev shook her head. 'It's a garden centre. I've never needed…' Her eyes widened at the realisation that perhaps now she did.

'I can organise it for you, if you like?'

'Would you? I could do it myself but…'

'You're in no state to do anything at the moment. Why don't you go home?'

'I can't. My staff… I'm needed here. But if you can contact someone about security, I'd feel better. You don't think he's finished, do you?'

'I doubt it. Right now, he's on his way to Sydney with my ex, but when he gets back…'

'Your ex?' Bev's eyes widened again.

'It's a long story and one for another time. I'll see what I can do about getting security cameras installed around the entrance and the perimeter. And I don't think you should be alone this evening. Why don't you join us for dinner? It's not how I imagined you meeting my granddaughter but needs must.'

Bev only hesitated for a moment. 'Thanks, it's kind of you – on both counts. Do you think they can be installed today?' She wrapped her arms around herself and shivered.

Thirty

'Bev, are you okay? I heard about the break-in. How are you....'

Bev looked up from her computer screen as Ailsa pushed her way into the office, stopping suddenly at the sight of a man she didn't know peering over Bev's shoulder.

'Hi Ailsa. What are you doing here? Who told you about my break in? This is Jason Black. He's been fitting CCTV around the centre. Iain organised him for me.'

'Oh, right,' Ailsa said.

'I think we're done. You should be right now,' Jason said. 'You have my card. Contact me if there are any problems.' He nodded to Ailsa and left.

'Well!' Ailsa said, watching him leave. Then she turned back to Bev. 'Are you okay? Will was at a council meeting when he heard about what had happened. He contacted Martin who told me. He said someone had trashed the place.'

'Not exactly, but they did make a big mess, ruined a whole batch of pots and plants and left them all over the place. I'm fine. I rang Iain. He was a big help.'

'You don't look fine. Why don't you come to us after work. It must have been a shock.'

'It was. Nothing like that has ever happened here before. I never thought I'd need any security. It's a garden centre, for goodness' sake, not a bank. And thanks for the invite, but I've already agreed to go to Iain's for dinner. He only lives a few doors up the boardwalk. He says I can meet his granddaughter.'

'Hmm. Sounds like there's more to this thing with Iain Grant than you're willing to admit.'

'Not really. He's only being kind.'

But was Ailsa right? He was the first person she thought to call… and he'd come straight away, ensured she was okay, and organised the CCTV to be installed that very day.

'Kind… that's one word for it.' But Ailsa had the sense not to press the point. 'Will said there had been an objection to your application. Do you think it was him?'

'Milton Harris? Almost certainly, but the police have put it down to teenage vandals.' Bev sighed. 'Looks like he'll get away with it again.'

'Again? You mean he's done this before?'

'Not here, but Iain got someone to do a bit of digging and discovered he has a history of this sort of stuff. But he won't get me to change my mind,' Bev said in a stronger voice. 'I'm not so easily scared.'

*

Despite her brave words to Ailsa, Bev was still feeling a little shaky when she walked up the boardwalk to Iain's house that evening. Her plants were like the children she'd never have. If Milton Harris could arrange to have the garden centre broken into, and plants destroyed, what else was he capable of?

As she pushed open the gate to the house, which was almost identical to her own, Bev heard a small voice call, 'There's a lady coming through the gate, Grandad,' and Iain's tall frame appeared in the open doorway.

'Welcome,' he said, coming forward to give her a kiss on the cheek. 'I'm glad you made it. How are you feeling now?'

'Better,' Bev said with a smile. 'Thanks for arranging the security so quickly.'

'No problem. Bryan said the cameras have been installed. Hopefully that'll be an end to it.' He frowned.

'You don't think so, do you?'

'Given his history, I doubt it. But I'm pretty sure nothing's going to happen tonight. Come in. Mia has been helping me cook dinner.

Mia, this is Ms Cooper. She owns the garden centre where your daddy works and she's one of our neighbours.'

'Hello, Ms Cooper,' Mia said shyly.

'Call me Bev. Ms Cooper makes me sound so old.'

The little girl giggled. 'Grandad and I have been making pizzas,' she said proudly. 'I put on the olives and the cheese.'

'I'm sure they'll be delicious,' Bev said with a grin. She was a delightful child.

'I hope you don't mind pizza,' Iain said. 'When she heard we were having a visitor, Mia wanted to help, and pizza is easy for her – and her favourite.'

'I don't mind at all.' It was an interesting insight into the man to see him here in his own home with his granddaughter.

'Bev.' Bryan walked into the kitchen. 'Good to see you.'

'Likewise. It was kind of your dad to invite me.'

'Dad's like that.' Bryan grinned. 'Those new cameras are looking good. Jason said they're top of the range.'

'No point in doing things half-assed,' Iain said. 'Now, how about a drink before dinner? Wine? Beer?'

'Wine, thanks. White if you have it.' Bev was ready for a drink. She was starting to feel uncomfortable and to wonder what she was doing here.

But, by the time the wine was poured and she was seated on the deck with Iain – Bryan having disappeared with Mia to hear her reading homework – she felt more relaxed.

'What do you think Harris will try next?' she asked during a pause in the conversation. The thought of that man and what he might be capable of was never far from her mind.

'Who knows?' Iain raked a hand though his hair. 'He'll probably keep quiet for a bit, wait to see what we do. I've met his type before. The destruction of your plants was a warning. He most likely didn't expect you to act as quickly as you did. I suspect he has friends on the council – or people he's bought.'

'Will said as much.'

There was silence for a few moments, then Bev said, 'You mentioned something about him and your ex?'

Iain gave a sigh. 'Ros, yes. She picks up men like there's no tomorrow.' He shrugged. 'But… she's sick. That's why she wanted to see Bryan and Mia.'

'Is it serious?' *This might explain his solicitous attitude on the esplanade.*

'Cancer. She's having surgery on Wednesday.'

Bev's hand went to her mouth. 'Oh, I'm sorry.'

Iain glanced cautiously towards the house. 'Bryan doesn't know, so please don't mention it. She wanted to wait until…' He cleared his throat. 'To wait. Anyway, she met Harris at the hotel when she was staying there, and he offered to fly her to Sydney in his private plane. Probably thought he was onto a good thing. I think Ros sees it as one last fling before…'

'But she's going to recover?'

'Hopefully. She's optimistic, but with these things, one never knows. She's scheduled for chemo after the surgery. She'd been hoping to stay in our Sydney house, but it's been sold.'

'So where will she go?'

Iain scratched his head. 'I hadn't thought about that, but it would have to be somewhere in Sydney where her treatment will be. Damn, if I hadn't been so quick to sell…'

Bev put a hand on his arm. 'You weren't to know. I'm sure she'll find somewhere.'

'Mmm.'

'What are you two looking so serious about?' Bryan walked out carrying a beer, followed by Mia with her class reader.

'Can I read to you?' she asked, sidling up to Bev.

'Of course you can,' Bev said, moved by the request. She held out her hand for the book, but Mia had other ideas.

'I need to sit on your lap. Put your wine down,' she instructed.

Amused, Bev did as she was told, and the little girl clambered onto her lap. The feeling of her small body, her soft skin and the scent of her hair brought Bev close to tears. If things had been different, this could have been *her* grandchild. She barely heard the words of the story as she thought of what might have been.

*

Dinner was more fun than Bev had expected. Mia kept them entertained with her stories of school and her descriptions of her morning at Nippers, and Bev shared her own tales of when she was a Nipper along with her twin brother and their best friend.

It was when the meal was over, and Bryan had gone to the kitchen to make coffee, that Bev's eye caught sight a small, silver bowl on the sideboard. 'Is that…?' she asked.

'Family heirloom.' Iain said. 'It's a quaich. A traditional Scottish drinking cup.' Clearly seeing Bev's puzzled look, he added. 'My family originally came from Scotland – hence the Scottish spelling of my name.'

'Oh.' Was this where Bev had seen it? But she'd never been in this room before.

'What's the matter?'

Bev shook her head. 'Nothing. We… Ailsa and I were talking about a two-handled drinking cup for her wedding ceremony. We were looking on the internet, and I thought I'd seen one somewhere.'

'It may have been in the kitchen last time you were here. I polished it recently. Came up rather well. Mia, can you bring over the silver cup to show Bev?'

Mia slid out of her seat to fetch it and handed it to Bev who took it carefully in both hands. 'It's beautiful,' she said, stroking the engraved surface.

'You said your friend and Martin want to incorporate one into their wedding ceremony. Would they like to borrow this one?'

'But it's a family heirloom.' Bev looked at Iain. His eyes held something that had nothing to do with their conversation, but everything to do with the pair of them. She looked away.

'I mean it. It's been sitting around since I've been a child, first in my grandparents' home, them my parents', now mine. It would be good to see it being used in a wedding ceremony.'

'Ailsa would be thrilled. Can I take a photo of it to show her?'
'Sure.'

Bev took out her phone and took a shot of the cup, then gave it back to Mia to allow her to replace it on the sideboard. 'Thanks,' she said.

'Now, Mia, bedtime for you,' Bryan said, rising from the table and picking up a giggling Mia. 'Say goodnight to Grandad and Bev.' He held her down to kiss Iain, then over to Bev.

The touch of the little girl's soft lips on her cheek almost brought Bev to tears again. 'I should be going too,' she said. 'Early start in the morning.'

'Let me walk you down the boardwalk,' Iain said.

'Thanks.' Bev relished the opportunity to be alone with him.

This time, when he took her hand, Bev didn't draw away. It felt good to feel his big, warm hand enclosing hers, as if nothing could harm her if he was with her. The spark she'd felt before was there again, but this time she didn't shy away from it. When they paused at her gate, and his lips brushed hers fleetingly, she felt a flash of something she'd never expected to feel again.

'Dinner, Saturday?' he asked, his voice thick with emotion.

Too overcome to speak, Bev merely nodded.

Thirty-one

Excited as she was about finding a loving cup for Ailsa and Martin's wedding ceremony, it wasn't till Wednesday that Bev was able to share the news with her friend.

She had arranged to meet Ailsa at the surf club. Martin, along with Will was attending a meeting about the triathlon, and the two women planned to have a few drinks before the men joined them for a meal. Cleo had promised to come along, too, but had been delayed by Hannah.

'I have something to show you,' Bev said, taking out her phone when the two were seated out on the deck with glasses of icy cold wine. It was a lovely evening. What they had first thought to be raindrops proved to be fireflies caught in the beam from the spotlight, turning the sky into a magical panorama.

Ailsa took the phone and looked at the photo Bev had taken of the quaich. 'What? We've already seen that.'

'Not this one. This is one I saw on Monday evening when I was having dinner at Iain's. It's a real one and…'

Ailsa peered at the photo more closely, then looked at Bev. 'Iain Grant has a loving cup?'

'It's called a quaich. Apparently, it's a family heirloom and… he's willing to lend it to you and Martin for the ceremony. What do you think of that?'

'Really?' Ailsa's face broke into a wide grin, then she peered at Bev. 'Wait a minute. You were at Iain Grant's house for dinner on Monday night. How did it go?'

Bev blushed. 'It was good. I met Mia. She's so lovely, Bev. And to think her mother died and left her. It's tragic.'

'And that's it?' Ailsa raised an eyebrow in disbelief.

'We're having dinner again on Saturday.' She blushed again.

'He kissed you, didn't he?'

Bev didn't reply.

'He did! Well, all I can say is it's about time. I'm glad, Bev. He sounds like a nice guy. What about his ex? Didn't you say she was visiting?'

'She's gone back to Sydney.' Bev didn't elaborate. She didn't think it appropriate to share what Iain had told her about Ros, especially since Bryan was unaware of his mother's illness.

'So, no competition there,' Ailsa said smugly.

'Sorry, I'm late. Children!' Cleo slid into a seat and took a gulp from the glass she was carrying. 'You think they've become independent, then…'

'Problems?' Ailsa asked.

'Nothing that couldn't be fixed with a bit of motherly TLC.'

Bev's stomach clenched.

'What have I missed?'

'Bev has found us a… what did you call it, Bev?'

'A quaich.'

'A quaich for the ceremony. It's a loving cup. Iain Grant has one and we can use it. Show Cleo, Bev.'

Bev took out her phone again and Cleo was admiring it when Martin and Will arrived.

'What's up?' Martin said, and the phone was handed round as Bev explained again. 'So, no need for a champagne flute,' was Martin's response.

Will only chuckled.

'So,' Ailsa said to the two men, 'how did the meeting go? Have you solved the problems of the world?'

'It was good. Will's a good chairman. There was none of the argy-bargy these groups often have. It's all systems go for the big day. We just have to liaise with the council on the road closures. But Will's onto that, too.'

'Speaking of the council,' Will said, turning to Bev. 'You heard an objection has been lodged to your application?'

Bev nodded. 'Iain told me. Milton Harris. He's got to be behind the break-in at the garden centre, too.' Her lips tightened. 'But I'm not going to let him stop me. Iain says…'

'We seem to be hearing a lot about what Iain Grant says these days. What gives, sis?' Martin asked.

Bev blushed. Martin wasn't normally so perceptive.

'Your sister has an admirer,' Ailsa said, chuckling.

An admirer – it sounded like something out of a regency novel.

'He's a friend and he's been very helpful,' Bev said. 'He's helped with the application to the council and helped organise CCTV for the garden centre. His son works for me.'

'Don't forget the dinner invitations,' Ailsa said.

'Really?' Martin's eyes widened. 'I didn't know about all this.'

'Well, you do now. Can we please change the subject?'

But Martin wouldn't let it go and it was only after some good-natured ribbing that they did start discussing other matters and ordered their meals.

*

It was the day of Ros's surgery, and she'd been on Iain's mind all day, ever since he'd dropped Mia off at school. He'd tried to settle down to some sketching but was unable to concentrate. Taking a walk up the boardwalk, he was outside Ted and Grace's home when he saw the couple sitting on the deck.

'Join us?' Ted called, holding up a mug.

Iain hesitated for a moment before pushing open the gate. 'Thanks.' He took a seat while Grace fetched another mug.

'I've asked for a valuation on the property,' Grace said. 'I should be able to let you know in a day or two.' She paused. 'Something wrong?'

'Thanks, Grace. Sorry, I'm a bit distracted today.' He dragged a hand through his hair, then, looking into Grace's kind and concerned eyes, found himself saying, 'It's Ros, Bryan's mother. She's undergoing surgery today.'

'Oh, I'm sorry. Major surgery?'

'Yes. Bryan doesn't know. She wanted to keep it from him till it was over, but…'

'You feel guilty not sharing it with him?'

Iain stared at her in surprise. Why hadn't he figured that out for himself. Besides his worry about Ros, he was consumed with guilt at keeping her illness a secret from his son. 'How did you know?'

'I'm a parent, too. It's hard to keep secrets from our children even if we know it's for their own good, and I guess Ros thinks it is. You may not agree with her, but you do need to respect her wishes.'

Iain knew she was right, but it didn't make him feel any better. What if Ros didn't survive the surgery? How would he admit to Bryan that he knew all about her illness, but kept it from him?

'Things are never straightforward where family is concerned,' Ted said. 'Take it from me. There have been a few times when Aaron and I have failed to see things the same way, and I know Grace has had similar challenges with her three – or at least two of them.'

Grace nodded. 'If the worst does happen, I'm sure Bryan will understand you did what you had to do, and that his mother was only thinking of what was best for him.'

Iain wasn't so sure. He knew Ros, and she could be devious at times. But he wanted to believe Grace. He hoped Ros would be all right. Bryan had suffered enough loss this year. He and Ros might not be close, but she *was* his mother. And Mia was just getting to know her grandmother.

'I hear your son is entering the triathlon this year,' Ted said. 'It's a good challenge and one of the highlights of our local calendar – that and the surfing championships.'

'He's been training hard,' Iain said, glad of the change of subject. 'It's been good for him after the loss of his wife to have something to focus on. Are you involved?'

'Not as a participant. Sadly. It's a younger man's game. But I am on the organising committee, and I'll be there at the start and the finishing line.'

'Couldn't keep him away,' Grace said with an affectionate smile. 'He and Will Rankin practically run the event.'

The conversation turned to Ailsa and Martin's wedding and the destruction at the garden centre and, before Iain knew it, he had agreed to stay to lunch, and it was time to pick Mia up from school.

Although he had stopped talking about Ros, she still wasn't far from his mind. So, when Mia disappeared to visit Libby and Milo, he picked up his phone to call the hospital.

It took him some time to get through to the correct section, and once he did, to manage to extract information about Ros's condition. He finally had to identify himself as her husband – something he never thought he'd do again – to be taken seriously, only to be told the surgery had been successful, she was as well as could be expected and he should call again the next day.

Glad the first part of her ordeal was over, but frustrated he wasn't able to talk with her, Iain debated what he should do, finally deciding Bryan deserved to know.

Fortunately, Mia was still at Libby's when Bryan arrived home.

'Good day?' he asked.

'Pretty good. At least there were no more dramas. The security cameras seem to be doing their work.'

'Can we talk?'

Bryan gave him a puzzled look. 'Let me have a shower first, Dad. I've been shovelling mulch all day.'

While Bryan disappeared to take a shower, Iain poured two measures of scotch and placed them on the table.

'What's up?' Bryan reappeared towelling his hair. 'Hey!' he said, catching sight of the scotch. 'Who's died?'

Not the best way to start the conversation.

'No one's died, but it's your mum.'

'What's she done now?' Bryan sighed, and flung himself down in a chair, the towel round his neck.

There was no way to sugar-coat this. 'She's sick, Bryan. Cancer. She underwent surgery in Sydney today. It seems to have been successful, but she'll have to undergo a round of chemo. She didn't want you to know until the surgery was over.'

Bryan shrugged, a white line appearing around his tight lips. 'And I'm supposed to care? Where was she when Nadia died, when *we* needed *her*?'

He threw the towel down onto the table and stormed out, leaving the scotch untouched.

That went well, Iain thought, picking up one glass and draining it. At least Bryan knew now. So why did he still feel guilty?

Thirty-two

Bev knew Iain's ex-wife was having surgery today and wished there was some way she could comfort him, but she wasn't sure how. Instead, she focussed on work and the preparations that still had to be made for Martin and Ailsa's wedding.

The one thing she had still to arrange was the wedding cake. It would have been easy for Cleo to have approached Ruby about it one morning when she was dropping off her regular supply of cakes, but it was something Bev wanted to take care of herself.

Leaving work earlier than usual after asking Julie to lock up, she went home, then slowly made her way up the boardwalk to the headland to speak to Ruby.

As Bev reached the white high-set weatherboard house she took a deep breath. Maybe she should have asked Ailsa to come with her, but her friend had assured her she'd be happy with whatever Bev and Ruby decided.

As children, they'd all mocked the woman who lived alone at the top of the boardwalk, often knocking on her door before running away to hide in the bushes and watch her peer out.

Bev had only been inside the house once before and, as she approached the door with its flaked white paint, the memory of that earlier visit rose up, almost choking her. It had been soon after she returned to Bellbird Bay to find her dad so sick. She'd gone up to the headland for a break, and Ruby had found her huddled on the edge of the cliff, sobbing. The woman, who seemed old even then, but couldn't have been any older than Bev was now, put an arm around her and led her inside where she gave her a cup of camomile tea and a slice of the most delicious cake.

The ambiance of the old house had wrapped its cloak around the girl, providing a much-needed comfort which allowed Bev to return home more able to cope with what fate had thrown at her. Ruby had asked no questions, merely provided her presence. Bev had never ventured inside the old house again.

'I was expecting you.' Ruby opened the door as soon as Bev reached it. Bev flinched, then decided the old woman had probably been peering through the window and had seen her coming up the boardwalk.

As soon as she walked in, the house enveloped her as it had before. It was easy to see why *Headland House* was a popular B&B, why holidaymakers returned year after year. It wasn't only Ruby's cooking that attracted them but the warm atmosphere of the house itself.

'I suppose you've come to ask me about making the wedding cake,' Ruby said when they were settled at the scrubbed wood table, seated in the old-fashioned ladderback chairs Bev remembered. She looked around the room. Nothing seemed to have changed from her previous visit.

Just as before, a large shallow pottery bowl filled with fruit sat in the centre of the table, an oversized fridge hummed in one corner and a double-sized gas cooktop and oven stood against one wall, at right angles to a deep porcelain sink. The kitchen surfaces were of polished wood and were home to the same blue and white striped canisters as before. It was like travelling back in time. But the Bev of today was a different person from the young woman who had sobbed her heart out all those years ago.

'Ailsa wanted me to ask you,' she said, taking a welcome sip of tea. 'If it's too much trouble…'

'Not at all. I'd be honoured. I remember you and your brother, and Will Rankin, too, when you used to come up here as youngsters to annoy the old woman. I suppose I've always seemed old to you. I was pleased to hear Martin and Ailsa decided to marry. It's as it should be. They've both had their troubles.' She nodded sagely. 'The cake will be baked and ready for their special day.'

'Thanks. I won't take any more of your time.'

'Time is all I have these days,' Ruby replied, but rose to see Bev to the door. Once there she stopped. 'You're a good woman, Bev. You haven't had an easy life either, I remember the day I found you crying your heart out and brought you inside. You've come a long way since then. And now you're at another crossroads. Just remember, there's no such thing as a coincidence. Everything happens for a reason.' She closed the door leaving Bev staring at it in surprise. She knew Ruby often spoke in riddles, but this really didn't make any sense.

*

The rest of the week seemed to drag for Bev but finally Saturday came around and with it, her dinner date with Iain. There was no sense in calling it anything but a date now, and the fluttering in her stomach was a sure sign Iain Grant was beginning to mean something to her. It was strange, after all those years of keeping her emotions in check, to be reminded of what it felt like to have a man in her life. It made her wonder what Phil would have been like if he'd lived, if he'd have turned into a carbon copy of the rigid military man his father had been, or if he'd have managed to retain his own personality, remain the man she'd fallen in love with.

Her life would have been very different if Phil and William had lived. It was doubtful if she would have returned to Bellbird Bay when her parents became ill. She would have had other responsibilities, been a married woman with a husband and child.

And *The Pandanus Garden Centre and Café* wouldn't exist.

Bev looked through her office door to where she could see customers wandering through the centre, enjoying its ambiance, selecting plants, to the staff in their signature green pandanus aprons busy tending to the plants. She sighed with pleasure at what she'd managed to achieve and thought of the improvements she still planned to make. There was no sense in fretting about what might have been. This was what she had established, and she'd done it all by herself, becoming a stronger person in the process. The woman who owned this garden centre, who had built it up from nothing, the woman who was having dinner with Iain Grant this evening was a very different person from the one who had fled Canberra to take refuge with her godmother in Sydney.

That woman had been a frightened twenty-year-old. Now she was in her late fifties and about to embark on a relationship which might change her life again. The thought filled her with a mixture of anticipation and dread. *Was she ready for this?* Her heart said yes, but her head was still undecided.

'Do you have time for coffee?' Ailsa popped her head into Bev's office, breaking into her thoughts.

'Sure.' This sort of thinking was unproductive. Coffee with Ailsa, who would no doubt want to talk about the wedding, would take her mind off it.

But, once they were seated in the café, it was Iain Grant who was the subject of Ailsa's conversation.

'I finally met your Iain,' she said with a grin. 'He's pretty dishy, isn't he? A bit like a younger Pierce Brosnan. Ooh, I loved him as Bond.'

'Ailsa! Listen to yourself.' Bev tried to play down her interest in Ailsa's opinion. 'Where did you meet him?'

'At the surf club. Martin and I were there for a drink before dinner last night when he came in with his son. He's pretty hot, too. They had his granddaughter with them. I think they were having dinner there. They start serving early and have a children's menu,' Ailsa continued, clearly oblivious to Bev's discomfort. 'She's a cutie. It would be nice to have a grandchild or two.'

'No sign of either of the boys tying the knot?' Bev asked.

Ailsa gave an exaggerated sigh. 'Not in this lifetime, though Pat and Vee have got together again – he's bringing her to the wedding – and I have hopes of Nate and Hannah, as I think I said. But the younger generation don't seem to set such store on marriage as we did – do. They seem content to live together. Though I do hope they change their minds before the children start to arrive.'

There it was again, the talk of grandchildren that sent a barb into Bev's heart. 'Talking of weddings,' she said. 'Are you happy with Cleo's menu?'

'It's perfect. I knew it would be. You have a gem, there, Bev. Hi, Cleo, just talking about you,' she said as Cleo came to join them.

'All good, I hope.'

'Just saying how much I like your ideas for the wedding menu. You have a gift. And I hear Ruby's promised to make the cake?' She looked from Cleo to Bev and back again. 'I guess we should add her to the list of invitees. In a strange sort of way, she did predict Martin and I getting together, back when…' Ailsa's eyes took on a glazed expression.

'How many will that make?' Bev asked, trying to remember how many chairs she'd asked Hannah to hire.

'Can I get back to you on that? Vee will be an extra, too.'

'Sure. Now I need to get back to work.'

'Have a good time tonight, Bev,' Ailsa said. 'Remember, you're never too old.'

Bev glared at her friend, but she knew Ailsa had her happiness at heart. She'd found love with Martin and wanted everyone to have the same happy-ever-after.

By the time seven o'clock came around, Bev was a nervous wreck. She'd decided to wear the same wide-legged pants as on their previous dinner engagement, but this time she matched them with a turquoise tunic top she'd picked up on a second visit to *Birds of a Feather*. She'd tried to do something different with her hair, tying it up into a bun on top of her head then wondering if it looked as if she was trying too hard. But it was too late to start again. She grimaced at her reflection in the mirror, her hand trembling as she applied a light touch of her favourite lipstick.

'Hello,' she said to Iain, suddenly feeling shy when she opened the door to him.

'You're looking lovely,' he said with a grin which put her at her ease. 'I booked a table at Harris's hotel. Thought we could check out the competition. I know he's in Sydney, so we're not in danger of running into him. I ate there when Ros was in town and the meals are excellent.'

'Oh, it's a bit upmarket, isn't it?'

'It's been quite a week. I think we deserve it.' He hesitated before adding, 'I want it to be special.'

'Oh,' Bev said again, unsure how to respond. She remembered Cleo and Will going there and reporting on the dim lighting and the romantic atmosphere, and her stomach lurched.

Iain looked pretty good himself, Bev thought, glancing at him out of the corner of her eye as they drove to across town to the hotel. Tonight, he was wearing a blue and white striped button-down shirt under a blue blazer, and in the closed atmosphere of the car, she could detect the slight aroma of a popular aftershave.

The fluttering in Bev's stomach went into overdrive when they reached the restaurant and Iain helped her out of the car. He took her hand as they walked through the plush entrance of the hotel, across the wide tiled foyer and into the restaurant, a room with subdued lighting, filled with small tables. A piano was playing softly. The whole place reeked of money. It was way out of Bev's league. She'd have been much more comfortable at the *Firenze* or in the surf club.

'I don't usually dine like this, either,' Iain said, sensing her discomfort. 'But, what the hell, let's enjoy it.'

The smile lighting up his face made Bev smile, too.

'Why not,' she said. 'Thanks for bringing me here. It demonstrates, as nothing else could, how ridiculous Milton Harris is to think I'm competition for this.' She waved a hand in the air to encompass the over-the-top décor, the waiters gliding silently around, not to mention the subtle background music.

The meal was delicious, and the sparkling wine Iain ordered to accompany it helped Bev relax. After a few sips she began to enjoy the romantic atmosphere, and Iain's anecdotes about his experiences dealing with difficult clients in his Sydney architectural practice led her to share some experiences of her own. By the time the meal was over, she felt as if she'd known Iain for years, and her initial worries had melted away.

'Coffee?' he asked, after they'd shared a dish of the red velvet soft cheesecake with amaretto crumb and raspberry sorbet Bev remembered Cleo telling her about.

'Why don't we have coffee on my deck?' she asked, daringly, stifling her former misgivings and remembering Ailsa's words. 'It will be lovely out there on an evening like this.'

Iain's eyes lit up again.

When they pulled up outside Bev's house, they turned to face each other, the buzz of the evening still there between them.

'Are you sure?' Iain said.

Bev knew he wasn't talking about coffee. 'I'm sure,' she lied, her heart thumping madly. It had been so long, over thirty-five years. What if...?

Then they were out of the car; she was fumbling with the key to her door. They were inside and suddenly Iain's arms were around her, his face so close she could feel his breath on her cheek.

'Coffee,' she said, pulling away and heading for the kitchen.

Iain followed more slowly, giving her time to regain her composure. He stood leaning against the kitchen bench as she made coffee and opened a packet of chocolate mints. Then he opened the door to the deck to allow her to carry out the mints while he followed with the coffee. They didn't speak.

Once outside, the gentle breeze from the ocean calmed Bev's flaming cheeks. What had she been thinking? She'd as much as invited Iain to… She was glad he was too much of a gentleman to insist on making good her thinly veiled invitation – or was she?

Thirty-three

Iain wondered if he'd misread the signs. The evening had gone well, better than he had anticipated. And when Bev had suggested coffee back at her place, while surprised, he'd been delighted at the indication she might be ready to take their relationship to the next level.

But here they were, actually drinking coffee on her deck. Had things changed so much in the years he'd been out of the dating game? Back then, coffee had been code for something more.

As Bev had said, it was lovely out here, the sound of the waves on the beach, the distant noise of a group of revellers down on the esplanade. He looked at his companion. Tendrils of hair were falling from the bun she'd obviously carefully constructed, a more sophisticated look than her usual ponytail, making her more desirable than ever.

What had gone wrong? There had been the moment in the restaurant when she'd invited him back for coffee – he'd have sworn she'd intended more than coffee – then the one in the car when their eyes had met. There had definitely been something. But, almost as soon as they were inside, her barriers had gone up again. He wished he knew what had happened to Bev to make her so afraid of letting go and giving into her emotions. She was a lovely woman, warm, intelligent, independent, ambitious. But there was something about her he didn't understand.

He looked up to see her watching him.

'How is your ex? Her surgery was this week, wasn't it?'

'It was, and she seems to be making a good recovery.'

'She'll stay in Sydney?'

'So she says. I expect she'll rent something close to the hospital till her treatment is over, then...' He spread his hands. He hoped she'd decide to stay there. She probably still had friends from when she lived there before, and she had been scathing about Bellbird Bay, so there was little chance of her coming here. 'Afterwards, she could go anywhere,' he said, realising it was true. Ros had always liked to travel. Though he wondered if her days of finding partners in different parts of the world were over.

'Will you go there... to Sydney... to see her?'

Was this what was bothering Bev? Did she think he still had feelings for Ros?

'No, she doesn't want me there. I would have gone to see her after her surgery if I'd thought it would help, but she was very clear she wanted to be alone.' *Or maybe she hoped Milton Harris would come to the party.*

'It must be difficult for her with no family around.'

'It's her choice, Bev. We all make choices for how we want to live. I chose to come here when Bryan's wife died, and it's proved to be a good move for us all. Bryan is happy at the garden centre, Mia is happy in school and at Nippers, and I've met you.'

Bev blushed and looked down into her mug.

Daringly, Iain took the mug from her unresisting hand. He placed it on the table. Then he took her hands in his. 'I like you, Bev. I like you a lot. I think you like me, too, maybe more than like. But each time we seem to become closer, you pull away. Is it me? Do I do something to upset you? If so, I wish you would tell me what it is.' He waited. At least she hadn't pulled her hands away.

'I'm sorry, Iain. I do like you – a lot. This is the first time I've felt this way for a long time. I guess I'm afraid, afraid of being hurt, afraid of giving in to my emotions only to find...'

Iain didn't wait for her to finish speaking. Releasing her hands, he drew her into an embrace and with her head on his shoulder, the scent of her hair filling him with yearning, murmured, 'I'd never hurt you. Bev. You mean too much to me. I never thought, when we came to Bellbird Bay, that I'd meet someone like you, someone who made me feel young again, someone who I could care for.'

He moved his head slightly and their lips met. It was as if he'd been waiting all his life for this moment.

Thirty-four

The last two weeks had been bliss. Bev had finally managed to put aside her fears and allow Iain to become close to her. They hadn't yet made love, but she knew it was only a matter of time. Ailsa's words kept repeating in her ears. *It's never too late.* She might be fifty-five, but she had lots of good years ahead and maybe, just maybe, she wouldn't need to spend them alone.

But today, she couldn't hide from the past. It was the one day each year when all Bev wanted to do was hide away from the world. It was the anniversary of her William's birth. She forced herself out of bed, showered, dressed, and managed to swallow a piece of dry toast and drink a glass of water, promising herself to have something more substantial later.

Once at the garden centre, she planned to stay in her office and avoid everyone. By ten o'clock hunger pangs forced her out and, as she made her way across to the café in the hope a cup of coffee and one of Ruby's cakes would sustain her, she heard the sound of voices coming from the work area. Peeking around a display of pots, she saw Bryan was the centre of the group and, as she watched, they began to sing *Happy Birthday* to him. Shocked, Bev turned back to shut herself in the office again. How could this be Bryan's birthday? It was too much of a coincidence.

Bev laid her head down on her arms, memories of the past threatening to overwhelm her. Her William would be the same age as Bryan Grant. What cruel fate had sent him here to torment her?

Until she'd met Bryan Grant, she'd had trouble summoning up Phil's image. Now he was there, in her garden centre, every day – a reminder of what might have been. No wonder some nights she had trouble sleeping. And now this!

Somehow, she got through the rest of the day and made it home without breaking down. But once in the safety of her own house, the tears began to flow, tears for the loss of the young boy who hadn't had the chance to live, for the lover who'd died too soon, for all those lost years.

When her phone rang and Bev saw Iain's number, she almost let it ring out, then taking a deep breath, she answered. 'Iain?' She tried to put an energy she was far from feeling into her voice.

'Bev. Sorry this is so last minute. It's Bryan's birthday today. We weren't planning to do anything special – it's a day when he misses Nadia even more – but Mia wants to have a small family birthday tea for him, and we wondered if you'd join us. Well, actually, it was Mia's idea to invite you. But she's right... will you come?'

Touched at Mia wanting to include her in the family celebration, Bev would have loved to accept. But not today. 'Sorry, I'm not feeling very well. Wish Bryan a happy birthday for me.'

'Oh, I'm sorry, Bev. Is there anything I can do?'

'I'm sure I'll be fine after a good night's sleep.'

'Are we still on for Friday?'

'Of course.' Iain was planning to take her to *The Beach House* for dinner, and there was an unspoken agreement this would be the night they'd finally make love. After much heart-searching Bev felt she was ready to let Iain into the part of her life that till now, she'd shared only with Phil, to take the risk of opening herself up to another person, to risk being hurt again.

*

Next day, Bev was still feeling fragile, but she had arranged to meet Ailsa and Cleo for lunch so put on a brave face as she closed her computer and headed to the café.

'Are you all right?' Ailsa asked after they had hugged. 'You look pale?'

'I'm fine. I didn't sleep well, that's all. You look blooming.' And she did. Bev had never seen her friend with such a happy glow, not even when they were both twenty, and Ailsa had been dating Bob.

'Thanks. Here's Cleo.'

The dark-haired woman joined them at the table she kept specially for Bev. 'I've been having fun in the kitchen this morning. I thought you could try out some of the dishes I'm planning to serve at the wedding – just a taster of a few.'

'Mmm, sounds good,' Ailsa said with a grin. 'I could get used to being the focus of attention. Maybe you and Will will be next?'

Cleo blushed but didn't reply, then disappeared into the kitchen, to reappear carrying a tray of small dishes.

As Cleo said, it was a series of tasters. The women sampled the tiny morsels of seared scallops wrapped in prosciutto, the tempura zucchini flowers filled with mushroom and ricotta, the barramundi fillet, wombok filled prawn mousse parcels, the tender pieces of lamb fillet infused with thyme, and the decadent chocolate mousse, each one more delicious than the other. Their tastebuds tingling, the three commented on each as they ate, trying to decide on their favourites.

They had finished tasting, complimented Cleo on her choices and had progressed to coffee when Cleo said, 'Did you see the awful news item on television last night? Those poor parents.'

'No.' Bev rarely watched the evening news, preferring to relax with her favourite pieces of music or to watch a favourite crime series.

'Oh, it's dreadful. Their babies were accidentally switched in the hospital. They only discovered the mistake when one was found to have a genetic disease which couldn't have come from either parent.'

A tight band gripped Bev's chest. She thought of Bryan Grant, who looked so like Phil, who had been born on the same day as her William. What if…? She shook her head to dismiss the notion which threatened to destroy her.

'Are you all right, Bev?' Ailsa asked, her eyes full of concern.

'I'm fine.' But she wasn't. All she wanted to do was to run home and hide under the covers. Instead, she made an effort to pull herself together.

*

Bev couldn't get Cleo's words out of her head. She was unable to concentrate on any work that afternoon and was glad when it was finally time to go home where she could be on her own to think about what Cleo had said. She closed the front door behind her, so relieved to be alone. A calming cup of tea was called for. She flicked the kettle on, grabbed a cup from the cupboard, and sat down at the kitchen table, waiting for the water to boil.

The whole idea of babies being switched was a strange one. It was difficult to believe it could actually happen in this day and age. But it had. And if it could happen once maybe it could have happened before. Bev thought back to her William's birth. It had been a difficult birth, but at the end of it, her baby had been put into her arms – a perfect baby boy with a reddish fuzz of hair just like Phil's. It was as if a tiny part of Phil had survived in this baby, in their child. She'd hugged the knowledge to herself, as she'd hugged her child.

Then things had begun to go wrong. The day after she'd given birth, she began to bleed heavily and developed a fever. For the next five days she was too weak to know what was happening. Later the doctors told her that her uterus hadn't contracted properly after the birth, and she'd suffered from postpartum haemorrhage. She'd almost died.

As soon as she felt well enough, the only thing Bev wanted was to see her baby, only to be told he had died. She remembered yelling at the nurses and medical staff, accusing them of lying. Her son couldn't be dead. He was all she had left of Phil. But gradually, she was forced to accept that, while she had been lying in bed suffering from a fever, little William had died. What devastated her even more was that his body was already gone. Unwilling to wait till she recovered, her godmother had arranged a small, private funeral. Although Bev had been able to visit his grave and see the memorial, she had never seen her dead child. For a time, she wished she had died, too.

Bev stared into space, at the steam coming from the kettle. If what Cleo said was true, was it possible Willian was alive? Was it even possible Bryan Grant was her William, that the babies had been switched around in the hospital, that it was Iain's son who had died? An overwhelming feeling of... *love*. That's what it was... *motherly love* came over her She shivered as the idea took root.

Thirty-five

Iain had been disappointed Bev couldn't join them to celebrate Bryan's birthday. But perhaps it had been just as well. It was a sad affair. Mia was the only one in party mood, Iain and Bryan just going through the motions. Iain had bought a cake, and there were presents to open, but the rest of the evening fell flat as Bryan was tormented with memories of his birthday the previous year when Nadia had organised for them all to go to dinner at the restaurant in Centrepoint Tower, and they had spent the evening eating good food and watching the views of the city as the restaurant slowly rotated.

Today, he intended to visit the council to see what he could discover about the objection which had been submitted by Milton Harris. He had arranged to meet Will Rankin beforehand. Being a member of the council, Will had offered to give Iain advice on how best to handle the situation. Although he had plenty of experience in dealing with town councils, it was always good to have local knowledge. It had been kind of Will to offer. Being an old friend of both Bev and Martin, he was eager to see Bev's application approved.

Iain was feeling cheerful as he strode down the boardwalk to *The Bay Café* where he was to meet Will. Despite the fiasco of last night's meal, Bryan had appeared more cheerful this morning and Mia had been her usual chatty self on the way to school.

The café was almost deserted. It was too early for the coffee crowd and the few tourists around who'd come for breakfast had already left. Will was seated at one of the sun-bleached wooden outdoor tables with a large mug of coffee.

'G'day, Will.' Iain took a seat and ordered a mug of his own, wishing he could look as good as Will after what had no doubt been an early morning surf. The man's hair, tied back in his customary ponytail, was still wet and his tee-shirt, bearing the logo of his surf school, was clinging to his damp body. Will Rankin couldn't be much younger than Iain, but he had kept himself fit. Iain found himself self-consciously pulling in his stomach.

'What can you tell me about this guy I need to see?' Iain asked, as soon as his coffee had been served. 'Is he likely to be difficult?'

'Hard to say. Brad Kelly has been in charge of development here for years. He's seen a lot in his time and tends to be pretty fair. But it's not only his decision. He has a committee to deal with.' He grimaced. 'That's where the problem comes in. From what I've heard, Harris had the ear of some of the committee members and…' he rubbed his chin, '…money may have changed hands or favours offered.'

'Ah.' It was good to know what he was dealing with, even though he might not be able to counteract it.

*

Well, that had been a waste of time. Iain fumed as he left the council chambers. The meeting with Brad Kelly had been pleasant enough, but he'd been unable to learn any more about how the council proposed to deal with Harris's objection to Bev's proposal – and he'd rejected Iain's suggestion that Harris might be using underhand tactics to get his own way.

'It's not unheard of,' Kelly said, 'but not here in Bellbird Bay. I don't know where you got your information, but Milton Harris is a respected member of the community. He's put a lot of money into Bellbird Bay and has some good friends on the council. In fact, I understand he intends to stand at the next council election. So…' he had spread his hands wide, '…I'm not sure how I can help. I can only suggest you submit a rebuttal to his objection.'

*

Iain spent the best part of the afternoon preparing the document for the council. Then he picked Mia up from school, her happy chatter managing to lighten his mood. 'How about we stop for ice cream?' he asked as they drove homewards.

'Yes, please, Grandad,' a delighted Mia replied. She was so easy to please. Iain wished everything in life was as easy to manage.

Mia was playing in the living room, and Iain was reading over the document for the council one more time before sending it off, when Bryan popped his head into the study. 'Got a minute, Dad?' he asked, a serious expression on his face.

'Sure. What's up, son?'

'I've been thinking about what you said… about Mum. I still can't forgive her, but she is my mother and Mia's grandmother and… what if she doesn't recover? Mia deserves to know her grandmother.' He paused.

Iain waited for Bryan to continue. He had no idea what Bryan meant. What he said next was a shock.

'Dad, I want to go to Sydney, to take Mia, to see Mum.'

'That's… quite a turnaround, Bryan. Are you sure? When were you thinking of going?'

'We'll fly down tomorrow evening and can be back in time for Mia to go to school on Monday and me to work. She'll miss Nippers, but I'm sure she'll understand.'

Iain wasn't sure how Ros might react to a visit from her son and granddaughter while she was in hospital. 'Don't you want to wait till she's been discharged?'

'What if things don't go well for her, what if…'

They were both silent, thinking the unthinkable. *What if Ros didn't make a good recovery?*

'It's a good thing you're doing, son.' Iain clapped Bryan on the shoulder. He just hoped Ros would appreciate the gesture and wouldn't antagonise Bryan any further. Maybe this would prove to be the reconciliation Ros had hoped for when she visited Bellbird Bay.

Thirty-six

Bev was still caught up in memories of the past when Ailsa and Martin appeared at her door. She hadn't bothered to shower or change and was seated at the kitchen table, an uneaten bowl of leftover pasta in front of her.

'You looked so strange at lunch,' Ailsa said. 'We had to come to check you out. You still don't look good.'

'I'm fine,' Bev repeated.

'You're not.' Ailsa put a hand on her arm. 'What's wrong. You're as white as a sheet. Was it something Cleo or I said?'

Bev took a deep breath. Maybe it was time she revealed her secret. Ailsa and Martin were her family. They deserved to know. 'It was a long time ago,' she began.

When she had finished, she was in tears, and Ailsa and Martin, far from looking shocked, appeared sympathetic.

'Oh, Bev. I wish I'd known.' Ailsa hugged her tightly. 'You went through all that on your own.'

'I did have my godmother.' Bev sniffed. 'And you were so wrapped up in Bob at the time, I didn't…'

'And I was off overseas,' Martin said with a frown. 'Didn't Mum and Dad know?'

'I couldn't tell them. Can you imagine Dad's reaction?' Bev thought about her religious father, his disapproval, and how ashamed her mother would have been. 'Anyway, Dad got sick, and they had more to worry about than anything I might have suffered.'

'So, you think perhaps…?' Ailsa asked.

Bev shook her head. 'I don't know, but… it seems too much of a coincidence. I don't know what to do.' Ruby's words came back to her. *There's no such thing as a coincidence.*

'Have you ever spoken to Iain about it?' Martin asked.

Bev shook her head again. There had been no need. How could she have told him his son resembled her love of long ago? And now, how could she tell Iain what she suspected? Bryan was his son, had been for the past thirty-five years. What would it do to him to learn a mistake could have been made? And what would it do to their growing relationship? 'I can't…'

'I think you have to,' Ailsa said. 'I know if there were doubts about Pat or Nate's parentage, I'd want to know. Luckily, they both look too much like Bob for there to have been any mistake,' she said, referring to her ex-husband. 'He seems like a reasonable person. I'm sure he'd be understanding.'

'Mmm.' Bev wasn't so sure. But she saw the sense of Ailsa's suggestion. If she didn't mention it to Iain, she'd never know. And the thought of living with the uncertainty was worse than the risk of losing the closeness that was developing between her and Iain.

It was late by the time Ailsa and Martin left, having extracted a promise from Bev she'd speak with Iain. But what could she say? She tried to imagine the conversation and, each time, came up empty-handed. How did you suggest to the man you were in a relationship with you might be the mother of his son? It was an impossible situation. Bev wished Cleo had never mentioned the news item. The idea her son might be alive, might be Bryan Grant had never occurred to her. Was it really such a coincidence? Didn't they say everyone had a double? And lots of people were born on the same day. But Ruby Sullivan's words rang in her ears. *There's no such thing as a coincidence.* And Bev was looking at two coincidences.

Still undecided, and in an attempt to put the problem aside, Bev went to bed. But once there, unable to fall asleep, she tossed and turned, only to fall into a light doze as dawn was breaking and to waken unrefreshed at the sound of her alarm.

To Bev's relief, she made it through the day without seeing Bryan, the prospect of her date with Iain filling her with dread. The evening she should have been anticipating with all her being ruined by the thought of what she was to say to him. She was about to turn his world upside down, to force him to question the last thirty-five years, to question whether Bryan really was his son, or if his son was dead. Once thing was for sure. They weren't going to end up in bed.

Bev's mind was in a whirl as she showered and changed. Tonight, she didn't care what she wore. She just wanted to get the evening over with. She pulled on the dress she'd set aside on her previous dates – the lemon linen one she'd last worn for Martin's first exhibition in Bellbird Bay over two years earlier. She'd intended to buy something new, but now it didn't seem to matter. Nothing seemed to matter apart from finding out the truth.

The Beach House was one of Bellbird Bay's best restaurants, fashioned from glass and timber, it was built on an outcrop of rock and seemed to stand on top of the sea. Normally, Bev would love to eat there, but tonight, the sight of the setting sun shimmering on the tall glass walls which faced the sea failed to move her.

'Wow!' Iain said, as they walked up to the glassed entrance. 'Wish I'd designed this. It's spectacular. Milton Harris, eat your heart out. His hotel, no matter how plush, can never compete with this prime location.'

Bev must have hidden her distress well, because Iain didn't appear to notice anything was amiss as he ordered a bottle of sparkling wine and with her agreement chose the fish of the day for both of them.

The meal progressed with Iain doing most of the talking. He described his visit to the council chambers and his subsequent email to argue the case for what was now called *Pandanus Weddings*. 'It has a good ring about it,' he said with a smile.

Then, as they waited for dessert, Iain became more serious. 'Bryan surprised me,' he said. 'He's on his way to Sydney to see Ros.'

Bev finally roused herself from the blue funk she'd been in all evening, while hopefully pretending interest in the conversation. Bryan was going to see his mother, or rather, the woman who might not be his mother. The poor woman was ill. What would it do to her to learn she might not be Bryan's mother? What would it mean to Bryan?

For the first time, Bev realised what a shock it would be to Bryan to learn Iain and Ros might not be his parents. Could she do that to

Bryan – and to little Mia? Would it be better to stay quiet, to keep her suspicions to herself and go on as if nothing had happened, as if Bryan's resemblance to Phil and his birthday on September fourteenth were just coincidences and nothing more?

But she knew she couldn't do that. Despite the risk of what she might uncover, the fallout to the people so closely involved, there was no way she could let it go. She had to know the truth.

Bev waited till their meal was over and they were back, seated on her deck. It was romantic out here and would be easy to keep her questions to herself, to enjoy the moment. This was supposed to be the evening when they took their relationship to the next level. And she was about to spoil it.

As Iain's arm snaked around her shoulders, Bev took a deep breath and steeled herself. 'There's something I want to ask you,' she said, 'but first I need to tell you a story, a story about a twenty-year-old girl in Canberra, a girl who became pregnant, whose lover was killed and who was told her child had died.' She pulled away from Iain and wrapped her arms around her body. 'I was that girl.' Her voice broke.

'Oh, Bev!' Iain made a move to hug her, but Bev warded him off. 'I was told my son died,' she repeated, 'but today…' she took a ragged breath, '…I learned that sometimes mistakes can be made, babies can become switched in hospital.' She met Iain's eyes which now held a puzzled expression. 'When I met Bryan, I was struck by his likeness to Phil – the father of my child… then his birthday yesterday… September fourteenth is the day my William was born.' She was shaking by now. 'I wanted to ask… I wondered if…'

Ian appeared stunned. Then he spoke quietly.

'Bryan's adopted.'

Thirty-seven

Iain's head was reeling, unable to take in what Bev was telling him. Could it be true? Part of him wanted to dispute what Bev was suggesting, another part wanted to comfort her. But now she had moved away from him, out of his embrace, her arms tightly wrapped around herself as if for protection.

Iain dropped his hands between his knees and stared at the worn surface of the deck as if it held the answers he was seeking. Then he raised his eyes to meet Bev's.

'He's adopted? You mean…? Then who…?' Bev pressed a fist to her mouth. Iain could see her eyes fill with tears. 'Does he know?'

'He's always known he was adopted.' Iain was shocked by Bev's revelation, by the unbelievable possibility Bryan could be her son. 'He's never been interested in seeking out his birth parents. I was the one who pushed for adoption,' he said. 'In retrospect it was foolish of me, though if I hadn't, I'd never have Bryan – or Mia – and I can't imagine my life without either of them. Ros wasn't able to have children, and although she didn't feel the lack the same way I did, she agreed to adopt Bryan. It was fine for a while, then… she became restless.' He dragged a hand through his hair. 'I guess she wasn't cut out to be a mother.'

He could see how his words hurt Bev and wanted to comfort her, but her arms were still firmly clasped around her body, as if to prevent him from touching her.

What if what Bev suspected was true? What if Bryan was her child?

What if there had been a mistake and it was some other child who had died?

'I need to talk to Bryan,' he said, wondering how his son would react. He'd already suffered such a terrible loss. What would it do to him to have to question his whole life? Would he even want to know?

Iain looked at Bev, her face now streaked with tears, and knew that for her sake, he had to find out the truth, regardless of the consequences. It was unfortunate this had come just as Bryan was attempting a reconciliation with his mother – his adoptive mother, Iain corrected himself. God, what a mess this could turn out to be. It was the worst timing, though there could be no good timing for this sort of news. He knew it was only a suspicion of Bev's at this stage, but he'd never believed in coincidences and if this was a coincidence he'd eat his hat – if he had one.

'I'm sorry,' Bev said. 'I've spoiled everything.'

'No, but it takes a bit of getting used to. We've always known the day might come when Bryan might want to look for his birth parents, but we'd given up worrying about it as the years went on. At least I did. I don't think Ros ever thought much about it. But this… isn't what I expected.' He ran a hand through his hair again. 'Mia's just getting used to having Ros as her grandmother,' he said.

'It's not my intention to turn all your lives upside down,' Bev said, scrubbing her eyes with a tissue. 'But you can see how I need to know.'

'Yeah.' Iain tried to put himself in Bev's position, to think what it must have been like for her… to grieve for her son for all these years, then to discover there was a possibility he was alive.

'I need a drink.' Iain rose. 'Do you have whisky, brandy?'

'Brandy. In the pantry.' Bev made no effort to rise.

Inside the kitchen, Iain found the brandy and took two glasses from the cupboard, then stood, his hands gripping the edge of the sink, staring into space, trying to work out what it would mean if Bev was right. He felt a jolt in his heart at the thought he and Bev might share Bryan… and Mia. She'd make a much better mother and grandmother than Ros ever had. And Bryan and Mia already liked her – a lot. But liking her as a friend was a different kettle of fish from discovering she was their mother and grandmother. He sighed. It might never come to that. In all likelihood, Bev was mistaken. It would all come to nothing, and they could all go on as before.

But could they? Earlier that day, he'd admitted to himself he was falling in love with Bev Cooper. He'd planned to take her to bed, to tell her how he felt in the hope she felt something for him, too. Now that wasn't going to happen. A thought occurred to him and began to curl through his head like a worm. Did she care about him at all? Had her interest in him been fuelled by the fact Bryan looked like the man she'd once loved. If Bryan did prove to be her son, would she drop Iain like a hot potato, having found the son she'd thought lost for ever?

When Iain returned to the deck, Bev hadn't moved. She was sitting exactly as he'd left her, head bowed.

'Here.' He handed her a glass, took a seat, and drank the measure he'd poured for himself.

'Thanks.' Bev took the glass. She held it in both hands but didn't drink.

'What do you want to do about it?' he asked.

'I don't know… check our DNA? It's the only way to find out… to be sure.'

'I need to talk with Bryan. We'd need his permission.' Iain had no idea how Bryan would react. 'He'll be back Sunday evening.'

'Right. Thanks.'

Iain wasn't sure what she was thanking him for. It would all depend on Bryan, and he wasn't looking forward to bringing this up with him. But it had to be done.

'I'll be in touch,' he said, putting the empty glass down on the table. He glanced at Bev, but she didn't meet his eyes before he walked away.

Thirty-eight

Bev didn't know how she got through the weekend. At least the garden centre kept her busy – and there was no Bryan to distract her. But when she came home on Sunday evening, all she could think of was Iain telling Bryan of her suspicions.

She wished she'd never heard about babies being switched, never thought Bryan might be her son. Her stomach churned as she imagined his reaction to what Iain was going to tell him. What if he became angry, decided he never wanted to see her again, resigned from his job? What if the whole family left Bellbird Bay, returned to Sydney? It was only when this occurred to her that Bev realised how attached she'd become, not only to Iain, but also to Bryan and Mia.

Little Mia. How would she react? Although there was no likelihood of her hearing anything about it unless… A tiny glimmer of hope began to grow in Bev's heart. What if it was true? What if Bryan was her son, hers and Phil's? What if Bryan accepted she was his birth mother? But where did that leave Iain, the man who was the only father Bryan had ever known – and Ros? Whatever her faults, she was Bryan's mother, Mia's grandmother. And she was battling what could be a terminal illness.

Bev was googling DNA testing, pleased to discover results could be obtained in less than a week, when there was a knock on the glass door in the kitchen and she saw Ailsa peering in.

When she opened the door, Ailsa immediately drew her into a warm hug. 'Thought you might be in need of company. Did you speak to Iain – tell him your suspicions?'

'Yes, I did.'

'What was his reaction?'

'Difficult to know. He agreed to speak to Bryan when he got back from Sydney, which should be...' she checked her watch, '... around now. Then he left. Oh, Ailsa, I feel I've just opened a can of worms and I don't know if it was the right thing to do.'

'It was right for you. You have to know.'

'Yes, but... that poor family. What will it do to them?'

'Was Bryan born in the same hospital as your son?'

'I don't know. He was adopted which makes it all the more difficult.'

'So... DNA?'

'I mentioned it, and Iain said we'd have to get Bryan's permission, which of course we would. Evidently, he's never expressed any interest in finding his birth parents so what are the chances?'

'This may be different.'

'Mmm. I've been googling, and it seems the test can be processed fairly quickly – if he agrees.'

'It'll be a shock. No idea how he might react?'

'Not a clue. We get on well as employer and employee, but this is something entirely different. I don't know what to do. What if...?' Her eyes widened as she thought again of the possibility the family might leave Bellbird Bay.

'Well, there's nothing you can do tonight, and you look in need of a glass of wine.'

'In the fridge,' Bev said without moving. Her hand had been hovering over the button to order the testing kit when Ailsa arrived. Now she closed the site, promising herself to check it again later.

'Thanks, Ailsa,' she said when her friend handed her a glass of wine. She'd deliberately avoided having one earlier, worried she might drink the entire bottle.

'It's not all bad,' Ailsa said when they had taken their drinks outside. 'It would be wonderful for you if Bryan did prove to be your son – and he was happy about it. Just imagine...'

Bev had. She'd imagined every possible scenario.

*

Further up the boardwalk, a difficult conversation was taking place. When Bryan and Mia arrived home, Mia was tired and irritable after the long journey, and Bryan had a face like thunder. There was no opportunity for Iain and Bryan to talk until they'd eaten, and Mia was in bed.

By the time Bryan came back to the kitchen, Iain had poured a couple of beers. 'It's a lovely evening. Let's sit outside,' he said, leading the way onto the deck, 'and you can tell me all about it. How is your mum?'

'She seems to be recovering well, but she's up to her old tricks,' Bryan said. 'Saturday was good. We had a pleasant conversation, and she chatted to Mia, asking her about school and Nippers. But when we went to visit again on Sunday, there was a man there, who says he knows you – or of you. Milton Harris.'

Iain blanched. 'What was he doing there? I knew she was flying down to Sydney in his plane, but…' He shook his head. Ros could still surprise him.

'They acted like they were good friends. She was talking about when she finishes the chemo, how they intend to see more of each other. He was very attentive.' It was Bryan's turn to shake his head. 'She seemed glad to see us again but was more taken up with him. It was Milt this and Milt that. It made me sick. Really, Dad, I felt the trip was a waste of time.' He took a gulp of beer. 'How was your weekend? Did you see Bev?'

'About Bev, son. There's something I need to talk with you about.' Iain's forehead creased. 'You've always known you were adopted.'

'Sure, and I always told you I didn't want anything to do with someone who didn't want me, who gave me away. Why bring it up again now?'

'What if they didn't give you away?'

'What do you mean?'

'It's something Bev told me.' Iain furrowed his brow again. 'When she was younger – much younger – she gave birth to a baby boy. She was told her baby died. Then, recently, there have been reports of mistakes being made, of babies being… not swapped exactly, but mixed up, switched.'

'What's this got to do with me being adopted?' Bryan looked genuinely puzzled.

'The fact is… it seems you resemble her baby's father, and…'

'So where is he? Did she marry him?'

'He died, too.'

'Well, I'm sorry for Bev. She's a good woman. But I still don't see…'

'Her son was born on the fourteenth of September, the exact same day as you.'

Bryan's eyes widened now. 'Wait, she doesn't think… You're not trying to say… No way, Dad. I bet lots of kids were born that day. There's nothing to say it could be me.'

'But it might be, Bryan. And if it is, if you are her son, wouldn't you want to know?'

'Don't do this to me, Dad. I've just been pissed off by the woman who *chose* me as her son. I don't need another woman trying to lay claim to me only to piss me off, too.' He thumped his empty glass down on the table and stomped inside, slamming the sliding glass door closed behind him.

Iain stared at the closed door. He hadn't handled it well. He'd had two days to get used to the idea which didn't seem too farfetched. Maybe Bryan would come around after a good night's sleep – maybe not. His son could be remarkably stubborn when he put his mind to it. He suspected Bev could be, too. That was one thing they had in common.

Now he'd had time to mull over what Bev had told him, Iain realised he could have handled things better with her, too. He'd left fairly precipitously, with no real indication of when he might see her again. For him, the evening he'd looked forward to so much had been spoiled. But what about Bev? It had been spoiled for her, too. It must have taken a great deal of courage for her to tell him her suspicions, because that's all they were at this stage. But the more he thought about it, the more he believed she might be right.

Thirty-nine

Next morning, Bryan had left before Iain got up. There was a note on the kitchen table to say he'd gone to training and wouldn't be going into work today. He "needed time to get his head together". Iain sighed, wondering what he could have done to avoid a recurrence of the sense of hopelessness from which Bryan had just been recovering. But Bev's hurt was real, too, and Iain knew he had to talk to her, to attempt to repair some of the damage his behaviour had caused.

It was the shock of her revelation. It had knocked him for six. All he could think of was what it might do to Bryan. He'd been right about that. But he'd ignored Bev's feelings when he left so abruptly.

On autopilot, he prepared breakfast and got Mia ready for school, deaf to her morning chatter as he tried to work out what he was going to do.

'Grandad, you're not listening,' she accused when he had ignored her several times.

'Sorry, sweetheart. What did you say?'

'I asked where Daddy is. He's usually here for breakfast.'

'He has a longer training session this morning.' Iain was wondering where Bryan was, too. Given his frame of mind last night, he suspected his son intended to keep out of his way.

When his phone beeped with a message, Iain grasped it eagerly, hoping it was Bryan. Instead, it was from *The Bay Gallery*. John Baldwin wanted to inform him several of his drawings had sold and asked if he had any more he could drop in. It was good news, but not the news he'd hoped for. While Mia was brushing her teeth, he packed several more of his sketches into his satchel. Once he'd dropped Mia off at school, he'd go to the gallery, then he'd head to the garden centre to see Bev, to apologise and try to mend the harm he'd done to their relationship.

There was a closed sign on the gallery door, but Iain could see the owner pottering around inside. When he tapped on the glass, John peered out, then opened it.

'Iain Grant, welcome. I'm glad to see you so quickly. You have some pieces for me? Your others sold well, as I expected. And with the triathlon coming up, there will be an influx of tourists. I always like to have plenty of artworks on display on holiday weekends.'

'It's a big deal – the triathlon?' Iain had assumed it was only a local event.

'My word. Entrants from all over Australia plus those who come from overseas. And an event such as this attracts followers, too. It's boom time for the local shops and cafés – and for the gallery.'

'I didn't realise.' It seemed there was a lot about Bellbird Bay Iain didn't know. He unpacked his satchel with his latest offerings.

'Good,' John said, examining each of the pieces in turn. 'These will go well, too. I'll have Mel arrange your payment for the first batch – and I may increase the price of these ones.'

'Thanks.' While Iain was grateful, his mind was elsewhere this morning. He was working out what he was going to say to Bev.

*

Bev didn't know whether to be relieved or worried when she listened to the message on the answering service in the garden centre office. Bryan wouldn't be coming in today. It was a brief message, giving no explanation. She tried to analyse his voice but couldn't work out if he was annoyed or merely tired after the trip to Sydney. *Had Iain told him of her suspicions? And how was Iain today?*

After a sleepless night, she'd risen early and taken out her box of mementos, tears filling her eyes as she looked again at all she had left of Phil and her son, and wondering anew if she had done the right thing by sharing her suspicions with Iain.

She was trying to keep her eyes open and work on her accounts when there was a knock on her office door and a familiar voice said, 'Bev?'

Bev looked up to see Iain Grant standing there, a sheepish expression on his face.

'I'm sorry for how I behaved on Friday. Can we talk? Do you have time for coffee?'

Bev swallowed, relieved at the olive branch Iain was offering. *Had he spoken with Bryan, did he have news for her?* 'Of course.'

Neither spoke as they made their way to the café. Pleased to see it was almost deserted, instead of her usual table outside the kitchen, Bev chose one at the other side of the café. It wasn't till they ordered – black coffee for Iain and a peppermint tea for Bev – that Iain spoke.

'I'm sorry,' he repeated. 'I acted impulsively on Friday. I should have…' He dragged a hand through his hair. 'I should have given more consideration to how you might be feeling. This can't be easy for you. I don't want to… I've come to care for you, Bev. It was a shock to learn you… Bryan… Hell, how are we going to do this?'

'You spoke to him?' *He must have.*

Iain nodded.

'How did he react? He left a message to say he wouldn't be in today. I guess he wasn't thrilled.'

'No. I timed it badly. I'm sorry. He and Mia had just returned from Sydney, from seeing Ros. It didn't go well. More on that later. But suffice to say he stormed out, and I haven't spoken to him since.'

'Oh!' Bev's heart plummeted. She thought she'd been prepared for this reaction from Bryan, but at Iain's words an uncontrollable shudder swept through her.

'Are you okay?'

'I think so.' Bev took a sip of her tea. But she wasn't okay. She might never be okay again.

'He… Bryan's been through a lot lately. I guess this, on top of everything else…'

'I shouldn't have brought it up. There was no need to…'

'No, Bev. There was. I've had time to consider your position, how you must feel, to realise the son you thought had died might be alive, might be Bryan. I think you could be right. There are too many coincidences. Give Bryan time. He's a good lad really. I'm sure he'll come round, see it your way, agree to the DNA test.'

'You mentioned it to him?' Bev gazed at him fearfully.

'I'm afraid I did. As I said, I could have timed it better.'

'It probably wouldn't have mattered,' Bev said with a sigh. 'He's not a boy. He's a man who knows his own mind. I'm not sure how I would have reacted in his place, probably have wanted to run away and hide. Where is he? Do you know?'

'No idea. He had left for training before I got up. He left a note. You may be right about him wanting to run away and hide. But where would he go in Bellbird Bay?'

'There are lots of places where a person can be alone – the beach, the headland, along the coast. Has he done this before?'

'Gone off on his bike? A few times. But I've always had some idea when he'd be coming back. This time…' Iain shook his head.

'So, we wait. You will let me know if… when you hear from him?'

'Of course.' Iain's eyes met hers and, despite the gravity of the situation, she felt a shiver of the attraction that had been there before. 'Bev, I don't want this to come between us. Everything was going so well till…'

'Till I spoiled it?' she couldn't help saying. How could they go back to where they were before? How could she have a relationship with Iain while his son was determined to avoid her, to ignore any discussion of what she hoped for with all her heart?

'Can we…?'

'Not now, Iain,' she said sorrowfully. 'I'll wait to hear from you.'

*

This was worse than she'd imagined. Unable to concentrate on anything, Bev told Julie she wasn't feeling well and went home. But once there, she was still unsettled. Remembering where her refuge had been all those years ago, and wondering if Bryan had taken the same route, she slowly made her way up the boardwalk towards the headland.

At the top, she stopped and gazed around, but there was no sign of Bryan, only a group of surfers in the distance and a flock of noisy seabirds. She was turning to return home when a gentle voice stopped her.

'I have a pot of camomile tea inside. You look as if you need a cup.'

Bev allowed Ruby to lead her inside, into the kitchen where she'd found comfort once before. She clasped the large cup of soothing tea in both hands, surprised to find she was shaking.

To her relief, Ruby didn't start chatting. Once she had handed Bev the tea, she continued with the baking she'd obviously been doing before Bev appeared. It didn't occur to Bev to wonder how Ruby knew she was there, or that she needed a place where she could be still. It was enough that she did, that she'd been there for Bev today, just like she had before.

Bev didn't know how long she sat there, while Ruby baked, but the results of her efforts had been taken out of the oven, the enticing aroma of freshly baked cakes filling the kitchen, before Ruby spoke.

'You think everything is ruined,' she said. 'I've been around a long time, and I've seen a lot. And one thing I know is that worry and regret will never change anything. What will be, will be, and I believe whatever is worrying you will work itself out. All will be well. You just need to have patience and let everything take its course.'

Bev gulped back her tears. She wished she could believe it was true, but today Ruby's words failed to comfort her.

Forty

Bev had no recollection of walking back down the boardwalk, but she must have done. The next thing she knew, she was wakening from the soundest sleep she'd had in days. *Had Ruby added a sleeping draught to the camomile tea she'd drunk, or had Bev just been completely exhausted?*

Whatever the reason, she was ready to go back to work, ready for whatever the day had to offer.

As usual, Bev was first to arrive at the garden centre. She loved it at this time in the morning, before her other staff members arrived, before it was crowded with customers. It was peaceful, the only sound the cackle of a pair of kookaburras on the fence outside her window.

When it came, the knock on the door was tentative. Bev turned from the window where she'd been watching a group of cockatoos feeding on the bottlebrush on the far side of the fence to see Bryan standing in the doorway.

He wasn't dressed for work. The normally neat and tidy young man looked as if he'd slept rough. He was unshaven and wearing shorts, singlet and a hoodie.

Bev wanted to throw her arms around him and pull him into a warm hug but knew it wouldn't be welcome.

Bryan was blinking rapidly and biting his lip.

'Hello, Bryan. Can I help you with something?' Bev tried to keep her voice even.

'Bev…' He shuffled his feet. He didn't meet her eyes.

Bev waited, something telling her this was going to be an important conversation.

'Can I sit down?'

She gestured to a chair and took a seat herself.

Bryan didn't immediately speak. He rubbed the back of his neck, and Bev could see his knee bouncing up and down. 'Dad told me… what you said… that you think…'

Bev held her breath.

'I couldn't handle it. I had to think. I haven't been home. I rode out of town, spent last night on a beach. White sand. Calm sea. But you don't want to know all that.'

Bev did. She wanted to know everything about him.

'It made me realise this isn't only about me.' He looked up to meet her eyes and her heart melted. It was as if Phil was looking at her. 'I'm sorry for the stuff you went through. It must have been hard. I know what it was like to lose Nadia.' His voice broke on his dead wife's name. 'I tried to think what she would have wanted me to do and…' he exhaled loudly, '…I think she'd have wanted me to find out for sure if what you think is true, if I'm…' he took a deep breath, '…if I'm your son. I'll take the test.'

Bev had trouble hiding her excitement, but knew Bryan was still hurting. He looked as if he was ready to flee at any moment. 'Thanks, Bryan. I appreciate how difficult this must be for you. It's not easy for me either. But I've known about the possibility for longer than you have. Your dad will have told you how much you look like my… like Phil.' She almost broke down, then rallied. 'I've checked out DNA testing and it appears to be quite a simple process. Now you've agreed, I'll send off for the test kit.'

Did she imagine it or did Bryan look relieved.

'I'll let you know when it arrives.'

'Thanks.' He looked down at his feet.

'I'm guessing you don't want to come to work today. You do want to continue to work here?' She held her breath.

'Yeah. I like it here. If you still want me after how I've behaved. I let you down.' He shuffled his feet again.

'Of course I do. You're one of my best workers. Tomorrow?'

Bryan almost smiled. 'Tomorrow,' he said as he rose to leave.

*

Iain had just returned from dropping Mia off at school and was debating whether to pack his sketching gear or set off to look for Bryan, when his son walked in looking more like a homeless person than the son he knew and loved. Unable to speak, he pulled him into a hug. 'I'm so glad to see you back safe and sound – and in one piece. You had me worried. I was about to call in reinforcements,' he joked. But there was a hint of truth in his words. He had considered reporting Bryan as missing if he didn't turn up soon.

'Glad to be back, Dad. I just needed time to get my head together. It was a lot to take in.'

'But you're right, now?' Iain held his son at arm's length and peered into his face. A pair of bloodshot eyes stared back at him from a bleary unshaven face.

'I've been better, but I'm getting there.'

'When did you last eat? I can make some scrambled eggs, coffee and…'

'Don't fuss, Dad. I'm not very hungry. I need a shower, then maybe I'll be ready for some food. Coffee sounds good.'

'Right.' Iain wanted to know where Bryan had been since he left yesterday morning but knew his son. Bryan would tell him in his own good time. Meanwhile he'd brew some coffee. He needed another cup, too.

When Bryan returned, washed, shaved and wearing a clean pair of chinos and a tee-shirt, he seemed a different person. 'Something smells good, Dad,' he said, taking a seat at the table as if it was a normal morning.

In addition to brewing coffee, Iain had made scrambled eggs, fried some bacon, and toasted a couple of slices of bread. Now he served them up before joining Bryan at the table.

'I spoke with Bev.'

Iain almost choked on his coffee. His eyes widened. He hadn't expected this.

'I thought about what you told me. I haven't been able to think of anything else. And I decided Nadia would have wanted me to find out the truth. I told Bev I'd go ahead with the test she wants.' He continued to eat his breakfast as if he hadn't made a startling statement.

'So what happens now?'

'She'll send off for the test stuff and let me know. It's probably all a mistake.' He shrugged.

And if it isn't? But Iain kept his thoughts to himself.

'I take it you're not going in to work today?'

'Not today. I need a good sleep.' Bryan yawned. 'It's surprisingly noisy on the beach and difficult to get comfortable. Sand can be pretty hard.' He grimaced.

So, he'd slept on a beach somewhere.

'I told Bev I'd be back tomorrow. Thanks for breakfast, Dad.'

'No worries.'

Bryan finished his breakfast, put his dishes in the dishwasher and disappeared to his room, leaving Iain shaking his head.

Alone again, Iain had lost the urge to spend the morning sketching and, with Bryan asleep upstairs, there was no need to go looking for him. He hated to think of him sleeping rough last night, but at least he'd come to his senses – and he was home now. Mia would be delighted. Iain had almost run out of excuses for him, stories of where her dad might be.

Iain's thoughts turned to Bev. How must she be feeling now Bryan had agreed to be tested? He should call her. About to pick up his phone, Iain changed his mind. He wanted to see her, to talk to her face to face. Maybe Bryan's change of attitude could change things for them, too.

Forty-one

It was almost a week since Bev had sent off the DNA test and she was on tenterhooks waiting for the result. Iain had been wonderful. After Bryan's agreement to go ahead with it, she and Iain had found common ground, both desperate to know the result. Having a common interest in finding out if Bev really was Bryan's birth mother seemed to have brought them closer, though Bev knew she had more of an investment in the result than Iain could ever have.

Each day, she checked her mail carefully, hoping today would be the day she'd see the envelope from the testing lab – and today there it was. But now it had arrived, she was afraid to open it. And what if it didn't have the result she wanted so much? What if it did?

She sat looking at the package for several minutes, then picked up her phone. 'It's come,' was all she needed to say.

Less than five minutes later, Iain was at her door.

Bev's mouth was dry. There was an empty feeling in her stomach. Iain seemed just as nervous as she felt.

'You haven't opened it yet?' he asked, seeing the sealed envelope on the table.

'I couldn't do it by myself.'

Iain pulled her into a hug, but his warm embrace did little to lessen the tension in the room. 'Are you ready?' he asked when he released her.

Bev nodded.

Iain handed her the envelope, his arm around her shoulders.

Nervously, Bev tore the envelope open, her eyes scanning the enclosed document. 'The probability of maternity is 99.99 per cent,' she read in a shaky voice, then collapsed into a nearby chair, tears streaming down her cheeks. It was true. After all these years she'd found her son, not William, but Bryan, Bryan Grant.

She raised her eyes to look fearfully at Iain. Her gain was his loss. But he was smiling.

'I'm so glad you have an answer at last. I can't imagine what it must have been like for you to be told your son had died, and the past week, waiting to find out.'

'But Bryan…'

'Bryan's been getting used to the idea. I think, until he actually did the test, he believed it was all going to be a mistake. But these last few days, he's been talking more about what it might be like if the test came out positive.'

'Really?' Bev smiled through her tears.

'Really. It's probably best if I tell him, then we can tell Mia, then… why don't I call you, let you know how it goes and, if all is well, you can join us for dinner?'

The next hour dragged, seeming to be three times as long, and Bev had almost given up hope when Iain's call finally came.

'Bryan's okay with it, says it'll take a bit of getting used to, and Mia's over the moon to have another grandmother. I've ordered pizza, and Bryan's opening a bottle of red. See you soon?'

Bev gave a relieved 'Yes' before picking up her keys and heading out the door.

What did one say to the man who had suddenly learned he was your son, Bev wondered as she made her way up the boardwalk. There was no blueprint for a situation like this, and it wasn't one she'd ever expected to encounter. At least she was lucky to already know Bryan and Mia – and to have Iain's support. But the situation was a strange one.

When she arrived and knocked tentatively on the glass door, it was Mia who came dancing towards her. 'Can I call you Nana?' she asked. 'I already have a grandma, so you can't be my grandma, but I don't have a nana.' She held up her arms for a hug.

'Of course you can.' Bev's voice was muffled by tears as she reached down to pick up the little girl. Over Mia's head she could see Iain and Bryan behind her. Iain had an encouraging smile on his face while Bryan was clearly trying to smile, too.

'Bryan,' Bev said, unsure how to approach him.

'Dad told us,' Bryan said, coming towards her and giving her an awkward kiss on the cheek. 'I can't… I can't call you Mum.'

'Bev is fine.' It was enough he was willing to recognise the relationship.

The pizzas arrived, the wine was poured and, eventually, a tired Mia was tucked up in bed with another hug for her new grandmother.

Iain poured them all another glass of wine and the three settled down in the living room.

'What was he like?' Bryan asked, 'My other dad.'

Bev sent an apologetic look toward Iain, who nodded. 'He was younger than you when he died,' Bev said, 'a student at the military academy in Canberra. He came from a military family and his future was mapped out for him. I don't think he ever considered doing anything else.'

As Bryan leant forward, she continued to tell them what she remembered of those days in Canberra, their decision to marry, the accident, and Bryan's birth.

'Do you have any photos?' Bryan asked.

'A few. I can show them to you.'

'I'd like that. Dad's okay with it.' He looked across at Iain.

'We've always known you had other parents out there somewhere,' Iain said, 'so this doesn't come as such a shock as it would have if we thought you'd been born to Ros and me.'

'I never felt Mum wanted me,' Bryan said. 'Was it all your idea to adopt, Dad?'

'Not entirely,' Iain cleared his throat, 'though I may have pushed her a little. She does love you, Bryan. She just has a different way of showing it. And she has always found it difficult to settle in one place.'

'You're being charitable, Dad. But it doesn't matter. Mum is what she is. She'll never change, I've finally accepted that. I may have rejected the idea of being your son at first, Bev. It wasn't about you. I'd never wanted to seek out my birth parents, content with the relationship I have with Dad. I was afraid they'd be like Mum. But you're different, and now you and Dad… Well, it's okay with me.'

Bev glowed, while Iain appeared amused.

Later, when Bryan had gone to bed, and Iain took her in his arms, she knew she had come home. At last she had a real family of her own, the family she'd always wanted.

Forty-two

It was only a few days since their lives had all changed. Bev was elated with the way Bryan had accepted the fact she was his mother, and they had spent several wonderful hours with her box of mementoes where she related stories about Phil and the times they spent together.

While awkward at first, they ended up hugging and clasping hands, and they both shed a few tears as they gazed at the picture of the handsome young man. For Bryan, it was almost like looking in a mirror. He was stunned by his resemblance to this man who was his father.

But once Bryan had gone, and despite her joyous mood, Bev was left with a niggle of dissatisfaction. Now she had proven without doubt that there had been a mix up at the hospital, she felt the need to at least attempt to discover how it had happened. Someone was responsible.

Along with everything else in the box she'd kept hidden for so long, was William's birth certificate. While she was so ill, her godmother had registered William's birth and there on the document, along with her name and Phil's was the name of the maternity hospital – Saint Bernadette's. It had been a small private hospital, Bev remembered, one chosen by her godmother for its promise of privacy.

Bev waited till she was in her office next morning, then, her heart in her mouth, she checked the internet only to come away empty-handed. There was no maternity hospital called Saint Bernadette's listed in Sydney, or anywhere in new South Wales.

Damn! What had happened to it? Surely it couldn't have disappeared off the face of the earth. But it seemed it had. Bev sat back and thought for a few moments. The one person who might be able to tell her what had happened to it – her Aunt Bea – was still alive, but she was very frail. These days, they only communicated at Christmastime. But Bev couldn't wait till then. She searched through her contact list and picked up the phone.

The receptionist who answered the phone in Fairview Nursing Home was unhelpful at first. But, after explaining who she was as slowly and carefully as she could, given her impatience, Bev was put through to the matron. Once again, she had to explain her relationship to Bea, but eventually, she found herself speaking to an assistant who agreed to carry a phone into her godmother's room, after warning her that Bea might not know who she was.

'Hello?'

At the sound of her godmother's frail voice, Bev was filled with guilt and regret. She should have been in touch before this. It would have been easy to pick up the phone and call Bea. But Bev had allowed her busy life to get in the way – and she had never completely forgiven her godmother for arranging to bury William without her knowledge. She had taken her godmother at her word and put it all behind her – including Bea herself. Now she needed her help.

There was silence on the other end of the phone as Bev haltingly explained about finding William, of how, while she was so ill, the hospital had made a mistake. 'I just need to find out how it could have happened,' she sobbed, suddenly overcome with grief for all the years she'd missed.

There was silence for so long Bev feared they'd been cut off, then she heard her godmother's voice, feeble but clear. 'You're too late, Beverley. Saint Bernadette's ceased to be a maternity hospital over twenty years ago. The building it was housed in is now Fairview Nursing Home where I've been living for the past fifteen years. I'm glad you've found your son, but I fear everyone who was here then, is long gone. I always wondered…' Her voice faded away.

'What? What did you wonder?' Bev almost yelled into the phone, only to hear the calm voice of the hospital assistant say, 'I'm sorry, but Bea has disappeared again into her own little world. You were lucky to catch her in one of her more lucid moments.'

Disappointed, Bev ended the call, resigned to the knowledge she'd never be able to discover the truth. At least she had Bryan – and Mia – she thought with a spark of her former happiness.

Forty-three

The morning of the triathlon had arrived and the house was filled with excitement as Iain prepared an early breakfast for his son and granddaughter.

'We were talking about the tri…*athlon* at school, Daddy,' Mia said, stumbling over the pronunciation of the word, 'and I said you were going to be in it. Some of the other dads are, too. Are you going to win?'

'No, sweetheart. I'll be happy just to finish. It's a tough race.'

Her little face fell.

'I'm proud of you taking part, son,' Iain said. 'It's been a tough year for you, for all of us, but mostly for you.'

'Thanks, Dad. There have been a few surprises, some good, some not so good. Bev was one of the good ones – for us both, I think.' There was a twinkle in Bryan's eye that Iain hadn't seen for some time.

'When does the tri… trithlon start?' Mia didn't manage it this time.

Iain and Bryan laughed.

'In just under an hour, sweetie,' Bryan said. 'You and Grandad can watch the start at the beach, then be at the finish line to see me crawl over it.'

'You're going to crawl over it?' she asked, her eyes widening.

'I hope not, but you never know. As I said, it's a tough course. Even entering as a novice, I have to swim fifteen hundred metres, cycle forty kilometres and run ten kilometres. It's not for the faint-hearted.'

'That's a lot,' Mia exclaimed. 'You'll be very tired.'

'That's why your daddy's been training every morning,' Iain said.

'Too right, Dad. I should go now. I may see you at the beach, but I'll be too busy to talk to you then.'

'Good luck, son, and remember, there's no shame in dropping out.' Iain gave Bryan a hug, then Bryan picked Mia up for a hug, too. 'See you later, princess,' he said.

*

Iain had arranged to meet Bev at the beach. Like most businesses in Bellbird Bay, *The Pandanus Garden Centre and Café* was closed for the duration of the race, and Bev was eager to see Bryan competing.

As soon as she saw Bev, Mia ran towards her with a grin. 'Hello, Nana,' she yelled. 'Have you come to watch my daddy, too?'

'Yes, I have, sweetheart,' Bev greeted the little girl with a hug and kiss.

It did Iain's heart good to see how quickly two of his favourite people had bonded. 'Do you have a kiss for me, too?' he asked, to be rewarded by a peck on the cheek from Bev and a chuckle.

'Later,' she whispered.

'Can't wait,' he whispered back, aware of how different this interaction was from one they might have had a few weeks earlier. The resolution of the business with Bryan could have gone either way. It was a miracle it had brought them closer. Once Bev had shared the story of her past with him, and they'd gone through the process of checking her and Bryan's DNA, he discovered the barriers which Bev always seemed to erect had disappeared.

'There are a lot of people,' Mia said, as they made their way through the crowds thronging the esplanade. 'I can't see Daddy.' Her lower lip trembled.

'Let me help.' Iain hoisted her up onto his shoulders as they found a spot close to the barrier.

'There he is!' Mia pointed to where a crowd of men and women were on the beach preparing for the first leg of the event.

'Come to watch the fun?' a voice in Iain's ear said.

'Ailsa,' Bev said. 'I see Martin and Will down there, too.'

'Martin's the official photographer and Will's in charge of the entrants. Nate and Owen are the ones competing,' Ailsa said. 'Nate said Hannah almost entered, too, but changed her mind at the last minute.'

'Wise girl. I entered a couple of times when I was her age,' Bev said, 'but I'd lived here all my life, I was part of the whole scene – and it wasn't as popular back then. Now, most of the entrants aren't locals. They come from far and wide. Their friends and family come too, so it's good for the local businesses.'

'Look, Grandad!' Mia broke into the conversation to point to the shoreline. 'They're going to start.'

The mayor sounded a horn, and they were off, several quickly pulling ahead of the others as they ploughed through the waves.

'There's not going to be much to see for a bit,' Bev said. 'Why don't we have an ice cream? We can come back across later when the first few return to the beach and pick up their bicycles. Then there won't be anything for spectators till later in the afternoon, unless you want to stand somewhere along the course. The professional guys should reach the finish line in around two hours, but for most of the entrants, it'll be more like three or more, if they finish at all.' She chuckled.

'I'll catch you later,' Ailsa said. 'I promised to keep my eyes on the swimmers. Nate's hoping to beat Owen in the swim heat.' She rolled her eyes. 'I think Owen's a lot fitter than my son.'

'Nana said ice cream, Grandad,' Mia said, taking Iain's hand and pulling him towards the kiosk where there was already a line of children and parents waiting to be served.

Several minutes later, each carrying an ice cream cone, Iain, Bev and Mia made their way back to the beach. As Bev had predicted, there was nothing to see. The swimmers were merely small black dots in the distance.

'This is boring,' Mia said. 'What are we going to do now?'

'Any ideas?' Iain grinned at Bev.

'I know a really nice beach,' Bev said. 'Why don't we go for a swim of our own?'

'Yay!' was Mia's response.

*

It was over an hour later when Bev, Iain and Mia climbed down the path to Dolphin Beach. As she'd anticipated, the beach was deserted, the stretch of white sand pristine and gleaming in the morning sunshine.

In addition to changing into her swimmers, shorts and a tee-shirt, Bev had packed a picnic lunch from some of the leftover food she'd brought home from the café the previous day. She had grimaced as she examined herself in the mirror while dressing. Her red and white bathing suit had seen better days. Going swimming with Iain wasn't something she'd expected to be doing – not yet anyway. But she had suggested it, and it would be a pleasant way to spend the day.

'Are you okay?' Iain asked, helping her down the slope. Mia had run ahead as soon as they got out of the car.

'I'm fine. I love this beach.'

'What a beautiful spot,' Iain said, stopping to admire the view. 'It's so untouched.'

'Thanks to Will Rankin and a few others,' Bev said.

'How so?'

'There was a plan to build an eco-resort here, cabins, water park, wave pool, the lot. Will was at the forefront of the group which foiled the plan. It would be sacrilege to spoil it.'

'What happened?'

'Dugongs. They feed on sea grass, and Will and his supporters were able to prove the resort would ruin the habitat for the marine animals.'

'Lucky.'

'Mmm.'

'Can we go swimming now, Grandad?' Mia came running back to meet them and stood with her hands on her hips. 'Why have you stopped?'

'We're coming, Mia.' Bev laughed. It was so much fun being a grandmother. She still couldn't quite believe this little person was related to her, her very own granddaughter.

Bev was still laughing when they reached the beach and set down a blanket and the picnic basket in a shady spot. Then, at Mia's urging, Iain began to undress to reveal a bronzed torso emerging above a pair of navy board shorts. Bev's breath caught at the sight of his naked flesh.

'Come on, Nana,' Mia called, when Bev didn't immediately follow suit to undress.

Slowly, she slipped off her tee-shirt and shorts, feeling very exposed and hoping Iain wouldn't be horrified at her sagging, middle-aged body. She hadn't envisaged his first sight of her undressed would be on a beach in bright sunlight with their granddaughter, preferring to imagine it might have been in a darkened bedroom where the signs of age wouldn't be so noticeable.

She needn't have worried. By the time she had undressed, Iain and Mia were both running into the ocean. She followed more slowly, diving into the waves as soon as the water was knee deep.

Being in the sea with a six-year-old was a new experience for Bev. They splashed around together, then Mia wanted to show off her prowess as a swimmer, before she left Iain and Bev, preferring to play in the shallows. Once they'd assured themselves she was safe, Bev and Iain swam farther out together. Bev enjoyed being in the sea again. These days, she tended to be too busy to make time for swimming – hence the age of her swimsuit. She'd had no need to update it.

She was surprised when, as they were returning to the shore, she felt Iain's hands on her skin, his naked chest against her, and his lips whispering in her ear.

'I've dreamt about this,' he whispered. 'Ever since we met, I've wanted to...'

'Grandad! Nana!'

'Damn!' Iain loosened his grasp on Bev who was still trying to come to grips with the unexpected jolt of desire his touch had triggered. 'What is it, Mia?' he said in a different tone as he and Bev waded to the shore to join the little girl.

'Look at this shell I've found.'

Iain and Bev examined the shell carefully, then the trio made their way back to their belongings, where Mia placed the shell in a corner of the basket. Bev was still trembling as she dried herself off and pulled on her shorts and tee-shirt.

Lunch was a selection of small quiches, sausage rolls, biscuits and cheese followed by fruit. There was juice and mineral water to drink. By the time they had finished eating, Bev was feeling calmer again, but she was very aware of Iain sitting close to her with his still naked chest.

'I wish we could do this every day,' Mia said when they began to pack up. 'Can we go to see Daddy now?'

'I suspect he might still be in the race,' Iain said, pulling on his shirt, 'but we'll head to the finish line to see what's happening.'

Iain was almost right. When they reached the place where the race was to finish, they caught up with Libby, Adam. Nick, Emma and Clancy to discover Bryan was with them.

'I didn't make it, Dad,' he said ruefully. 'But I had a good crack at it. Next year…'

'You have a whole year to train,' Nick said, slapping him on the shoulder. 'You did well to last as long as you did.'

'Thanks. Nick was one of the first contingent to reach the finish line, Dad,' Bryan said.

'Hey, I grew up here. I've been in this event since I was in my teens. I had a head start on a newcomer like you.'

'Nick and Emma have invited me and Mia for a barbecue. Okay with you, Dad?' Bryan asked.

'You're very welcome to come, too,' Emma said to Iain, 'unless you have other plans.' She looked from him to Bev and back again with a smile.

'Thanks, but I'll decline. I do have other plans.' Iain glanced at Bev whose stomach began to churn as she remembered Iain's whispered words.

Iain didn't say much on the way home in the car, but when he stopped outside Bev's house to drop her off, he said, 'I'll go home and shower, then I'll be back. Okay?'

'Okay.' Bev smiled, relieved to have some time to herself, time to shower and pull herself together before he returned. But once inside and in the shower, all Bev could think about was how it had felt to have Iain's body close to hers. She had never imagined feeling this way again.

Showered and dressed in a pair of cut-off jeans and a loose pink and white striped shirt, her hair in its usual ponytail, her face free of makeup apart from a smear of lip gloss, Bev was checking the fridge to see what she could make for dinner when Iain tapped on the sliding glass door. He had changed, too, and was now wearing a pair of chinos and a white shirt, the sleeves rolled up to the elbows. He looked… hot. She swallowed and looked away.

'I brought wine,' he said, holding up a bottle of chardonnay.

'I'll fetch glasses.'

They both seemed to be finding it difficult to speak. It was as if the encounter in the ocean had affected them, making ordinary conversation impossible.

They carried the wine out to the deck and settled onto the chairs. Iain filled their glasses, then held up his. 'To us… to the future.'

Bev lifted her glass and took a sip, wondering exactly what he meant, her heart thumping madly.

'Oh, blast this,' Iain said, laying his glass down, moving closer to Bev and taking her glass from her. 'I don't want to waste time drinking wine when all I want to do is…' He took her in his arms, his lips trailing across her forehead, eyelids and down to meet hers in a searing kiss.

Bev quivered with anticipation as she met his urgency. 'Not here,' she murmured, slipping out of his arms to lead him to the bedroom.

Forty-four

For the next few days, Bev moved around as if in a dream. She could barely believe what had happened to her, only surfacing to complete the daily tasks necessary to keep the garden centre functioning before returning home where Iain would be waiting for her.

She didn't enquire how he explained his absence to Bryan and Mia but realised Bryan must have a good idea of what was going on. Cleo, too, had an inkling of Bev's new-found happiness, but she managed to keep her thoughts to herself, only telling Bev she looked glowing. Ailsa was too caught up with her forthcoming nuptials to have noticed any change in Bev, or if she had, she'd chosen not to mention it.

It was just over a week till the wedding, and the plans were all in place. Ailsa had finalised the numbers which now included Iain, Bryan and Mia, and Hannah had organised the hire of sufficient chairs with a few to spare. She'd promised to be there to set them out, and Nate and Owen had volunteered to help. Cleo's storeroom was now packed with cases of sparkling wine and beer in readiness for the big event, and Bryan and Dean had built a perfectly formed arch under the plexiglass roofing. Everything was ready for the big day.

The icing on the cake was that Will reported he'd heard a decision was about to be made on Bev's application to add a function facility to the garden centre. He said there was a good chance of Milton Harris's objection being dismissed in favour of Bev's application. It seemed Iain's latest submission might prove successful.

It was still dark when Bev's phone rang in the early hours of the morning on the Thursday before the wedding. She and Iain were lying in bed curled up together, having made love while they were still both half-asleep.

'Leave it,' Iain murmured, his lips in her hair.

While tempted to do exactly that, Bev reached out to pick up the phone and glanced at the screen. 'It's the security people,' she said, frowning. 'What do they want at this time in the morning?' Her heart sank imagining the worst.

'Bev speaking,' she said, sitting up in bed and trying to become fully awake.

'There's been a report of damage at the garden centre,' a deep voice told her. 'Your security system issued an alert…'

Bev's heart plummeted. She pushed herself up. 'What happened?'

Hearing her tone, Iain stroked her back.

'There was a security breach on the perimeter of the centre on the side farthest from the entrance. One of our team drove over to check but couldn't see anything. You might want to check when…'

'Thanks. I'll go right now.' Bev was already climbing out of bed and searching for the clothes she'd thrown off in the heat of passion the evening before. 'It's the centre,' she said to a puzzled Iain. 'The bastard has done it again.'

*

All was quiet when Bev and Iain pulled up outside the garden centre just as dawn was breaking. 'Maybe it was a false alarm,' Bev said hopefully as she opened the gate, then the door to the office where she switched on the computer.

They waited while the system loaded, then played back the film from the last few hours. At first there was nothing to see then… 'Look there,' Iain said, pointing to the approach road where a gang of youths could be seen boldly making their way towards the fence line, before picking up rocks and hurling them over the fence. Then, with a few high-fives they ran off again. There was no sign of Milton Harris.

'I bet he's behind it,' Bev said, enlarging the images. 'These guys didn't think of this by themselves. What are you doing?' she asked Iain, seeing he'd taken his phone out.

'Calling the police.'

'They weren't much help last time. Let's check the damage first.' Bev tried to subdue the sinking feeling in her gut. The spot where the vandals had been tossing rocks was just on the other side of the place where Ailsa and Martin's wedding was to be held in two days' time.

Hands tightly clasped, they made their way to where yesterday the wedding arch sat proudly under the translucent roof panels, ready to be decked out with flowers.

'Oh!' Bev's free hand went to her mouth.

They stopped and stared. The ground was strewn with rocks and several panels of what had once been a beautiful roof were badly damaged, shards of the roofing material lying on the ground.

'What are we going to do? The wedding's on Saturday,' she wailed.

Meanwhile, Iain had stooped down to pick up a piece of card. It had writing on it. 'Look at this,' he said, reading out, '"No Pandanus Weddings". This was no idle vandal attack. Didn't Will say the committee were going to make their decision tomorrow?'

'Yes, and he predicted it would be in our favour. Surely Harris doesn't think he can intimidate me into withdrawing my application?'

'That's exactly what he does think. I'm assuming he believes that, by ruining Saturday's wedding, you'll change your mind.' Iain took out his phone again.

'You're calling the police now?'

'I am.'

Bev heard a heated exchange before Iain ended the call. 'They'll send someone out. They were about to dismiss it as another act of teenage vandalism till I told them about the message.' He took up his phone again.

'Who are you calling now?'

'Colin. With a bit of luck, he'll be able to fix the roof and the wedding can go ahead as planned.'

'Oh!' Bev said again, feeling the tension of the past hour drain out of her. 'Do you think so?'

Iain held up one finger as he spoke to Colin. 'He's on it,' he said, when he hung up. 'He knows how important it is for you and will send his guys over this morning to assess the damage and work out what can be done. He's confident it'll be all good by Saturday.'

'Thanks. I don't know what I'd have done without you.' Bev hugged him, taking comfort from his strong arms encircling her.

'I'm pretty sure you'd have managed, but glad I was here to help. Let's get rid of the mess before your staff and customers arrive.'

'Thanks.'

They were still removing rocks and splintered pieces of roofing when Bryan and Dean arrived for work and Bev had to explain what had happened. Next, the police arrived, forcing her to explain all over again. This time, she was able to show the computer images to the police officers who managed to identify a couple of the miscreants. Although they were dubious about Iain and Bev's claims Milton Harris was behind it, they did take away the card containing the message and agreed to question the offenders.

Gradually things were back to as normal as could be, given the damage, and the garden centre opened for business. The police had called back to say they were arranging to pick up the youths who they'd recognised.

'Will you be okay?' Iain asked, when Bev and he had downed a cup of coffee, Bev had swallowed a few bites of croissant and Iain demolished one of Cleo's special mushroom and chorizo omelettes.

'I'll be fine, now, thanks,' she said, giving him a kiss on the cheek. 'What are you going to do?' She could see from the way Iain's lips tightened that he had something in mind.

'I'm going home to shower and change. Lucky Mia had a sleepover with Clancy last night. Emma is taking them both to school. Then there's someone I need to see.' His expression was grim.

'Take care,' Bev said, sensing he might be about to get into trouble.

*

Showered and dressed more smartly than usual, Iain's heart was pounding as he drove across town to where he knew he'd find Milton Harris at this time of day. He was in no doubt who was behind the attacks on Bev's garden centre, and if the police wouldn't question him, Iain would.

'Good morning. Iain Grant, isn't it, Roslyn's ex?' Milton Harris greeted him with a smarmy smile.

Iain's anger rose. He clenched his fists, tempted to wipe the smile from Harris's face. 'Why are you harassing Bev Cooper?' he asked, making an effort to contain his wrath.

Harris smirked. 'Harassing? Do you have any proof of that? I think you'll find there's no evidence of my involvement in the unfortunate incidents which have occurred in her garden centre. She needs to realise it's no place for weddings, not like this,' he stretched his arms to encompass the hotel foyer in which they were standing. 'Now *this* is a wedding venue. *The Pandanus Garden Centre* and the so-called *Pandanus Weddings*... that place will never be suitable.'

Iain wanted to punch him. If he was a different sort of guy, he might have. But he'd never hit anyone in anger and wasn't about to start now. 'You don't know what you're talking about,' he said. '*Pandanus Weddings* will get council approval – and will be no competition to you. I have no idea why you've taken against Bev in this, apart from a desire to be difficult and make a point... though I have no idea what it might be. I can only hope you're finished. The police know the youths you've paid to do this. I don't think they'll be so keen to do your bidding again.'

Milton Harris didn't respond, leaving Iain no alternative other than to leave, feeling dejected. He'd come here in an attempt to force the man to confess he was behind the vandalism to the garden centre and failed miserably. He could only hope the police would have more success if they continued to interrogate the youths who had done Harris's dirty work for him.

Iain was feeling despondent when he arrived at Bev's that evening. He'd wanted to have good news for her, to be able to tell her he'd forced a confession out of Milton Harris, had persuaded the man to stop harassing her, to withdraw his objection to her application and accept what she planned was no competition to him. Instead, he had the impression Harris had enjoyed the encounter.

'Did you go to see Harris?' Bev asked as soon as he arrived. 'What did he say?'

'What we might have expected. He wouldn't admit he was behind the vandalism, has no intention of changing his mind, and reiterated *Pandanus Weddings* would never get off the ground. I'm sorry, Bev. I thought I could make a difference.' He dragged a hand through his hair.

'Thanks for trying.' She hugged him, and they stood entwined for a few moments before pulling apart.

'Have you heard from the police?'

Bev nodded. 'They called me, very polite. They've picked up the two youths they recognised from the CCTV and taken them in for questioning but haven't been able to link them to Harris. Neither of the youths they questioned would admit who had put them up to it, only referring to being well paid to wreak as much damage as they could and to leave the message. It's like your mate said. He's too wily to get caught. I guess we'll just have to wait for the council's decision.'

Forty-five

Next day, Bev was on edge waiting for the council's decision. Will had told her the committee wasn't meeting till midday, so she knew there would be no word till the afternoon. But it didn't prevent her from worrying about it.

The first indication there was any news was when Iain arrived at the garden centre unexpectedly at two o'clock. When he'd left Bev after breakfast, they'd made arrangements to meet for dinner. He had hinted at "secret men's business" he had to see to during the day.

'Have you heard?' he asked, grinning from ear to ear.

'What?' Bev's stomach lurched.

'Harris is leaving town.'

'He's what?' This was the last thing she expected to hear.

'I just had a call from him. Not sure why he felt the need to let me know, but I guess he wanted to rub my nose in it.'

'Sorry, Iain, you've lost me.'

'He and Ros. It seems it was more serious than I thought. He's kept in touch with her and, now she's been discharged from hospital and looking at making a good recovery, she's moving into an apartment he owns in Sydney overlooking the harbour. It seems she's struck gold this time.' He pulled on one ear. 'Ros always managed to pull the guys, but this time it's got me beat. Harris wanted to let me know he was taking care of my ex. Don't know what he expected me to say.'

'What *did* you say?'

'I wished him luck. Ros has never stuck with one man for long.

Maybe this time it'll be different. Maybe this illness has been a wake-up call. But Milton Harris!' He shook his head.

'So, what does that mean for *Pandanus Weddings*? Has there been a decision?'

'You haven't heard?'

Bev started to shake her head when her computer beeped with an incoming email. 'This may be it now,' she said, her mouth going dry. While the news about Milton Harris and Iain's ex was interesting, it had no bearing on her own future. Taking a deep breath and with Iain's hand on her shoulder, she opened the email.

Ms Cooper,

With regard to your application for a change in the stated purpose of the Pandanus Garden Centre and Café to include the provision of a venue for weddings.

As you know, an objection to the application was submitted which was followed by a rebuttal from you. Bellbird Bay Council take all such documentation very seriously and have been concerned by the recent incidents at the garden centre and the accusations made against a member of our community.

Taking all this into account, at its meeting today, the council determined your application be accepted, and the change of purpose of The Pandanus Garden Centre and Café be approved, dependent on certain conditions being met.

The conditions attached to this approval are as follows…

Bev didn't need to read any further. She turned into Iain's arms. 'It's gone through,' she exclaimed, her eyes wet with tears.

'Hey, why the tears?' Iain gently wiped them away with one finger. 'It's good news.'

'Sorry, I'm just so happy. Do you think that's why Harris called you?' she asked when she'd dried her tears. 'Did he hear about the decision before me?'

'We'll never know. But he does have friends on the council. And he's the sort of guy who hates to lose. I guess his call to me was some sort of last-ditch attempt to get his own back – and it didn't work. He and Ros deserve each other.'

'It seems a bit odd,' Bev said reflectively. 'No offence to Ros and her undoubted charms, but Milton Harris doesn't seem to me to be the sort of guy to go quietly – to be with a woman he's only just met. I wonder if there's more to it?'

Bev didn't have to wonder for long. Her phone rang, and Will's number appeared on the screen.

'Have you heard?' he asked before she could speak.

'About the council's decision? Iain's with me and we've just read the email.'

'No, about Milton Harris?' There was a gleeful note in Will's voice. 'He's going to Sydney.'

'Already gone. It was becoming too hot for him in Bellbird Bay.'

'What do you mean?'

'It seems the police weren't completely satisfied with his innocence. They began to wonder about your and Iain's allegations of bribery and corruption and leant on several council members. At first, they were adamant there had been no untoward dealings, but one finally cracked, and an examination of bank accounts revealed large sums paid into four accounts which could be traced back to Harris. My guess is that he fled interstate to avoid arrest. But he won't be able to avoid it for long.'

'Unless he leaves the country,' Iain, who had been listening on speaker phone said. 'He and Ros make a good pair. My bet is she'll be off overseas again, too, as soon as she's able.'

'Well, at least he won't bother us again,' Bev said with a sigh of relief. 'Thanks, Will.'

She ended the call and turned to Iain who took her in his arms.

Now they could look forward to the wedding without anything to worry them.

Forty-six

The day of the wedding finally arrived. Although a lot had happened in the past two weeks, it was finally here, and the garden centre was ready to host it.

The morning was a whirl of activity as Colin and his crew put the final touches to the repair of the roofing. Then in the early afternoon, Hannah, Nate and Owen arrived to organise the sound and set out the seating, and Bev decorated the arch with fresh flowers.

Now, as she slipped into the dress, which was unlike anything she'd ever worn before, Bev was glad she'd given in to Ailsa's pleading to make time for a trip to Brisbane and a visit to a high-end wedding boutique. While a simple design, the A-line, V-neck chiffon dress in ocean blue shimmered in the light and swirled luxuriously around her calves when she turned to admire herself in the mirror. A pair of matching high-heeled strappy sandals – also purchased at Ailsa's insistence – complemented it and completed the outfit.

Bev touched her newly styled hair, wondering if perhaps with this, she had gone too far. Ailsa had made the appointment for her, and Bev had left work early, after she'd made sure everything was ready for the ceremony. Now her fading blonde hair was fashioned into an elaborate topknot studded with tiny flowers. She looked like a different person. She looked… feminine and elegant. But, she reasoned, it was the wedding of her brother and her best friend, and she was willing to do this to please them.

When Iain arrived to drive her to the garden centre, he stood staring at her for a moment before saying, 'Wow, you look beautiful,' and pulling her into a hug, taking care not to mess her new hairstyle. Then he added, 'But I think I prefer the more natural version of Bev Cooper.'

Bev laughed.

As Bev slipped into the car to take her seat beside Mia, the little girl touched her dress reverently. 'You look like a princess, Nana,' she said breathlessly. Then added proudly, 'Daddy says I'm his princess.'

'And so you are,' Bryan's voice came from the passenger seat.

When they reached the garden centre, it was dusk, and Bev was stunned by the scene that met her eyes. Even though she'd planned for this day and had only left the centre a few hours earlier, the place seemed to have been transformed into a magical grotto. Nate had worked wonders with the lighting which illuminated the flowered arch, and there was the faint sound of music drifting in from somewhere unseen.

Most of the seats were already filled, and Bev could see Martin, accompanied by Will, standing under the arch waiting for his bride.

'Excited?' she asked Ailsa who was waiting with Nate. She was wearing a dress similar in style to Bev's, but hers was of cream lace. She looked stunning.

'I keep wanting to pinch myself. I can't believe how my life changed when I came here, how Martin and I met, and...' Ailsa kissed Bev on the cheek. 'Imagine if I hadn't accepted your invitation.' She shook her head in amazement.

'I'm so glad you did. You're my best friend, and now you'll be my sister, too.'

The music changed, a sign it was time for Ailsa, Nate and Bev to make their way towards the arch. Emma, who'd been waiting beside them with an excited Clancy, pushed the little girl forward and, carrying a basket of rose petals, she walked along, scattering petals as the music changed again to the Beatles rendering of *All you need is love*.

Bev couldn't keep the smile from her face as she walked behind Ailsa and Nate who had brushed up well in the white dinner jacket, blue bow tie and cummerbund which matched those worn by Martin and Will.

Having left Ailsa's side to sit with Iain, Bev was touched by the simple ceremony, her eyes moistening when Ailsa and Martin pledged their love and made their vows. Then there was the ceremony with the quaich which took everyone by surprise. When Iain's hand reached out to clasp hers, Bev had a sense of belonging she hadn't felt since she and Phil… But, this time, there was no mounting grief, only a faint sadness for what might have been, tempered by the hope of what might be to come.

All too soon the ceremony was over, and drinks were being served along with Cleo's famous nibbles while a photographer snapped the happy couple with other members of the bridal party and Ailsa's sons.

It was a relief to Bev when this part of the proceedings was over, and she could return to join Iain and Mia. Bryan was already enjoying a beer with Nick and Owen.

'Glad it's over?' Iain asked, seeing Bev's expression. 'The wedding went well. I'm sure there will be many others who want to book a Pandanus Wedding now, too.'

'It did go well, didn't it?' Bev gazed around. It was a small crowd, but everyone appeared happy.

Suddenly, there was a loud shout, 'Attention please' And in the ensuing silence, Nate announced, 'As I'm told is the tradition, the bride will now throw the bouquet. Mum…' He moved aside to allow Ailsa to take his place.

With a mischievous glance in Bev's direction, Ailsa hurled the small posy she'd been carrying into the air.

Of their own volition, Bev's arms reached up to catch it. Then she blushed. She had no idea why she'd done this. Why hadn't she waited till Cleo… or Hannah… or even Vee had caught it?

There was loud cheering and applause, then, as people began to move away, Iain's arms were around her. 'I think this is a sign, don't you?' Iain whispered into her ear.

Bev looked up to meet his eyes. They were filled with such love, her stomach began to churn with excitement. Her breath caught. Did he mean…?

'I love you, Bev. I've never felt this way before. I want…'

He was interrupted by a little voice.

'Can *I* be a flower girl at *your* wedding and scatter rose petals, Granddad and Nana?' Mia asked with a winning smile.

Bev felt her heart leap as Iain smiled down at her, his eyes twinkling as if they held a secret. 'What do you say, Bev? We can't disappoint Mia, can we?'

Bev nodded, her heart too full for words. In this man, she had found something she didn't know she was looking for. She had found a refuge from the memories, found her son, and found a forever love.

The End

If you've enjoyed Bev and Iain's story, a way you can say thank you to me is to leave a review on Amazon and/or Goodreads. A few words will suffice, no need for a lengthy review. It will mean a lot to me and help other readers find my books.

The next book in the series, *Escape to Bellbird Bay*,
features Ali Wells who first appeared as Adam Holland's
long-lost sister in Christmas in Bellbird Bay, and Neil Simpson
the son of Harry Simpson who owns Bay Books. It's book six
in this series but, like all my other books, it can be read
and enjoyed as a standalone novel.

When successful university lecturer Alison Wells' life unexpectedly falls apart, she follows in her brother's footsteps and escapes to the coastal town of Bellbird Bay on Queensland's Sunshine Coast.

Neil Simpson loves teaching and his position as principal at a prestigious boys' school in Brisbane. But when scandal rocks the school, and he learns his father's health is failing, he has no choice but to return to his hometown of Bellbird Bay.

Determined not to be a burden to her brother and his new partner, Ali is considering her options when her world and Neil's collide. Having avoided commitment all her life, Ali is unprepared for the force of her attraction to the man who is trying to come to terms with the upheaval in his own life.

As fate conspires to keep them apart, can this small town work its magic on these two lost souls?

A heartwarming tale of family, friends, and how a second chance at love can happen when you least expect it.

You can order it here https://mybook.to/EscapetoBellbirdBay

From the Author

Dear Reader,

First, I'd like to thank you for choosing to read *Finding Refuge in Bellbird Bay*. I hope you've enjoyed this trip to Bellbird Bay as much as I've enjoyed writing it. From the time I wrote *Summer in Bellbird Bay*, the first in this series, I knew I would have to write Bev's story. It just took me some time to work out what it was!

I'm really enjoying writing about my fictional town in the part of Queensland where I live and populating it with characters who I hope you will come to love. It's the fifth book in this series, but like the others, can be read as a standalone.

If you'd like to stay up to date with my new releases and special offers you can sign up to my reader's group.

You can sign up here

https://mailchi.mp/f5cbde96a5e6/maggiechristensensreadersgroup

I'll never share your email address, and you can unsubscribe at any time. You can also contact me via Facebook, Twitter or by email. I love hearing from my readers and will always reply.

Thanks again.

Acknowledgements

As always, this book could not have been written without the help and advice of a number of people.

Firstly, my husband Jim for listening to my plotlines without complaint, for his patience and insights as I discuss my characters and storyline with him, for his patience and help with difficult passages and advice on my male dialogue, and for being there when I need him.

John Hudspith, editor extraordinaire for his ideas, suggestions, encouragement and attention to detail, and for helping me make this book better.

Jane Dixon-Smith for her patience and for working her magic on my beautiful cover and interior.

My thanks also to early readers of this book – Helen, Maggie and Louise for their helpful comments and advice. Also, to Annie of *Annie's books at Peregian* and Graeme of *The Bookshop at Caloundra* for their ongoing support.

And to all of my readers. Your support and comments make it all worthwhile.

About the Author

After a career in education, Maggie Christensen began writing contemporary women's fiction portraying mature women facing life-changing situations, and historical fiction set in her native Scotland. Her travels inspire her writing, be it her trips to visit family in Scotland, in Oregon, USA or her home on Queensland's beautiful Sunshine Coast. Maggie writes of mature heroines coming to terms with changes in their lives and the heroes worthy of them. Maggie has been called *the queen of mature age fiction* and her writing has been described by one reviewer as *like a nice warm cup of tea. It is warm, nourishing, comforting and embracing.*

From the small town in Scotland where she grew up, Maggie was lured to Australia by the call to 'Come and teach in the sun'. Once there, she worked as a primary school teacher, university lecturer and in educational management. Now living with her husband of over thirty years on Queensland's Sunshine Coast, she loves walking on the deserted beach in the early mornings and having coffee by the river on weekends. Her days are spent surrounded by books, either reading or writing them – her idea of heaven!

Maggie can be found on Facebook, Twitter, Goodreads, Instagram, Bookbub or on her website.
>   www.facebook.com/maggiechristensenauthor
>   www.twitter.com/MaggieChriste33
>   www.goodreads.com/author/show/8120020.Maggie_Christensen
>   www.instagram.com/maggiechriste33/
>   www.bookbub.com/profile/maggie-christensen
>   www.maggiechristensenauthor.com/

Lightning Source UK Ltd.
Milton Keynes UK
UKHW012042310123
416280UK00007B/82